Chloe's Sanctuary

Sophie Dawson

May your life be a story in faithful living.

~~~~~

Dedication

So, who do I dedicate this book to? You, the reader, who have embraced my humble efforts with enthusiasm and good will.

I thank you.

Acknowledgements

Just as with awards ceremonies on TV many people need to be thanked for contributing in some way to the writing of Chloe's Sanctuary.

First and foremost, my loving Father who gave His only Son so we could be reconciled back to God through the death and resurrection. Without Him I could do nothing.

My husband, Ivan, who supplies the wear withal so I can eat not having to depend on the income from my writing.

The other authors who share the Barnabas Room on Slack who give me encouragement, love and laughter. Word wars and edit wars help move the work along with fun rather than drudgery (especially the editing part).

Of course, no acknowledgement and thanks would be complete without mentioning George McVey. He's been a steady source of spiritual support throughout my writing career. His ability to take my truly awful book blurbs and turn them into interesting paragraphs capturing readers for my novels.

~~~~~

This is a work of fiction. Most of the places within the story are fictitious but some are real. You will most likely recognize those which are. Those you don't are made up by me. The people, unless you recognize the name of a real historical person, are not real. They, too, have been created by me or by my friend and author George McVey. This is true of Nugget Nate and Penny Ryder who may or may not show up in this book. Even if real historical people are mentioned their lives may or may not adhere strictly to documented historical reference. In other words, what they do or say has little bearing in fact and they probably didn't do or say it. This is a fictional story after all.

~~~~~

Books By Sophie Dawson

<u>Cottonwood Series</u>

Healing Love

Lord's Love

Giving Love

Redeeming Love (With George McVey)

Stones Creek Series

Leah's Peace

Chasing Norie

Love's Infestation

Mold and Marriage

Single Books

Seeing The Life

Rescued By Love (Novelette)

A note from Sophie

I hope you enjoy **Chloe's Sanctuary**. Please take a moment to leave a review on Amazon. For independently publishing authors like myself, the reviews are extremely valuable in getting our work noticed. When you flip the page Amazon is going to give you the opportunity to rate and review this book. If you take just a few minutes you could help someone else find their next favorite book.

If you'd like to be notified of upcoming releases please sign up for my newsletter. It only comes to you when there is actual real, news about my books. You need not worry that your information will ever be released to anyone in any way for anything. I hate spam as much as you do.

Oh, here's the link for you to sign up. http://www.sophie-dawson.com/subscription.html

Thank you.

Sophie

If you enjoy this book and would like to find other great Christian Indie Authors reads, follow the link below. Christian Books in Multiple Genres, Join Christian Indie Author ~ Readers Group on Facebook. Opportunities for free books and giveaways.
https://www.facebook.com/groups/291215317668431/

~ ~ ~ ~ ~

Bonus Story: The Prequel to Chloe's Sanctuary

Chloe's Choice

Stone's Creek Series
Copyright 2015 Sophie Dawson

~~~~~

Chloe bent over and set the bucket of water on the ground as the tightness in her belly grew. Softly panting, she waited out the contraction then picked the bucket up and set out once more for the shack. Glancing at the porch, Duncan, her eight year old son, stood staring at her.

Holding the bucket, Chloe walked slowly so the water wouldn't splash on her shirts. The reservoir already held two buckets and she wanted two more before. Who knew when she would be able to haul water again.

"Mama," Duncan's shaky voice pulled her gaze from her steps and to the dirty face of her son. "The baby's coming now, ain't it?"

"Pretty soon." Chloe climbed the steps putting the bucket on the floor. "We're going to be okay. As soon as we can, we're leaving here. We'll find a town to live in."

"Mama, are the gang coming back?"

"No, they all went to..." Her voice trailed off. She didn't know where they had gone nor did she truly care. They had said something about heading south and finding battles going on in the War of the Rebellion. All she knew was they left her and Duncan at this shack in northwestern Iowa. Or maybe it was southwestern Minnesota. The important things were; they were alone, it was late September, and Chloe was about to give birth with only her barely eight year old son in attendance.

Another contraction hit nearly causing her to fall to her knees. They were close enough together Chloe knew she should be inside preparing to deliver. When the pains passed she carried the bucket in and poured the water into the tin tub. Just two more. I just want to get two more. Chloe thought as she caught her breath.

Duncan, who had followed her into the house, picked up the bucket she had set on the floor and started toward the door. "I'll get some water, Mama."

"No, I'll get it. I don't want you falling into the creek."

Duncan frowned but set the bucket down. "I want to go with you case something happens. I need to protect you."

Chloe smiled and nodded. She wondered where the idea of protecting a woman had come from. He most certainly didn't learn it from the men of the outlaw gang she'd lived with for so long. She shook away the memory and held out her hand to Duncan. "You carry the bucket and hold my hand while we walk." She was gratified when the boy smiled and did.

"Look," Duncan said as they carried the full water bucket between them. They managed, between contractions, to fill two more buckets. A dust trail was coming quickly up the lane toward them.

"You go hide in the wood box. Don't come out until I tell you. Hurry now." Chloe gave Duncan a little shove causing his hand to release the bucket handled. Water splashed onto her skirt. "Go."

She continued her walk to the shack as Duncan run around the side of the building then out of sight. He would climb into the lidded box situated just a few steps from the back door. She couldn't try to hide or get away. She was in labor and getting very close to giving birth. Chloe only hoped whoever was coming would help instead of hurt her.

Another contraction, stronger than the previous, brought her to her knees before she reached the three steps leading up to the sagging porch. Chloe closed her eyes gasping small quick breaths. The sound of a buggy or wagon became louder but she couldn't lift her head to see who approached.

"Nate, she's in labor. Pick her up and bring her in." The woman's voice held an eastern accent. Heeled boots sounded with each step she took as she walked past Chloe and up the steps and across the porch.

"Come'n girl." This voice was male and in no way as refined as the woman's. Strong hands and arms scooped Chloe up, flipping her upright. A little gray sprinkled through the light brown beard on the man's weathered face. On his head was a coonskin cap. "You's safe now. Penny 'n me, we'll help you whelp that young'un."

Before Chloe could think of a reply she was in the shack with Penny unbuttoning her dress and asking questions a mile a minute.

"How far are the contractions apart? Is this your first? Where's your husband? Where are the diapers and clothing? What's your name?"

Chloe was barely able to think of the answer to one when the next was fired at her.

"Penny, m'love. Ya be a letting the girl answer afore ya ax her another." The man named Nate interrupted the string of questions.

"You are right of course. You were in so all fired a hurry to get here I haven't slowed down yet." Penny lifted the dress over Chloe's head leaving her standing in a threadbare chemise and petticoat. Chloe blushed at being so scantily dressed in front of a strange man but not sure why. It's not as if she hadn't been before. Well, maybe not nine months along.

"You go fetch some wood, Nate. We need to boil some water. Get my sewing kit from the coach, too. I'm not using your knife to cut the cord."

"It be nice 'n sharp. Would slice through like butter." They heard Nate mutter as he left by way of the back door.

"You get on the bed. You said you've had babies before?"

Chloe got the first good look at the woman called Penny as she knelt on the straw mattress divested of sheets and blankets. Tall and lean her clothing was obviously high quality and expensive. She removed her hat by pulling a long hat pin topped by a large green stone.

"Yes." That was all Chloe was going to tell her at this point. Along with the contraction her stomach knotted at the thought of the man, Nate, finding Duncan. Memories started flooding her. Chloe covered her eyes with her hand for a moment to force them away.

"Well then, we should have an easy time with this one coming." Penny bustled around the room picking things up and putting them out of the way. "I was skeptical when Nate said we needed to come this way. I mean, we were in northern Minnesota. We are staying away from that war. Nate doesn't believe in slavery in any way shape or form. Still, he does not like the idea of brother fighting brother. So we've spent the time as far from the war as possible."

"Lookie what I done found in the wood box, Penny my love." The tall man stood in the doorway with Duncan in his arms. The boy struggled against him

with all his strength but Nate didn't seem to notice.

"Mama," Duncan hollered, his voice sounding both fearful and protective.

"I think it's okay, Duncan. They are here to help me have the baby."

Duncan stopped struggling and stared fiercely at Nate. "You better be good to

my mama or I'll string you up on the nearest tree and use you for target practice."

Chloe breath caught. It was a threat made to Duncan, as well as adults in the gang, and he had heard it often. Her eyes widened when Nate threw back his head and laughed loud and long.

"The day ya ken do that, boy, 'ill be the day I hangs up my guns an' hatchet fer good." He set Duncan on his feet but kept a strong hand on his shoulder keeping him in place. "We be agoin' ta fetch wood now. We'll be stayin' outta yer way. Birthin' ain't no place for menfolk. Ya jest call iffen ya be a needin' me, my love."

"Make sure you put water on to boil before you make your escape, Nate," Penny called to his back. A long arm rose high in acknowledgement as Nate and Duncan turned away. "Birthing makes Nate so nervous. He has fainted the few times I've helped with this before. Don't tell him I told you. It doesn't fit the Nugget Nate legend." Penny grinned and placed a hand on Chloe's stomach as the next contraction began. "Lord, it's... Forgive me but what is your name?"

"Chloe, Chloe Ashburn."

"It's Chloe and me trying to help one of your precious little ones into this world. I need your help, Lord. I'm not trained but have the little experience you've given me. Please make this birthing easy and safe. Bring this babe into our arms and love soon. Thank you, amen. Now we've covered this in prayer so you can give birth."

Penny's imperious tone took Chloe by surprise. It was if the woman gave her permission to deliver the baby. "I think the baby will come when it wants to."

"When Nate told me he had a calling and it was a woman in need of help I knew it was for a birth. I asked God to keep the baby from being born until we got here and were set up. He honored that and so now's the time."

A contraction hit that was many times harder than any of the previous. Chloe let out a moan that turned into an anguished cry of pain.

Nate and Duncan had built up the fire and put the water on to boil. The wood box by the stove was full. Now they were a ways away from the shack with Nate showing Duncan how to set up a snare to catch a rabbit.

"That's jest right, boy. Yous gonna make a fine mountain man when yous done growed up. I ken teach ya all sorts o' ways ta catch animals, how ta skin 'em, make buckskin from the hides."

"Can you teach me to fight and shoot a gun?"

"Yessiree, I ken do that too." Nate smiled at the boy kneeling beside him. "I ken teach ya about the most important thing of all. Lovin' the Lord wif all your heart, soul, mind, 'n strength."

"My ma don't truck with the Lord. She says he done nothing but hurt her all her life."

"Hum." Nate thought for a moment. "Well, boy, Penny 'n me'll jest hafta see iffen we can change her mind a bit on that score."

Just then a scream came from the direction of the shack. Duncan leapt into Nate's arms throwing his around his neck. "I hate this part. Makes me scared all over." Duncan's voice was muffled since his face was tucked against Nate's chest.

"Me too, but it be part of the curse God done put onta Eve. Ya will be a birthin' yer babes in pain. It also let's us menfolk know it's all about done. Let's be aheading back and see what kinda baby yer ma done had."

Penny stood on the porch as they approached the shack. The smile on her face told Nate all was well. "A little girl. Simply beautiful with lots of dark hair. Chloe is sleeping."

Nate jumped onto the porch skipping the steps. He took hold of Penny and gave her a big kiss. "See, my Callin' were right."

"I never question your Callings, my dear." Penny's eyes showed her adoration of the tall man.

Duncan hadn't said anything. He glanced around for the boy. Duncan stood near the edge of the clearing around the house and looking intently at the ground. "Duncan, whatcha be adoin'?" He and Penny left the porch and walked to where the boy stood.

"I'm looking for a place to bury the baby."

Penny knelt beside him and took hold of his hands. "The baby and your mother are fine. No need to worry over her."

"She'll die just like the others. Mama and me, we pick out the spot together. I thought I'd do some looking so I'd be able to suggest someplace."

Chloe woke up to an infant's cry. A soft voice cooed and she heard the sound of the baby being picked up. Opening her eyes, Chloe watched Penny give the soft cheek a kiss.

"Oh good. You're awake. This little one needs something in her belly." Penny approached the bed and waited until Chloe sat up against the wall at the end before handing the baby to her mother. "She's such strong little thing. And look at those eyes."

The baby opened her eyes. They were large with dark lashes and a deep blue. Chloe smiled. "They are pretty." A few moments of silence reigned as she settled the baby to nurse. Looking down at the tiny head nestled against her breast Chloe sighed. She didn't want to bury another child. Each time she did the ache in her heart became larger. Tears slip down her face unnoticed. One dropped onto the baby's cheek.

"Why the tears?" Penny was sitting next to Chloe carefully brushing the tangles from her hair. She pulled a handkerchief from her sleeve and gently wiped the tears away, first from Chloe's face, then the baby's. "She's strong and healthy. She'll be fine."

"No," said Chloe. "She will die like the others. There's no way I can feed her and Duncan. We have no one and no where to go. Winter is coming. We need to head to a town so I can find work. No one will want to hire a nursing mother. All I can to do is wash clothes, a little mending, and cooking. Not enough of such work to support me and the children."

"God will provide and protect, so don't you worry. I understand it sounds like platitudes but it's truth."

"He hasn't so far in my life. I don't think he'll start now."

The defeat in Chloe's voice broke Penny's heart. Childbirth should be a joyful time, not a time of such hopelessness and worry. She finished loosely braiding Chloe's hair and tying it with a ribbon.

"There," Penny said laying the braid over Chloe's shoulder. "See how the red ribbon is so pretty on your black hair."

The baby was on Chloe's shoulder being burped. Penny had hoped the brushing and braiding would sooth the young mother. Instead she broke down sobbing. Penny took the sleeping infant, quickly changed the diaper, then placed her in the crate swaddled in a clean but faded and tattered blanket.

"There, there, now. Everything be all right. What caused this?" Penny sat beside Chloe and took her in a close embrace. The red ribbon now rested against Chloe's cheek as she held the braid in her hand. Penny rubbed gentle circles on the young woman's back until her sobs became ragged breaths.

"My mama... a red ribbon... It was what she tied in my hair that day. A new one. Papa had brought it from town a few days before. I'd gone out to show Papa how pretty it was. We were in the barn when they came. We went out to see who was coming. It was them." The last words were nearly unintelligible as she began crying again.

Penny held Chloe until she lay exhausted on the bed. "You rest now. Let Nate and I take care of things right now."

Once Penny was sure Chloe slept she went to the stove and gave the stew a vigorous stir. Father, something terrible happened to this young woman. You know all of what happened and her needs now. Give Nate and me the wisdom to do your will and help Chloe, Duncan, and the precious newborn.

Penny was sitting on the porch holding the baby when Nate and Duncan came out of the woods. The look of adoration on the boy's face made Penny smile. He gazed up at Nate listening to who knew what tall tale her husband was telling him. Three rabbits were tied to his belt. Their snares had worked well.

Duncan saw her and came running. "Missus Penny, we caught rabbits. Mister Nate's gonna skin 'em and show me how to tan the hides. He says I can make stuff from them, like mittens. I'm gonna keep one of the feet for luck."

"You did well. We can add the meat to our stew. It'll taste so much better." Penny ruffled Duncan's hair. She would bathe him later and get it washed. No need to tell him yet. That fuss could wait until later. "Do you want to meet your sister?" Penny lay the baby along her lap and drew back the blanket.

"She's sleeping."

"Yes, she's very tired from being born."

"Is Mama awake?"

"No, she's very tired too."

"Oh... Is she gonna be okay?" The shakiness in Duncan's voice revealed his

fear for her.

"Yes, but she's tired. How about you go around to the back and get some

wood for the stove?" Penny gave Nate a glance telling him to stay put.

"Okay." Duncan was as enthused about the chore as any eight year old boy

would be.

Once he rounded the side of the shack Penny eyed Nate. "The girl's had a

hard life. She's needing our help. She doesn't have a man or any family that I can figure. I think we should take them to Sanctuary Place."

"I done thought the same thing." Nate untied the rabbits from his belt and laid them beside the Kentucky rifle he'd placed on the porch. "Dunc done tole me 'at they used ta run with a gang o' no count men. They went ta find 'at dad burn war. T'other women goed with 'em. Chloe got left a hind cause she were 'spectin'.

"I'm not surprised. There's something else in her background. I don't know what but hopefully we can get her to talk about it."

Nate nodded. "How soon'll she be fit fer travelin'?"

"A few days yet. She's nearly sick with worry." Penny told him about Chloe's breakdown and what she had revealed.

"Gives me an' Dunc a chance ta get more friendly like. I's a thinkin' he could help cornvince his ma ta go with us."

"I hope she won't need much convincing, Nate."

Late in the evening after Duncan was asleep on a pallet near the stove and the baby had been fed, Nate sat straddling a straight chair leaning on the back. Penny sat at the end of the bed. Chloe leaned against the wall at the head.

"Penny, done tole me yous ain't got nobody but Dunc an' the babe. We be a fixin' ta help yous get ta a place y'all ken live an' learn an' be safe."

Penny began fiddling with the edge of the tattered blanket. "Sanctuary Place is a small community set up for women like you. A place where women, and their children if they have any, can go and learn to read and write, learn arithmetic, and a way to earn a living when they go back into a town or city."

"I don't understand."

"Penny my love, I's a thinkin' plain talk'd be best." When she nodded Nate continued. "It be fer girls what got in the family way an' the low down scum don't marry 'em. Girls what got throwd outa their family. Widders 'at ain't got no means o' supportin' 'emselves. Now, Penny an' me, we's be athinkin' yous might jest fit purty keen."

"Why? Why would you do that for me?" Chloe looked from Nate to Penny and back to Nate.

"'Cause it be a part a what God set fer me ta do. He done give me a Callin' ta come an' help ya. Not jest fer the birthin', but fer ever'thin' ya need. An' I's a be thinkin' Sanctuary Place w'd be jest the place fer ya."

"God called you here?" Sarcasm filled Chloe's tone. "God's the one who didn't care enough about me to protect me thirteen years ago. Why would he care now?"

"Oh Chloe, God loves you more than anything in this world,"

Penny said.

"Then why did he let me be raped and kidnapped when I was ten and used by the gang all those years? When Lloyd died, why did he let all the rest leave me and Duncan here with barely anything to live on? Why did my Pa think God didn't want him to fight the men who did this to me and Mama?"

Nate rubbed his hand on his beard as he watched his wife take the sobbing young woman into her arms. It was so hard to explain God's love to someone who had been hurt in so many ways. In her voice was devastation of the betrayal of Chloe's father who had such a messed up idea of who God was.

"I's a knowin' you been hurt a passel in yer life. Ya done had a real hard life. But God ain't the one what done it to ya. It be man an' his selfish, wicked ways. The Good Book says troubles 'n trials 'll be a heaped onta us our whole lives. It'll happen ta the wicked 'n the good.

"God, he done 'llowed that there dev'l ta take 'way ever'thing ole Job had. Took his chillens, an' his stock, his wife mose likely too. Ole Job jest kept on saying he wast gonna believe God 'n praised him. Job knowed God was a watchin' 'n a listenin' and a weepin' right 'long side him.

"Jesus told' us we was gonna have troubles. He knowed what life's like. He said we's ken count on him ta hep us whilst we's a sufferin'. Said it'll make us more like him iffen we let it."

Chloe snorted. "To not even fight to protect your wife and child from rape and kidnapping because God hates violence more than he loves us? What kind of a God is that?"

"It's not God, Chloe," Penny said taking Chloe's face gently between her hands. "It's man not understanding who God is and his true character. God wanted your father to fight for you. Jesus didn't let the men stone the adulterous woman and she was guilty."

"That was Jesus," Chloe argued. "And he just spoke and the men dropped their rocks. The gang wasn't going to stop because Pa told them to."

"You's right. But jest standin' there lettin' them hurt 'n take ya t'weren't right neither. He should a fought 'em with all his might. With his rifle 'n knife, yellin' out Jesus' name as he done it." Nate's voice rose as he stood up pulling a Bowie knife out of its sheath and a hatchet from his belt.

"Shh, Nate. The children are asleep." Penny grabbed his buckskin shirt and pulled him from the fighting stance he assumed.

"Oh, sorry." Nate could feel Chloe's eyes on him. Could feel her fear as well as wonder at his fierceness. He sat down putting his weapons away as he did.

"It's all right, my love," Penny said as she leaned over giving him a kiss on the cheek. "I know how injustice and violence against innocents riles you up."

Nate looked Chloe straight in the eye. "The trouble with sinnin' is 'at ya never sin alone. Yer sin spills over on t'others. It be kinda like the sinner throwed a rock inta a pond. Them ripples spread out away from that there center an' it done flows over inta 'nother person's life and jest messes 'at life up. A whole bunch a ripples done crashed t'gether inta yer life, Chloe, whenst ya weren't nothin' but little girl. 'N all 'at sin jested messed up yer life somet'in fierce."

As he spoke he saw Chloe's eyes filled and the tears slipped over the lids down her cheeks. "T'ain't yer fault yer sufferin' fer so long. It be them there men what 'bused ya. God, he been a watchin' over ya and yer boy all this time. He knowed all ya been a goin' through. He done give me a Callin' ta come an' get ya an' the youngin's sose Penny 'n me could git yer babe born 'n hep ya ta git ta a safe place."

"That's right," Penny said. "Sanctuary Place is for women who want out of the situation they are in and into a new life. A safe place to live for a while and learn about how to live a better life. More importantly, they learn about the Lord and his love for you. How he wants you to understand the love that had Jesus giving up his place with the Father and becoming a man who lived a sinless life and died to take the punishment of every person who ever lived."

"An' he done rose again defeatin' death an' 'at old serpent the devil. 'Cause o' what Jesus done, we's ken git right with God an' be saved from the fiery pit o' hell. Iffen we cornfess 'at we's a sinner an' cain't fix it ourselves an' ax Jesus' blood ta cover our sin, 'en God'll fergive us an' assept us as one o' his chillens. Then we's a gonna lif with him in heaven ferever an' ever."

Again, Penny was pulling on Nate's buckskin shirt urging him to sit down and be quiet. He gave his wife a sheepish grin and settled back onto the chair.

"Chloe, we's don't want ta railroad ya inta somet'ing ya ain't a wantin'. We's a wantin' ya ta be safe an' cared fer. Yous an' yer little ones too. We's offerin' ya a chanst atta new life. A safe place ta raise yer youngin's."

"A sanctuary where you can learn to be the woman God wants you to be." Penny patted Chloe's hand. "You sleep now. We can talk some more in the morning."

Nate stood and swung the chair around placing it by the rickety table and prayed silently for Chloe and her children while Penny tucked the young mother in with a kiss on her cheek.

Chloe lay staring at the rafters above her head. Tears slid from the corners of her eyes, down her temples and into her hair. The God Penny and Nate talked about was so different from what she was taught as a girl. Nate had gotten so angry as he thought about what was done to her. Her pa would never have lifted a knife and ax intent on fighting for anything, especially his daughter and wife.

"Lord, I don't know if you are listening. Penny and Nate are sure you are. I just want to be safe and my babies to be safe and grow up to be good people. What they offer seems too good to be true. A place to live and work and learn. A place where the baby will be able to live. I can't lose her. Not another one. There isn't any other option really. We'll all die here if we stay. Lord, I hope you are listening because I need you. I can't do anything else. Just, Lord, just show me you are there. Something to let me know you hear me and you want me to go with Penny and Nate."

Chloe turned on her side and closed her eyes. The feeling of arms wrapping around her and a soft kiss on the cheek was followed by a peace Chloe hadn't felt in years settling on her as she fell asleep.

Nate was helping Penny down from the coach the next morning when the swish of skirts was heard and steps on the porch. Chloe was coming down the steps with the baby on her shoulder and holding Duncan's hand. Penny and Nate walked toward them. When they met in the yard Penny held her breath. The look on Chloe's face said her decision was made.

"Penny, Nate, thank you for coming here and all of your aid to us. About your offer to take us to Sanctuary Place. We are ready whenever you want to leave."

Chloe's Sanctuary

CHAPTER ONE

Chloe pulled Duncan closer to her with one hand while holding Lil-Pen's with the other. They were standing with seven other women and a number of children on the train depot platform of Stones Creek, Colorado. The July day was hot and they were all sweating in their wool travel outfits.

"Ma, I wanna go stand with Ozzie," Dunc, age thirteen, said. "We're all going to the same place. I won't get lost."

Chloe nodded and released her son. He was right. As soon as all the luggage was removed from the train the group would be taken to Sanctuary House, the new boarding house built for the women coming from Sanctuary Place for Women in Iowa. Each woman had her own story of abuse or neglect. All had been accepted, taught skills and presented the Gospel while living in the safety of Nugget Nate Ryder's mission.

A large group of men were building a mountain of trunks and cases at the other end of the platform as the items were removed from the train. Each man looked at the women as they moved from the growing pile of baggage back to the train to fetch another piece.

Chloe fought the urge to grab her daughter, Lil-Pen, into her arms and run back to Iowa. They had come to Stones Creek for the opportunity to become wives to the men living here and in the area. Women were scarce in the West. Just as many of the men had come here to begin new lives and have greater opportunities, the women standing huddled together were hoping for the same.

She hoped they would be accepted by the townsfolk. The past hadn't been kind to any of the women and the choices made by or inflicted upon them were not those readily accepted by polite society.

"You'd think we were a bunch of saloon girls with hardly nothing on, the way they's looking at us," Myra said with a chuckle.

Chloe bit back a giggle. Myra was an ex-saloon girl who had run away when her madame wanted her to have an abortion. Her son, Troy, was about the same age as Lil-Pen who was four and her best friend, most of the time.

Myra's comment eased the tension building in Chloe's stomach. Yes, the men were interested, very interested, in the women. Who could blame them? Each one, or most at any rate, was hoping to attract one of the women into marrying him. Still the idea of being with a man, being married and belonging with one made Chloe extremely nervous. She could sense Myra eying her.

"Relax," Myra said. "Nate and that pastor, I forget his name, set up them rules to keep us from marryin' a no-account. I feel pretty safe with that an' the Lord protectin' us. 'Sides, no set time when we got ta be married. Maybe I'll just take my time in choosin'."

Chloe laughed and gave her friend a hug. "No, you'll be married real quick like. I know you," she said with a smile. "Can't wait to get to the benefits of marriage and a man."

"Well, that's one of the things I miss," Myra's eyes twinkled then became serious. "But I want me a good man. One who'll stick to me like glue an' be faithful an' work hard an' treat my Troy as his own. Ain't gonna have a man what'll be mean to him. No way, no how. Don't have to neither. Nate done made sure we can all work to support ourselves." Myra's slight southern accent betrayed her Tennessee origins.

Chloe gave a small smile then looked at the other end of the platform. A tall man and two women were walking toward them. One held a baby. The chatter of the women and children stopped as they neared.

The man cleared his throat. "I'm Sheriff Newt Riverby and

these ladies are Mrs. Noah Preston and Mrs. Eli Steele. They are the wives of our pastor and doctor who couldn't be here because of an emergency out on a ranch. You'll meet them later today or tomorrow." The sheriff seemed to run out of words and looked at the ladies standing beside him.

"Welcome to Stones Creek." It was the blonde haired woman holding an infant. "We are very glad there will be more women here. Maybe the men will stop staring at the sight of one of us walking down the street."

The speaker looked sternly at the men unloading the luggage who had stopped their work and were gawking. They quickly went back to their task.

"I'm Vernie Preston and this little lady is Dorothy Mae. We call her Dottie. But let's head to Sanctuary House. I'm sure you are all anxious to settle in, eat something and rest. Boys, you grab up those bags and come along. No dawdling."

Vernie pointed and the boys whose ages ranged from thirteen to five picked up various carpetbags and totes. The girls did the same. At least those who were old enough. The four-year-olds, Troy, Lil-Pen and two-year-old Susan each clutched a small stuffed toy. The sheriff led the way up the dusty street. Vernie and Leah mingled within the seven women who had come with him.

Sanctuary House was several blocks away from the station and one street back from Main Street which was dirt and rutted from wagon and horse traffic during wet weather. Along the way they passed the livery, Cutler's General Store, a tailor shop, gunsmith, barber and bathhouse, and bakery on one side of the street. A feed store, the jail, a blacksmith, doctor's office, bank and the Stones Creek Hotel were on the other. Sanctuary House backed up to the gunsmith, barber and bathhouse, and bakery.

Chloe wasn't surprised at the handsomeness of the building. Nugget Nate never did anything halfway. Instead of being built of clapboard it was red brick. A porch wrapped around three sides. The porch, doors and windows were painted white. Chintz flowered draperies hung on the first floor windows. White curtains shielded the ones on the second and third floors. As they entered the children dropped the bags and scattered to explore.

"Ladies," Mrs. Steele said. "You'll find this floor is divided into two rooms to the left and right of the stairs, a parlor and dining room. The kitchen and laundry, bathing room are to the back. Upstairs are enough rooms for each of you. You can either have your children stay with you or they can stay in rooms across the hall. Each floor has a sitting room and one to house the necessaries."

A black woman came from the room Mrs. Steele had indicated was the kitchen. She smiled, but Chloe saw a look of unease was in her eyes. Leah wrapped an arm around her.

"This is Mrs. Thomas Wilson, the very best cook you will find, I'm sure. She owns Almeda's Bakery that we passed, but was gracious enough to volunteer to cook for you today. You will need to divide up the chores after today. The men of the town and surrounding ranches wouldn't be pleased if they didn't have their doughnuts tomorrow."

Everyone laughed. Blanche Basking, the oldest of the women at thirty-five said, "Thank you, Mrs. Wilson. We appreciate all your work. I'm sure there are others we should thank, also. The house is wonderful and I'm positive we will be very comfortable here." Blanche walked over to the three women who lived in Stones Creek and gave each a hug.

Chloe saw the uncertainty leave Mrs. Wilson's expression. She understood a little of what Mrs. Wilson felt. Each of the women who had come to town today did. Each had been rejected and treated as worthless by the general public. Mrs. Wilson, because of her dark skin, would have had it much worse. The possibility of more such treatment was always there for her.

Chloe thought of the verse in Galatians, *There is no Jew or Greek, slave or free, male or female; for you are all one in Christ Jesus.* Chloe decided to make sure Mrs. Wilson knew that was how she viewed her.

"You ladies go on up and choose your rooms. The luggage will be here shortly, and the men will want to know where to take it," Vernie said. "By then supper should be ready. It sure does smell good, Almeda."

With murmurs of agreement they trouped up the stairs.

CHAPTER TWO

Chloe chose a room on the second floor in the front next to the sitting room. Lil-Pen would stay with her on the trundle bed. Duncan and Ozzie and Will Basking wanted to be in a room together on the third floor. Blanche Basking's room was across the hall from theirs within easy hearing distance. John, her five year old would be in the room with her. Nancy, Blanche's seven-year-old daughter, was rooming with Ruth's daughter Kathryn who was eleven.

The trunks arrived and were distributed to the various floors and rooms chosen by the ladies and their children. Soon the sounds of sheets snapping as beds were made and mothers' voices instructing their offspring where to place clothing being unpacked filled the formerly empty house. Children's footsteps ran up and down stairs and hallways. A small body tripped, fell and was soon soothed in loving arms.

The children became peckish and grouchy as the fragrances of the food drifted up the staircases. Once the hubbub of the luggage coming was over they decided to have the meal Almeda had prepared. It was late afternoon and the meager lunch, of the last of the food they had brought on the train, hadn't filled any of them.

Chloe left Lil-Pen with Myra and went to the kitchen, towing Dunc, Ozzie and Will along. "You'll help with serving."

"Ah Ma, how come we have to? What about Eddie and Mark and Kathryn?" Dunc complained.

"Don't worry, they will have their chance. You know how it is.

We just haven't divvied up the chores yet. Be grateful the meal is ready and you don't have to help fix it. That will change quickly enough."

That silenced the complaining. Everyone at Sanctuary Place learned to cook, clean, sew and do laundry; boys and girls alike. It was one of Nugget Nate's rules, although Penny had been the one to insist he make it one.

The smells that met them as they entered the kitchen made mouths water. Stew, cornbread and apple cobbler would fill the bellies of the hungry women and children. There was a very large black man bringing firewood in through the back door.

"This is my husband, Thomas. I hope it's okay for him to come eat. We can eat here in the kitchen," Mrs. Wilson said.

"No," Chloe said. "You both will eat in the dining room with us. I think you'll find none of us cares about skin color. We've had a tiny taste of what you go through. Besides, under the skin we all look pretty much the same." Chloe held out her hand to Thomas after he had placed the wood in the box. His smile when he shook her hand held relief and friendship.

"Just call me Almeda. I don't think I'd answer to Mrs. Wilson." The ladies invited her and Thomas to call them by their first names also. Then Almeda said, "Come on now. Let's fill these hungry bellies." Almeda began ladling stew into bowls and indicated the boys take baskets of cornbread into the dining room. "Can they handle trays or pitchers?"

"Dunc and Ozzie can. If the pitchers aren't to big or full, Will can."

Eleven-year-old Kathryn Naylor came into the kitchen when the boys returned. "Can I help?"

A squeak came from a basket sitting in an out of the way corner of the kitchen. Almeda hurried over to it and lifted out an infant. Smiles broke out on the women's and girl's faces.

"Oh, Almeda. He or she is so cute," Chloe said.

"He's Abraham after President Lincoln. He's free born because of him. Just about two months old, he is." Almeda's face shone with joy and pride as she snuggled her son against her breast.

"Can I hold him while you all serve the meal?" Nancy asked.

Chloe introduced her to the couple and set the children to taking the trays and pitchers to the other room. Nancy sat down at the kitchen table and gently rocked back and forth as she crooned softly to little Abe. Thomas, who had washed, carried a large coffee pot and began filling cups. Soon everyone was served and Almeda and Thomas were sitting at one of the tables.

Blanche stood up. "Normally we have a schedule of who does what, but since we haven't set it up yet I will say grace." Everyone folded their hands and bowed their heads. "Our gracious and heavenly Father, we thank you for bringing us here safely. For the food and the hands who prepared it. Please bless Almeda and Thomas for their sacrifice of time and effort in having this meal to welcome us to Stones Creek. May we use it to the benefit of your kingdom. Thank you, in the name of your son, Jesus."

A hardy, "amen," followed and spoons clinking in stew bowls quickly commenced.

~~~~~

With the children settled in their beds later that evening, the eight women met in the parlor on the first floor. They were discussing schedules for chores and first impressions of the town.

Chloe was in the kitchen getting coffee and tea pots to refresh cups when there was a knock on the front door. She heard men's voices identify themselves as Pastor Preston and Dr. Steele. Then the voice of Leah Steele whom they had met earlier that day. Chloe placed three more cups on the tray before heading to the parlor.

Placing the tray on the low table, Chloe stood back. Blanche, the leader of their group, would make introductions.

"I'll take coffee," Dr. Steele said. "And Leah will take tea, thank you."

Chloe quickly poured the cups and handed them out as she was introduced to the doctor. They were sitting on a settee next to Cora.

"The pastor will take coffee, Chloe," Blanche said. Chloe poured the cup and straightened, turning around to hand it to the man standing behind her next to the fireplace. "This is Mrs. Chloe Ashburn."

Chloe glanced up at the tall preacher. His face made her heart drop. Her trembling hand rattled the cup in its saucer, sloshing coffee over the rim. She quickly lowered her gaze as the man swiftly took the clattering cup.

"Thank you. I'm sure the coffee's cool enough without cooling it in the saucer." Pastor Preston smiled, but Chloe was oblivious to his quip.

No, it couldn't be. This man was too young to be her pa. Chloe's mind shut down to all thought. He was tall with dark hair and brown eyes. A mustache hid the shape of his mouth and his cheeks were more chiseled, his face more oval.

"Noah Preston, ma'am. You met my wife, Vernie earlier." His voice was low with a slight gravel.

Chloe dropped her eyes to look at the floor. "P...p...pleased to m...meet you." She turned and fled to the other side of the room choosing a straight chair away from the lamplight. Sitting down she adjusted the chair slightly to make sure her face was in shadow.

No, no, no, Lord. How could you do this to me? Noah. My Noah. My little brother. How could you bring me to the town he is pastor to? Chloe's thoughts were in a whirl. How could she stay? No, he wouldn't recognize her. Yes, he would. How would she explain the children? Where could she go? Each of the women had a bank account in their name with thirty dollars in it.

Chloe thought about where such a large amount of money would allow her and the children to go away from Stones Creek. No, they could not take more than one dollar out of the bank at a time without giving good cause. It was a safe guard Nate had put in so none of the women wasted what he had given them. The conversation was simply background noise to her confused thoughts.

"Chloe? Chloe, would you like some tea?" It was Myra standing in front of her holding out a cup. There were questions written in her expression.

Chloe lifted a shaking hand then let it drop again to her lap. "Please set it on the table," she said, indicating the small side table.

Myra reached out picking up Chloe's hand and giving it a slight squeeze whispered, "It'll be fine," then she returned to sit in her place.

Looking over the people in the room, Chloe saw smiles on the women's faces and acceptance from the two men. Noah blushed at the mention of the birth of his daughter three months before, but the twinkle in his eyes told her he was accepting of Leah's teasing.

"Now that I've been thoroughly discredited as the pastor of this mangy town, I will invite you all for Sunday services. They begin at nine-thirty. You may not have noticed the church today. It's just a ways further along the road. We're in the process of getting ready to raise a school building. It will be beside the church." Noah smiled, then said, "Now we'll leave you. I'm sure you are all tired from the trip and moving in. We hope you find living in Stones Creek a blessed and fulfilling life. Let's have a moment of prayer."

Chloe tried to find peace in the words her brother lifted to the Lord but her agitation kept it from coming. During the leave taking she was able to keep to the background avoiding contact with either the doctor and wife, or the preacher by gathering the cups and saucers and piling them onto the tray. She escaped through the door leading from the parlor to the washroom and through it into the kitchen.

Chloe was standing at the sink gripping the edge with white knuckled hands when someone began rubbing her back. She dropped her head and released the tension in her shoulders.

"Okay, so who is he?" Blanche asked.

Chloe simply shook her head. There was no way she could utter a word around the lump in her throat. Another hand was placed on her shoulder.

"Is he one of the men?" This time Myra spoke. "Don't worry, the other ladies are all upstairs. We told them we would help with the dishes."

Chloe opened her mouth to explain but only a ragged sob came out. Blanche spun her around and pulled her into a tight hug. "Go ahead. Get the tears out."

For several minutes it was beyond Chloe to control her weeping. Finally, she pulled in deep shuttering breaths, stepped back and opened her eyes. Myra and Blanche watched her with worried expressions.

"He's my younger brother. The last time I saw him was as I looked back when I was being taken away. He was in the woodpile. I remember his eyes, so big and terrified. He reached out a hand to me and yelled my name. He was only six, but he did more than my pa did. Pa was standing facing the barn not even looking as they took me away."

"Oh, honey." Blanche pulled a handkerchief from her sleeve handing it to Chloe.

"What're ya gonna do?" Myra asked.

"I don't know. I'm going to pray and see if God gives me any answers. That's all I can do right now." She told them of her thoughts earlier and how confused she was.

"Well, let's pray right now and do these dishes. The day's been long and tiring. We need to get some sleep. The children will be up and ready to go at the normal time." Blanche said as she took the hands of the other two ladies and bowed her head.

~~~~~

Chloe stared into the darkness. She'd tried to fall asleep but each time she closed her eyes she'd see Noah looking from the woodpile reaching out to her. Then he'd morph into an adult who knew what she had done during the years they'd been separated, and he'd frown and turn away.

Tears slipped from her eyes, down her temples and into her hair. Oh, how she had wanted a new start, a new life. She'd decided to release her fears to the Lord, yet He'd brought her to face her shame with the one person she'd never thought to see again.

CHAPTER THREE

McIlroy, the blacksmith of Stones Creek, stopped on his way to Doc Eli's office, holding his hand wrapped in a bloody rag. He looked across the street at the group of women bustling along the boardwalk and into Cutler's General Store. They looked like fine women to him. Then he shook his head and continued on and into the clinic.

"Morning, Doc. Got time to tend this hand?" McIlroy asked.

Eli looked up from his ledger and shook his head in mock admonishment. "I told you I didn't need your help with my income. People are paying me just fine. Haven't been offered a kitten or child as payment in a long time. I get a chicken now and again but I've gotten them to make sure they are dressed and ready for Leah to cook."

It was a standing joke between the two men. McIlroy was continually hurting himself doing his work and Eli teased the blacksmith about making sure he had enough income to stay in town.

"Okay, I won't pay you this time. That should fix you." McIlroy laughed.

"What'd you do this time?"

"Aw, just didn't move my hand out of the way of a breaking pump handle I was working on. One hit too many I suppose." McIlroy allowed Eli to unwrap the injured hand as he spoke.

"Well," Eli said as he examined the hand. "It's going to take some stitches. You ready or do you want a drink of whiskey before I start?"

"Nah, Doc. I probably won't feel much." McIlroy had injured his hands so many times the nerves were pretty well gone. He barely felt anything when Eli began cleaning, then stitching the slice to the back and side of his hand.

"I saw the ladies who came in on the train yesterday going into Cutler's as I came here just now. Looked to be about half a dozen of them."

"There are eight women and a number of children. Met them last evening. Noah, Leah and I went over. We were supposed to meet them at the train yesterday but there was an emergency out at the Triple K Ranch. Cletus got bucked off and stepped on. Noah and I went out to tend him. He'll be all right but it'll take a while."

They were silent for a while as Eli continued placing stitches along the cut. Then Eli said, "Are you going to try for one of the ladies?"

McIlroy twitched causing a pull on the stitch Eli was placing. "Sorry. Didn't mean to jerk. No, I'm not gonna try for one of them. Let the younger men have them. I'm too old and set in my ways."

"You're what? Thirty-five? That's not too old. I'm sure one of the ladies wouldn't be adverse to your grizzled face." Eli stepped back a bit and eyed McIlroy with a raised eyebrow. "Well, maybe if you cleaned up a bit and trimmed that beard."

"Beard stays. I ain't going to go sparking any lady." McIlroy's gruff reply had Eli looking at him sharply.

"Well, okay. There," Eli said as he clipped the last thread. "Let's get this wrapped up and you back to your forge. Come back in a week."

"Yeah, Doc. I know the drill. I'll be back to get the stitches out. Could most likely do it myself and save you the trouble."

Eli clapped McIlroy on the shoulder. "You probably could, but then I'd have to charge you half price."

McIlroy laughed and left the clinic. He had intended to go straight back to his shop but found himself crossing the street instead. He needed coffee didn't he? He'd just go to Cutler's and buy a couple of pounds.

When he walked in, the sound of feminine laughter caused

him to stop with his hand on the doorknob. His chest tightened. It wasn't that he hadn't heard women laugh. It was one particular voice that caused the reaction. He was just about ready to open the door and leave when Ben Cutler, the store owner, called his name.

"McIlroy, don't just stand there. Come and meet the new citizens of Stones Creek. A few of them anyway."

Now he was stuck. He let go of the doorknob and moved up the aisle to the counter at the back of the room. There six ladies observed each step as he approached. McIlroy tipped his Stetson and stood tongue tied.

"Ladies, this is McIlroy, the blacksmith in town. He's also the best patient of Doc Eli's as you can see from the bandage on his hand."

McIlroy, who had been holding the hand against his chest to keep the throbbing down, whipped the hand behind his back and his cheeks warmed with a blush.

"Tis nice to meet you, ladies. Ben, I'm needing a couple of pounds of coffee." McIlroy realized he'd made a mistake when Ben looked at him and blinked. Then he remembered. He'd bought two pounds of coffee just a couple of days ago. Ben had ground it himself. "No, not coffee. I need, um, sugar. Yeah, that's right, sugar. Two pounds."

The twinkle in Ben's eyes told McIlroy he wouldn't escape with the sugar that easily. "How about I introduce these fine ladies to you while I measure up that sugar?"

Ben lifted the lid of the sugar barrel as he introduced the ladies. "This lady in the blue bonnet is Miss Ruth Naylor. Mrs. Laura Duffle is next to her. Miss Cora Sepal is the lady in green. Myra Hope is next to her. Mrs. Chloe Ashbury is in the dark blue and Miss Birdie Pullman is in the brown."

As each was introduced they greeted him. When the one called Chloe spoke he knew her voice was the one he'd noted before. It happened again. His chest constricted and the ache he had thought was over resurfaced. Along with it came the longing.

Ben had wrapped the parcel of sugar in brown paper and just finishing tying the string. "Nice to meet you all. I'll just take that and be getting out of you ladies' way." McIlroy grabbed the package from Ben and walked swiftly down the aisle and out the door. He didn't stop until he was in the room where he lived above his blacksmith shop.

McIlroy sat on his bed and held up his hand. It was shaking. The low voice of the one called Chloe saying she was pleased to meet him brought beads of sweat to his forehead as he recalled her words. She sounded so much like… No, he wasn't going to think about that. He had started over here and wasn't going to remember.

A shout from the forge room calling him pulled McIlroy from his thoughts. He tossed the unneeded sugar onto the table in the center of the room and called that he was coming. He took a moment to dip a bandana into a bowl of water and wiped the sweat from his face. Taking a deep breath he headed down the stairs.

~~~~~

Chloe watched the man stride away. He was tall and broad with a dark bushy mustache and beard below shaggy dark hair. He could use a trim. He was definitely nervous around them. She put him out of her thoughts as Laura started telling Ben what was on their list.

Nate had set up an account for Sanctuary House with Ben so the ladies could purchase the needed items to keep the place running. Enough for a day or two had been stocked at the house but they had made a list of what was needed in the way of food and cleaning supplies. The women had come to carry what they could back. There would be a return trip with the older boys to pick up the rest later in the day. Truth be told, all of the women wanted to see the general store. Those not here now would be coming with the boys.

"Ooo, look at this." Cora had wandered down an aisle. She was holding up a pretty pink gingham fabric. "Wouldn't my Susan look pretty in this?" Susan was her two year old daughter.

Several of the women, including Chloe, hurried to the aisle with the fabrics. Each adult and child had been supplied with one set of Sunday clothes and three everyday wear. One pair of shoes, several pairs of stockings, undergarments and a coat or cloak finished out the wardrobes. The mothers would have to make or purchase future needs.

With the skills they had learned at Sanctuary Place in Iowa they were able to make clothing and knitwear for themselves and their children. Some had more expertise than others. Myra was very talented with needle and thread, being able to do fine embroidery and complicated designs. The young woman was hoping to find work with Leah Steele who owned the dress shop.

Cora looked at Chloe. "What do you think of making my Susan and your Lil-Pen each a dress from this fabric? I think they would like having identical outfits."

Chloe examined the fabric finding it of good quality. She smiled. "I think that's a good idea. We can make them with puff sleeves now and add long sleeves for fall."

"Here's some pink ribbon." Cora held it up.

Soon they had all the supplies they wanted bundled with the food stuffs from the list. Several of the others had picked out things either for their children or themselves.

These purchases necessitated a trip to Stones Creek Bank since none of the ladies had the cash to make their purchases. Soon they were back at Cutler's General Store with their coins and promptly paid. They then left, heading back to Sanctuary House, chatting and laughing as they went.

~~~~~

McIlroy stood in the doorway to the smithy and swallowed. The new ladies in town were heading back to Sanctuary House. He kept the one named Chloe Ashburn focused in his sight. Shaking his head, McIlroy turned back and picked up the next piece of iron he was going to work on. He couldn't let his mind wander to include a woman in his life.

CHAPTER FOUR

After Duncan, Ozzie, Will, and Eddie dumped the last load of wood in the box and topped off the water tank, they headed out the kitchen door. Ozzie grabbed Duncan's shirt and skidded to a halt. "We got to make our beds or get skinned alive."

Soon they snuck out the kitchen door and ran down the alleyway between Sanctuary House and the building behind it. They were going to investigate the town. The woodbox was full, as was the water tank, their specified chores for the morning. Now they had until noon to check out all the businesses and the surrounding area.

It wasn't that they weren't allowed out of the house or free time. It was more fun, however, to pretend they were escaping the Indians or sheriff or outlaws so they peered out around the door jamb. Alley clear of varmints, they snuck out the kitchen door and slinked down the back wall, eyes and ears peeled for danger. Any would do.

"Let's go around this way. It smells real good," Dunc said. They turned left at the end of the building and ran to the steps leading up to the boardwalk. The smell was even better here.

They passed an empty storefront and stopped. The window display of the shop held the boys enthralled. The open door delivered the tempting aroma of baked goods. Four noses pressed up against the window. They looked at the cookies, breads and a cake artfully arranged before their eyes.

"Would ya look at all that." Will's voice held awe. "I know we have lots when all the cooking gets done, but still. Those are fancy."

The other boys nodded. The breads were braided, the cookies, not just the drop kind, were shaped and decorated. The cake, oh the cake. It was frosted with icing flowers on top and around the base.

The boys stood with mouths watering and didn't notice the woman in the bakery coming to the door. When she stepped outside and cleared her throat four boys jumped and turned to face her, their eyes wide with fear they would be scolded for messing up the window with nose and fingerprints. Will raised his arm and wiped at the smears with his sleeve.

"I'm Mz Almeda and met you all yesterday. How would you each like some cookies?" Her dark smiling face relieved their fear and the boys' jaws dropped as they nodded their heads. "Well, come on in and choose some."

They trouped in and surrounded her as she held out a tray with a variety of cookies laid out in rows. "You can each take three. That shouldn't spoil your dinner. You boys always seem to be starving."

Eddie quickly grabbed three different cookies. "Thank you." The others followed suit and all soon had crumbs stuck to their faces.

"Now, this is a one-time special. If you'd like to do some chores for me sometimes I can pay you in cookies or coins. Now scoot on outta here. I got work to do." Almeda smiled and made shooing noises. The boys took the hint.

"She's real nice," Will said with a cookie in each hand. "She cooks real good, too."

"Yeah, come on." Ozzie headed along the boardwalk. A man sat in front of the shop his chair tipped back against the wall, a Stetson shading his face. A sign was above the door.

"Barber and Bathhouse," Eddie read.

The man lifted his hat and let the chair down to rest on all four legs. "Yeah, that's my business. Name's Hank Johnson. Ya be new in town. You boys come with the women from Sanctuary Place?"

"Um, yes." Dunc's tone was uncertain.

"Well then, tell me who you are and how old you be." Hank's

smile put the boys at ease.

"I'm Dunc Ashbury and I'm thirteen."

"I'm Ozzie Basking and I'm twleve. This is my younger bro.."

"I can tell my own name, Ozzie," Will interrupted punching his brother in the arm. "I'm Will and I'm ten."

"Eddie Duffle's my name and I'm nine and three quarters."

Hank laughed. "Pleased ta meet you. Any of you needing a haircut or a bath?"

"No," four voices said in unison as each boy took a step back.

Hank laughed again. "Well, you just tell your ma's that I'm just around the corner when they decide you boys need my services." Then he leaned back in his chair and tipped his hat down again to shade his face.

"Look," Will pointed to the window of the next shop. In black painted letters were the words 'Preston's Gunsmithery'.

"Let's go in." Dunc jogged down the boardwalk. Soon they were standing just inside the door of the rather dim shop. A tall dark-haired man with a mustache was standing behind the counter spinning the cylinder of a six shooter as he inspected it. He was dressed in black with only the white of his shirt relieving the severity of his clothing. The black of his hair, mustache and beard mirrored that of his clothes. He looked just as each boy thought a Western gunfighter would look like.

"Morning, boys. Looking to buy a gun?"

The boys looked at one another. Finally Dunc, as the oldest, chose to speak. "Um, no sir. We're just investigating the town. We just moved here."

"Well," Noah snapped the cylinder in place and laid the gun on the counter. "Tell me who you are."

Each boy said his name.

"I met your mothers last night. I'm Noah Preston, gunsmith and pastor of Stones Creek."

Four mouths dropped open. Noah smiled. He loved the dichotomy of his two professions and the reactions of people when he told them.

"So, will you be in church Sunday?" He made eye contact with each one as he picked up the revolver again and spun the cylinder.

"Yes, sir," came the synchronous response.

"Good, now how about you boys come over here and look at the guns I have."

Suddenly the atmosphere in the room changed from threatening tension to welcome and camaraderie. The boys crowded around Noah, deeply interested as he showed them each gun and there features. As he was taking a gun apart he noticed Dunc's confused look. "You have a question, Dunc?"

"Uh, yeah, I suppose so. How can a preacher be a gunsmith? I thought you had to be against guns to be a preacher."

Noah looked at Dunc. "Some do think that way. Think that God doesn't want anyone to fight. But what if someone was to come and threaten your mother or brother or sister? Would you just want to stand there and let them?"

"No."

"Well, maybe Nancy…" Ozzie said. Will punched him. "Okay, even her."

"God wants justice doesn't he?" There were nods from all heads. "Is it justice to let someone be hurt when you can prevent it?"

"That's what Nate says. He can get real worked up when he thinks someone is being treated wrong," Dunc said. "You know Nugget Nate? He found me an' ma when she was birthin' Lil-Pen. He and Missus Penny. They took us to Sanctuary Place."

"Yes, Nugget Nate and Penny. Mighty fine people. He's an uncle to Ben Cutler who owns the general store."

Noah chuckled at the awe in the faces of the four boys crowded near him. It was obvious they held Nate in high esteem.

Just then the light from the doorway dimmed as a man entered. "Noah, I need… Oh, I didn't realize you had customers."

"Eli, these are four of the new residents of Stones Creek. Boys, this is Doc Eli Steele. He'll be the one who fixes you up when you hurt yourselves or are sick." Noah went on to introduce the boys to Eli who shook each of their hands.

"Pleased to meet you," Eli said. "Welcome to Stones Creek."

"What can I do for you?"

"I'm taking Leah out for target practice this afternoon and

need some ammunition."

Noah turned and reached up to a shelf and took down a wooden box. "How many do you want?"

A bell began ringing from outside. The boys came alert.

"We gotta go. The bell calls us all home right now. If we don't, we get in big trouble. Bye," Eddie said as he followed the others out the door at a run.

Noah and Eli looked at each other.

"They are well trained to that bell aren't they?" Noah chuckled.

"Yes, indeed."

~~~~~

"Did you know Nugget Nate is the uncle of the man who owns the general store?" Dunc asked as he ran into the dining room and up to his mother. "Did you know the preacher is a gunsmith and sells guns and bullets? Did you know I could do chores for Mz Almeda and earn cookies or coins?"

"Slow down," Chloe laughed. "I couldn't tell one question from another. First though, go wash up and come help me with the bread baskets." She watched Dunc run to the washroom. The other boys had gone there first so they were filtering out.

"Mama, I'll help with the bread baskets." Lil-Pen tugged on Chloe's skirt.

"I have a special job for you." They went into the kitchen and Chloe handed her four-year-old daughter a stack of cotton napkins. "Will you go place one by every plate, please?"

Lil-Pen's blue eyes lit up. "That is a important job."

"An important job," Chloe corrected. It was Lil-Pen's first chore. At nearly five years old she would have a chore to do every time Chloe's task was bread, rolls, butter, jam and linens at meals. She had decided the move to Stones Creek was a natural time to set her daughter doing the small chores she would be able to handle. Lil-Pen carried the stack carefully as she went into the dining room.

Noah was a gunsmith? She had heard that as Dunc fired questions at her. What did that mean? She could understand him being a preacher. Even as young as he was when she'd been kidnapped Noah was more spiritually minded than many adults.

What confused her was the firearm aspect of his life. The only thing their father had used a gun for was hunting and killing varmints that came around the house and barn.

"Ma."

Chloe turned around and looked at the hands Dunc held out to her, turning them so she could see both sides. At her nod Dunc picked up the baskets of sliced bread and carried them into the other room.

"Are you all right?" Blanche asked. She was putting mashed potatoes in several serving bowls.

"Uh? Oh, yes. Just thinking about something Dunc told me. Here, let me take those." Chloe picked up two heaping bowls of potatoes and escaped to the other room before Blanche could ask anything else. She needed to think about this revelation about her brother.

CHAPTER FIVE

Sunday morning found Chloe's stomach knotted. She was terrified the pastor would look at her and recognize who she was. She'd spent some time studying her reflection in the mirror on the wall in her room trying to determine if she resembled her parents at all. The black haired woman gazing back at her was tall and thin. Dark brown eyes in a heart shaped face spoke of sadness and hardships in her past.

After breakfast everyone went up to change into their best clothes. The new dresses for Lil-Pen and Susan were finished thanks to the help of Myra's sewing skills. Everyone met in the dining room, the only room large enough to hold all the women and their children.

Blanche raised her hand and the chatter quieted. "There are, no doubt, some people who don't want us here. They will think we are not as good as they are. We know better, don't we? Our Lord Jesus died for us just as he did for them. The Bible says that all have sinned and turned away. We know where we come from. We have been blessed to have the opportunity to begin new lives here in Stones Creek."

Blanche looked each child in the eye, lingering longer on the boys. "We need to all be on our best behavior. We need to be quiet, respectful and listen to the sermon. We will meet many people today who don't live in town. We want to make very positive impressions. Doing so will make it so much easier to be accepted here in Stones Creek. Now, do we have everything? Okay, let's go." With those words they trooped out of the house and headed to the church.

<center>~~~~~</center>

"I don't think it was a good idea to build that Sanctuary House and let those women come." Traci Fugard sniffed, lifting her nose just a bit higher.

"I agree. We have enough loose women in town at the saloon." Jeanne Brook nodded her head. "Look, here they come, looking all pious. My, what a lot of children."

"I suppose that is to be expected."

McIlroy, who had been standing behind and to the right of the two women, looked at the Sanctuary House occupants walking toward them. He thought they looked just like any other group of people. They were clean and the children were all well behaved. He swallowed the ache in his throat.

He saw the Steeles and Vernie Preston who was carrying Dottie, coming behind the group. He walked forward to greet them.

"Morning, Doc, Leah, Vernie. How's the little one?" He smiled at the baby who grinned toothlessly at him.

"Just fine," Vernie grinned.

McIlroy leaned in. "The missus Fugard and Brook have been expressing their displeasure at the newcomers to Stones Creek."

"I hope they don't make a scene. They seem to be very nice women. Noah told me several of the boys came into his shop the other day and were quite well behaved." Vernie went on to tell of how they had run out as soon as they heard the bell ringing.

Just then the bell in the steeple began chiming and the various groups of people visiting in the church yard began filtering into the building.

Chloe took a deep breath and let it out slowly as she climbed the few steps and walked through the door. She was holding Lil-Pen's hand with Duncan following behind. Her stomach knotted tighter than ever. The tension in her shoulders caused an ache in her back.

The interior of the church was whitewashed with a waxed pine wood floor. A number of rows of pews began in the front. Behind them were rough benches. Three sets of windows on each side lit the space. Being open, they also provided a welcome breath of air on the warm July day.

Esther, who had entered first, led the way to a row of benches about half way back behind the pews. The rest followed, filling that row and the next. Each child sat next to their mother or siblings.

Chloe noticed that Duncan and Ozzie had managed to sit next to each other. She tapped his leg. When he turned to her she gave him a look that promised retribution if needed. Lil-Pen and Susan were sitting between Chloe and Cora holding hands. Even though Susan was two years younger they liked each other and played fairly well together.

"Welcome to the house of the Lord." Noah's voice rose above the low murmurs causing silence to fall on the congregation. "Please rise. We will open today's service with 'Just As I Am Without One Plea.'"

Someone with a pure sweet soprano voice began singing. Soon the rest of the congregation joined in. The church had piano or organ leaving the voices alone to lift the hymn to God.

Chloe watched Noah lead worship. She marveled at his ease as he prayed, made a few announcements then stepped to the pulpit and began to preach.

~~~~~

Noah looked over his congregation seeing several disapproving expressions. He knew the arrival of the women from Sanctuary Place would bring out the critical spirits. He'd planned for that with the Scriptures he was using for his message.

"Today I want to talk about sin. The sin that separates us from God. Our Scripture for today is Romans 2:23-24. *For all have sinned and fall short of the glory of God, and are justified by his grace as a gift, through the redemption that is in Christ Jesus.*

"So just what does this Scripture mean?" Noah looked over the congregation. "It means that everyone one of us, including me and each of you, have sinned. We have all done what God doesn't want us to do. That's what sin is. Doing what God disapproves of. There has only been, and will only be, one person who never sinned. That person is our Lord Jesus Christ.

"Some people think different levels or seriousness of sin exist. That's not correct. In the eyes of God sin is sin. Remember that

He tells us in Isaiah 64:6 "*For we are all become as one who is unclean, and all our righteousness are as a polluted garment: and we all do fade as a leaf; and our iniquities, like the wind, take us away.*

"Whatever you think someone else does or did is just the same in His eyes as what you have done. He sees no difference.

"The consequences can be vastly different. Here, in this life, some of our sin results in harsher consequences than others. When we make the choice to sin we choose those consequences. They can also spill over into other people's lives.

"The choices we make, whether good or bad, impact others and can result in benefit or harm for more than just us. I've known a number of cases where someone sinning has hurt not only themselves but their families and others as well.

"Let's take gossiping, for example. We've seen in our community how that can damage a person's reputation. Make the rest of the community look at them in a bad light. It doesn't just effect the person gossiped about and ruin their reputation. It also effects the reputation of the person doing the gossiping.

"When you get a reputation as a gossip monger, people tend to avoid you. They make sure you don't know their business. They might refuse to talk with you or not invite you to something they are hosting. Which leads to damage to your reputation in town as well as loneliness.

"We need to remember that Jesus went to the cross for each and every one of us. He is the judge, not us. He is the one who is perfect, not us. He is the only way back into relationship with God that we broke with our sin. He paid the price. Anyone who has accepted the gift of his payment for our sin is redeemed and no longer guilty.

"If you look at others as guilty of sins God has already forgiven them for, then you are pretending you don't sin and are placing yourself above God. That is sin. Original sin. Thinking you are god or your ideas and thoughts and actions are perfect. You cannot be. I cannot be. No one but Jesus can be. That's why we need Him.

"So, look to yourself for the actions you need forgiveness for. Don't look at others. They and their actions aren't for your thoughts. You, your choices and your relationship with God and

Christ are.

"Remember, all have sinned and fall short of the glory, but Christ came and paid the price for all sin for all people for all time. Perhaps what we need to do is offer grace and mercy to those we think are sinners just as our Lord Jesus Christ did for us."

CHAPTER SIX

Chloe and Blanche walked along the front of the building looking in the window. The large room was empty all the way to the back wall. Light entered through windows on the left and back walls as well as the large display windows they were peering through.

"What do you think? The space could be divided into two rooms fairly easily, couldn't it?" Chloe pulled her hand down from where it had been shading her eyes as she'd pressed against the glass.

"I think so. Just a wall with a door and maybe a window to pass plates through." Blanche kept studying the space. "We'll have to talk with that banker though about how to borrow money to purchase what we need."

"How much do you think a stove, sink, cooking equipment and tables and chairs would cost? We don't have much money to start with."

"I don't know."

"Morning, Mz Chloe, Mz Blanche." Almeda's greeting had both ladies turning toward the bakery where she stood.

"Morning, Mz Almeda," Chloe said with a smile.

"Oh, lands, you ain't needing to Mz Almeda me."

Chloe chuckled. "Then you don't need to Mz Chloe me."

"Nor me," said Blanche. "In fact, you might be able to help us with some information." Blanche walked over and linked arms with Almeda then entered the bakery with her. Chloe followed.

There was a small table near the window and Blanche steered

Almeda to the chair and had her sit. She took the other one and Chloe pulled one from the end of the counter. Soon they were seated around the small table. Almeda was looking nervously from one to the other.

"You've got a wonderful little business going here. Chloe and I are interested in starting one ourselves. Unfortunately, we really don't know anything about doing that. Would you be willing to help us with how you got started?"

"What kind of business are you talking about?" Almeda's tone was cautious.

"We're thinking about a cafe. We don't want to compete with you so we've talked about buying your breads and desserts, but those are just details for later. We need to learn how to get financed and what some of the cost of things would be."

"Like a stove, sink, pots, pans, etc. You've done so already. How did you get the money to open?" Chloe asked.

"That new banker, Mr. Ritter, done invested in the bakery. He bought the stove and had the wall and counter built. He gets a portion of sales and I pay him back for the costs so eventually I'll own the bakery."

They continued to talk about getting financing and what was needed to start a cafe. They were often interrupted by customers coming in to purchase or order the baked goods Almeda offered.

Most were men who wanted the pastries and cookies displayed in the window and glass-fronted case. Often they were cowboys in town for supplies needed on the ranches where they worked. All looked at Blanche and Chloe with interest and eyes filled with a different kind of hunger. Soon there were several men in the shop with a number more loitering outside on the boardwalk.

"That's enough, boys. Leave the ladies alone. If you're interested in courting you know who you have to discuss it with before you approach them." Noah Preston's voice had the men finishing their purchases and scattering from the bakery.

Chloe started at the sound of his voice though she'd been uncomfortable being stared at by so many men. It had been a long time since she'd been looked at in such a manner. She hadn't missed it at all. She knew what they wanted.

Filled with insecurity, one thing Chloe knew for certain. Never again would she be used by a man for his purposes. She had value now. She was one of God's daughters and He had loved her enough to die for her.

Marriage would be the only way Chloe would ever be in a bed with a man again and that man had to be worthy of her.

She understood her worth now. Was sure she had been washed clean of the sin of the life thrust upon her at the age of ten. Those years were over. Stones Creek was offering her the chance for a life as an upstanding citizen and possibly a good, honorable husband who would treat her right.

Still, Noah's voice stabbed her heart. Shame coursed through her. As Noah entered the shop Chloe's lungs seized and she could barely breathe. She looked down at the table hoping her bonnet brim shielded her face from his view.

Chloe wasn't sure if she resembled her parents or not but didn't want to take the chance the pastor might make the connection. She had to look at him some to keep him from being suspicion of her actions.

"Sorry about that, Almeda, ladies. I noticed what they were looking at and figured out why they were standing around. I'll keep an eye out and break up such gatherings sooner."

"Thank you, Pastor," Blanche said. "I suppose we'll become used to it. Or it will fade as marriages occur."

"Don't hurry yourselves to avoid such. We want you to find the best match for you and your children."

Chloe tried to smile at Noah but it must have appeared forced as he gave her a quizzical look. She wanted to say something but couldn't force words from her lips.

"Blanche and Chloe's thinking of opening a cafe next door and we was talking about how to go about it." Almeda had finished handing a small sack to a cowboy and come back to the table.

"A cafe. That'd be a good addition to the town. Hotel's the only place to buy a meal but a bit expensive." Noah paused and was obviously thinking. "Almeda, what are you going to do once the baby gets older and begins moving around? How will you manage the bakery?"

"I been thinking on that but haven't come up with a plan. I

just place the basket in the corner right now and he stays put. Won't last much longer doing so."

"If you don't mind my input on your discussion…" Noah left the thought hanging.

"Go ahead." Blanche waved a hand in encouragement. "We're just getting started with planning."

"What about cutting a doorway between the bakery and cafe? You'd be able to help and cover for each other as needed. Massot owns the building and would be happy to do any remodeling needed."

"Massot happy? I'll believe that when I see it," Almeda groused. "Might be able to save on your costs, too, using my stove for the cooking. Kitchen is really more than I need. Might be needing to expand later though."

Chloe was flabbergasted. "You'd open your kitchen for us to cook for our cafe? Wouldn't that be too inconvenient for you?"

"I'm seeing God's hand in this. How was I going to tend the baby and keep up with my baking and all? You ladies coming in today is an answer to prayer. That is… if you don't mind partnering with me? Maybe we could just have the cafe and bakery as one."

The doubt in Almeda's voice was evident. Chloe heard the fear of rejection because of her skin color in the other woman's voice.

Blanche reached over and hugged Almeda. "I, for one, would love to partner with you. We all have children who need care, and have other chores to tend to. Having one more person to share the load with will make it all the lighter. Right, Chloe?"

Chloe smiled and grabbed the dark hand resting on the table. "Of course it's fine with me. Blanche and I were talking this morning as we did the breakfast dishes how much work this was all going to be, the cafe, Sanctuary House, the children. Joining forces with you makes the plan that much stronger. A cord of three strands can't be broken and we'll have four. You, Blanche, me and God."

Almeda's eyes filled with tears.

"Now don't you go crying or you'll have us all bawling like babies." There was general sniffing and eye wiping from the three ladies, then Blanche cleared her throat. "I'm thinking we need to talk with that banker and Massot, and get this show on the road."

"Ladies, before I take my leave and let you discuss the business, let's take a minute and pray for your new venture," Noah said.

After he left, Chloe tapped her fingers on the table as she thought. "Blanche, do you think Ruth might be interested in having one more child to watch?" She looked at Almeda and explained. "Ruth's job is going to be watching the children while the rest of us work at other things. You don't need Abe away from you at the bakery now, but soon you will. Ruth could probably use the extra income and Abe would be safe and cared for while you were working."

"That's a good idea, Chloe," Blanche said. "How about you come to the House after you close today and speak with her? We'll talk with her ahead so she knows you're coming."

"Thank you for thinking of this. I'd a never thought to ask a white woman to tend my child."

"Ruth loves babies. I think she'd want to take care of him if he was purple with green polka dots." All three ladies laughed.

CHAPTER SEVEN

Myra paced back and forth in front of the dress shop nervously. She didn't know Leah Steele much at all, just from when they had arrived in Stones Creek and that evening when she, Dr. Steele and Pastor Preston had come to visit. She'd seen the couple at church the past Sunday but only greeted them in passing.

Over the last few days Myra had vacillated on whether to approach Leah or not about working at her dress shop. Myra knew she had to do something to support herself. The thirty dollars wouldn't keep her and Troy forever. She didn't want to become desperate and marry some man who might abuse her. She'd had enough of that from thugs of the madame who owned the brothel she'd run away from.

Ending up in the brothel hadn't been what Myra planned when she'd left the Tennessee home at age seventeen with the boy who promised to marry her when they got to the county seat. After taking her virginity and abandoning her, Myra had little choice but to sell her body to survive. She wasn't going to do that again.

Nugget Nate had found her a couple of years later, pregnant and homeless after she'd run away when the madame tried to force Myra into an abortion. Troy, now five, was born at Sanctuary Place. Myra desperately wanted a safe, stable and secure relationship.

Still trying to put together what she would say to convince Leah Steele to hire her in the dress shop, Myra pivoted to pace back toward the general store that occupied the same block. Looking up stopped Myra in her tracks.

Leaning against the corner of the building was Sheriff Newt Riverby. Tall, rugged, star badge pinned to his vest gleaming in the sunlight, one jeans-covered leg bent, boot toe against the boardwalk, the sheriff raised his eyebrows causing the Stetson to lift as if questioning her reason for being in front of the dress shop.

Spurred into action Myra grabbed the door knob and entered. The bell on the door jangled causing Myra to jump, adding to her discomfiture.

"Coming."

Myra recognized Leah Steele's voice echoing from the back of the shop. She twisted her hands together, her palms sweating into her gloves. Quietly she closed the door then stepped more into the center of the room.

Shelves against the wall held several bolts of fabric. A rod held a couple of dresses along with men's white shirts and buckskin vests. There was a model with sort of loose legged pants. Myra wasn't sure who would wear them. Men preferred tighter legged britches. Women wore skirts.

"Oh, hello. You're Miss Hope, aren't you?" Leah said as she came through the drape dividing the front room from the rest. "Welcome. What can I do for you?"

Myra opened and closed her mouth. Cleared her throat and opened and closed her mouth again. She'd never asked anyone for a real job before. The Creep, as she called the madame, had offered her food and a place to stay when she'd found her huddled in the doorway in the rain.

She had done day work cleaning or weeding after she'd run away from the brothel. Nate had found her seven months pregnant trying to haul bags of feed from a shed to load onto wagons for a lazy mill owner. He had loaded up the wagon then given the man 'what fer' for having a 'little slip of an expecteratin' woman doin' work he should o' been doin' hisself.'

"Afternoon, Mrs. Steele. Call me Myra. Ain't no need fer the miss. I'm, uh. I got some…" Myra cleared her throat again and started over, rushing the words past her lips. "I got some talent with a needle and was wonderin' iffen you'd be a willin' to hire me to do some sewing fer ya?" She rubbed her gloved hand across her forehead wiping the few beads of nervous sweat away.

Leah looked at her silently causing Myra's stomach to clench. There must not be work for her. Now what would she do? Sewing was the only thing she did well. Her only skill. Myra's shoulders slumped. "I understand. I'll get out of your hair now." She turned to go.

"Wait. No. I just was thinking how you are an answer to prayer. Come, let's go back to the workroom. I have seating there and we can talk." Leah pulled the drape back and made a sweeping motion with her arm.

Tears filled Myra's eyes. She hastily blinked them away as she walked past Leah heading to the back of the shop. Soon they were sitting at the tall work table with cups of tea.

"So you know how to sew? Do you do fancy work or just basic?" Leah asked.

"I can do just about any handwork. I made them dresses Susan and Lil-Pen was wearin' at service Sunday. Cora and Chloe got the fabric at the general store. Worked them up real quick like."

"I noticed they had matching outfits. Looked like they fit well."

The conversation continued with Leah quizzing Myra on her sewing skills. Soon they were laughing about different failures each had created over the years.

"I must say, you seem to be God sent," Leah said. "I'm busier than I had ever intended to be with sewing for not only women but men. I'm also going to be busier and unable to work for a while in about six months. You being here will enable the shop to stay open."

Myra realized this was Leah's way of telling her she was expecting a baby. Many women were reticent about speaking of such a delicate issue.

She smiled. "Congratulations. I got a little boy, Troy, who's just about five. Ya ain't gotta worry none about him being underfoot. Ruth, she's gonna be a watchin' the children whilst the rest of us work at jobs in town. We's gonna pay her a wage so she don't gotta find work."

"That's a good arrangement. How many children are there between all you ladies?"

"Eleven. Blanche's got four but Esther an' Birdie ain't got none. Esther can't. Birdie got lucky that Nate found her afore some man made her a whore. She got kicked outta her family when she was eleven cause they was too many kids and she weren't a boy. That's prime age fer gettin' into the business."

Myra saw Leah's discomfort and quickly apologized. "Sorry. With our backgrounds we tend ta talk perty plain. I forget and run my mouth sometimes."

"Don't worry about it, but that's all behind you now. Some of the ladies in the area would take exception to the topic. Let's get the details of your employment all worked out. How about you start next Monday?"

~~~~~

Myra was excited as she closed the door to the dress shop behind her. She was going to be sewing for a living. How could anything be better? Honest work. Even the possibility of moving into the apartment above the shop when Leah and Doc Eli got their house built.

"You think you have enough money to hire Leah to make dresses for you?" The deep voice of Sheriff Riverby broke into her delightful thoughts.

"Pardon me?" Myra looked up. Being short she was used to that but Riverby was taller than most men. And he was standing just a bit too close making her feel even smaller.

"Can you afford to have clothes made? Didn't Nate supply you with enough clothing that you don't need new dresses?" Disapproval was thick in his voice.

"I weren't orderin' a dress. I was gettin' hired to make 'em for others. I'm gonna do sewin' for Miss Leah. Not that it be any of yer business. Now iffen ya'll excuse me, I got things to tend to." Myra turned on her heel, sweeping her skirt indicating her irritation with the man. She stomped along the boardwalk and down the steps, turning between the buildings heading back to Sanctuary House.

CHAPTER EIGHT

Laura Duffle pinned the last of the laundry to the clothesline strung in the narrow yard behind Sanctuary House and eyed the building across the way. The alley separated it from the building that faced the main street of Stones Creek. The pastor's gun shop, the barber shop with its bath house, the bakery and a soon-to-open cafe filled the building. The second story was divided into apartments. She knew the barber lived in the one above his shop. The others were unfinished as Massot was busy building houses.

Laura was a widow who had two small children and no prospects when her husband died. She'd moved from Illinois to Sanctuary Place to have a safe place to raise her two boys. During the six years she'd lived there Laura had been in charge of the laundry. It was what she knew.

Knowing the goal was to have the women become self-sufficient so they wouldn't have to quickly marry just any man, Laura hoped to start a laundry service in Stones Creek. Now she just had to work up the courage to speak with the barber. He was key to her gaining clientele.

"Mark," Laura said. "You go and let Ruth know I'm heading over to talk with the barber, please, and you be a good man for me." Ruth had taken the job of watching the children so the other women could find work. Each of the women would pay her once they were earning wages. At the moment, they did more of the chores of the house since Ruth was watching the children.

The older boys tended to disappear as soon as their daily assigned duties were finished. They'd show up at noon to eat, then disappear again. So long as they weren't getting into trouble the mothers had decided to give them a few weeks of freedom to learn about their new home.

Her Mark was seven, too young to go with the older boys but too big to play with those who were younger. The only other child his age was Nancy Basking who liked to play with dolls. Laura hoped to find a boy closer to Mark's age who lived in town. This being just the second week the possibility was still there.

As Mark ran around the side of the house heading for the front yard, Laura untied her apron and flipped it over the clothesline. She tidied herself in front of the small wall mirror in the bathing room then practiced the short speech she planned to make to the barber.

She just wished she could remember his name. Laura was terrible with names. She was lucky she remembered all the names of those she had moved to Stones Creek with. Hopefully the man's last name was written on the sign for the barber shop.

Laura pinned her straw hat onto her head and left through the back door. She hurried down the alley and around to Main Street and up onto the boardwalk. The chair outside the barber shop was empty allowing Laura to check the sign.

Rats. It just read Barber and Bathhouse. No name. Now what should she do? Laura didn't want to talk to him without knowing who he was but didn't want to ask him either. It was so embarrassing.

"You just loitering, Laura, or do you want to come in for a chat?" Chloe's amused voice startled her from her musings.

"Oh, I'd forgotten you were working to get the cafe going." Laura followed Chloe back into the bakery. "Show me what you're doing."

Between Chloe, Blanche and Almeda she got the lowdown on the modifications Massot was making to the building. A large archway had been cut between the bakery and cafe spaces. The kitchen was being expanded with another stove having been ordered. Once the construction work was finished several tables and chairs would be moved in. Everything was used or repaired but the ladies didn't care. It was new to them and would serve the purpose well.

"We're working on our menu now. We'll have regular offerings and a daily special. Right now we plan to be open for breakfast and dinner. Or maybe dinner and supper. We can't quite decide. We think two meals a day is what we can manage at least for the start. What do you think?" Blanche asked.

"Hum. I'm not sure. Don't most people eat at home for breakfast then come to town?"

The three ladies looked at each other. "I suppose so," said Almeda. "But I have a lot of orders for early morning donuts."

"That's true. That's men heading out to work?" Chloe asked.

"Probably. Most of the men take either half or a dozen. Do you think they'd eat breakfast in the cafe if it were open?"

They heard the door of the barber shop open and close with a bang. "I need to go. I'm wanting to start a laundry and thought I'd ask the barber to pass the word. I don't think he has a client now so maybe it's a good time."

Chloe took hold of Laura's hand and gave it a small squeeze. "We'll pray he's willing to help."

"Thanks." Laura turned to go, then turned back. Her cheeks blushed. "What's his name, Almeda? I can't remember."

"Hank Johnson. He's a nice man. Single." Almeda grinned broadly.

Laura's cheeks turned more red. "I'm just wanting to start my laundry service, not find a man." Then she chuckled a bit. "At least, not yet."

All the ladies laughed as Laura, with a sweep of her skirt, made a grand exit.

~~~~~

Hank leaned back in his chair, resting it against the front of the building and tipped his hat over his eyes. He loved being a barber. It and the bathhouse made good money and he had time during the day to relax. Besides, the conversations kept him up on all the local news. Not that he was a gossip, but it suited him to be in the know about almost everything that went along in Stones Creek. He'd been one of the first to learn when the ladies of Sanctuary House were going to be arriving.

Hank wouldn't mind courting one or more of the ladies, but the men of the area had been warned that no suiters would be allowed for at least a month. The ladies needed time to settle in. He'd noticed them at church last Sunday and met a few of the boys. That was one drawback. They nearly all had children, as far as he could tell.

Footsteps, not male footsteps, approached and stopped. Hank waited for them to resume and pass by. They didn't. What would a woman want with him?

"Excuse me, Mr. Johnson. Might I have a moment of your time?"

The voice was definitely female. Hank lifted his hat as he settled the chair back onto its legs. Deciding he needed to be polite he stood. "Ma'am. What can I help you with?"

The young woman was just about average in height with ash brown hair pinned up under her straw hat. A few strands were escaping. Since he hadn't seen her before he figured she was one of the new ladies living in Sanctuary House. She wasn't overly slim which probably indicated she was one with children. There was both determination and hesitancy in her brown eyes.

"My name's Laura Duffle and I'm new in town. I'm looking to start up a laundry here in Stones Creek. Since mostly men will need my services and your customers are mostly men I was wondering if you'd be so kind as to spread the word. I'm experienced at doing laundry for hire and pretty fast. I'd be much obliged to you. If you'd help me."

Hank suppressed a chuckle. The words had tumbled out of her mouth so quickly he'd had to listen carefully to catch them all. "I'd be happy to help you, Miss Duffle."

"Actually, it's Mrs. Duffle. I'm widowed."

That surprised Hank. He'd thought all the ladies who had moved into Sanctuary House were from rather notorious backgrounds.

"Can you give me a few more details about your business? How much you charge? The time it will take for you to finish? Where you plan to do the work?"

"Oh, I hadn't thought about how much to charge. What do

you think?" The totally puzzled look on her face made Hank smile. Mrs. Duffle might know laundry but she didn't seem to understand much about business.

"I thought you said you'd done laundry for hire before. What did you charge then?"

"Well, um. I may have fudged that a bit. I did do laundry for other people, but it was more a barter type arrangement. At Sanctuary Place we traded labor or labor for items. I've never actually charged money for my work. What do you think would be a fair price?"

The trusting look on her face as she asked the question caught Hank off guard and his heart gave a sudden squeeze. His pondering of the topic a few minutes before took on more seriousness in his mind. Maybe he'd just get to know Mrs. Duffle a bit more. Maybe he could get the jump on the other men by helping her.

"How's about I bring out another chair and we can discuss your venture in comfort?"

"That'd be just fine, Mr. Johnson." The smile that lit up her face did the same to his heart.

~~~~~

"I must say, Mr. Johnson really helped me figure out all I needed to think about to start my laundry. He's going to be my first customer, too." Laura was so excited she was bouncing as she told about her afternoon later that evening at supper. "That way he can give recommendations. I'm going to do his first batch for free. That will pay for the sign I'm going to make for his window and his word of mouth advertising. He told me he knows several men in town who will most likely be interested in my doing their laundry. I'm going to do Mr. Johnson's tomorrow. I need to go to the store and buy my own laundry soap. I don't want to use the house soap."

"We're so happy for you," Blanche said. "It looks like several of us have already figured out ways to make a living."

"I don't want to spoil your plans but what are you going to do for wood to heat your water? You can't expect to use the house wood." This came from Ester Fuller.

"Oh, I hadn't thought of that. Thank you for thinking about

it. No, I don't want to use it. I'll have to pay for someone to chop wood for me." Laura was at a loss.

"It might be a good job for some boys to make some money," Chloe said. She was looking straight at Dunc as she spoke. Even though he was a couple of tables away he seemed to realize his mother was speaking about him since he looked over at her.

Blanche looked at her boys, too. "I think you're right. We can talk about it after supper."

Laura wondered if she was charging enough to cover her expenses as well as make some profit. She'd go and talk it over with Mr. Johnson in the morning when she picked up his clothing.

CHAPTER NINE

Blanche wiped down the table set in front of the window. They were opening tomorrow morning. The Creek Cafe. Breakfast and lunch would be served with the cafe and bakery closing at two in the afternoon. The menu wasn't huge but was filled with meals hungry cowboys would enjoy.

Ruth had agreed to watch Abe for Almeda. He stayed at the cafe/bakery sleeping until after the mothers and children of the House had breakfast. Then she would come for the baby. When he needed to be nursed Ruth or one of the other children came across the alley to tell Almeda. She'd then go to the House and nurse him.

Blanche looked out the window and saw a man on crutches moving slowly along the boardwalk in front of the hotel. Something about his slightly hunched form seemed familiar. That was silly. She hadn't met anyone who was missing his lower leg. Poor man. He must have lost it during the war. So many did.

Pastor Preston and Doc Steele were walking toward the man. They greeted him but were rebuffed, it appeared to Blanche. They stepped aside and allowed him to pass. Blanche watched Doc shake his head and walk away, shoulders slumped. He seemed dejected.

"Blanche, are you finished in there?" Chloe called from the pass through window.

"Yes, everything is wiped down and ready to go. I'm so excited. We're actually opening tomorrow. Between the three of us we should be able to balance the work load here and at home."

Almeda, Chloe and Blanche split the work into shifts with Almeda coming in earliest to start the breads and doughnuts rising. Blanche would then arrive and begin breakfast with Chloe coming in after she helped at Sanctuary House with breakfast, chores and children. Almeda left just after one and Chloe finishing up by doing any preparation for the next day after she and Blanche cleaned up after they closed at two.

"Do you think I need to come in early tomorrow just in case we are too busy, it being the first day and all?" Chloe asked as she folded napkins.

"Might be good, if you can. I'm hoping we have a crowd." Blanche smiled. "Several people said they were planning on coming to try us out tomorrow. I hope they plan to come for lunch rather than breakfast. We'll have the stew and meatloaves already cooked in large batches. Breakfast is more individual meals."

"I'll send Dunc over as soon as he gets up to see if you need me. I'm sure I can find someone to cover for my chores." Chloe set the stack of napkins on the shelf by the serving window.

They had done everything they could think of to prepare for the next day. The vegetables for the stew were cut and in the pot they would cook in. The meat was cut up and in a bowl in the ice box, as were slices of ham, bacon and the ground meat for the meatloaves. Potatoes were sliced for frying and cabbage waited to be shredded in the morning for slaw. Almeda would be making bread and rolls in the morning as well a cake and a couple of pies. They had made and rolled out the dough ready to fill.

Blanche let out a big breath. "I think we're as ready as we can be. I wish Almeda was here. I think we need to pray."

"I know what you mean. Let's you and I pray now then you and she can pray before you start in the morning." Chloe took Blanche's hand. They bowed their heads and thanked the Lord for the opportunity He had given them. The took care to ask for His guidance and support in their venture.

~~~~~

"My, we've served a mess of men this morning," Almeda said as she plopped into a chair by the kitchen work table. "I need me a break before we start on lunch."

"Let me pour you a cup of coffee." Chloe patted the black woman on the shoulder as she passed by, reaching for the coffee pot. "You sit too, Blanche. I'll fix you two something to eat then start the slaw. I'll put the vegetables in the stew, too."

"I must say my feet do hurt. I've been on them since four o'clock." Blanche slowly lowered herself into a chair and reached over to squeeze Almeda's hand. "I'm so glad we partnered with you. I'm not sure the two of us could have done this without you."

"You'd a managed, but I'm glad, too. It's more fun cooking and baking with others. I must say. I hated being a slave, but there were always others around you could talk to whilst you worked. I didn't realize I missed that when I started the bakery."

"Now you own part of a bakery and cafe. Pretty far from being a slave." Chloe grinned as she set the coffee cups on the table.

Almeda smiled. "Yes, tis at that."

The front door opened and a strange thumping sounded. Almeda and Blanche had half risen to look through the pass-through window and saw a man on crutches entering the cafe. Blanche sat back down her hands coming up to cover her face. "No, no, no. It can't be. No, no, no."

Chloe and Almeda looked at her.

"I'll go take his order," Chloe said. She patted Blanche on the shoulder as she passed. "You stay here. It'll be okay."

Chloe wiped her hands on a towel, then walked into the dining room. The man was sitting at the table nearest to the door with his back to the rest of the room. He had on a dark suit and his crutches were leaning against a chair. She noticed that his lower leg and foot were missing.

When she came to face him she noted his scowl. His face looked vaguely familiar. His hair was dark salt and pepper but his eyes were what she took notice of. They were amber, such an unusual color. Chloe couldn't think off hand who had amber eyes, but there was at least one person she had met with them.

"Good morning. What can I get you?" Chloe smiled hoping she wasn't staring at him.

"Coffee. Eggs, over easy, ham steak, toast." He didn't look at her just continued gazing out the window.

"Would you like fried potatoes as well?"

"If I'd wanted fried potatoes I'd have said so." His growled words had Chloe stepping back.

"Okay, I'll bring your coffee right away." She fled back to the kitchen. "My, what a grouch," she muttered to Almeda and Blanche. Almeda was already at the stove placing a ham steak in a skillet.

Once she'd served the man's coffee Chloe helped Almeda prepare the rest of the meal and took it out to him. Then she came back and sat next to Blanche who was as white as her name suggested. Tears were flooding her eyes and she just kept whispering, "No, no, no."

Not wanting to start the conversation that was needed while he was in the cafe, Chloe simply sat beside her friend holding her hand for comfort. Shortly, she went to the man so he could pay for his breakfast and help him with the door as he left. His growled thank you didn't imply sincerity.

Gathering up the dirty dishes, Chloe entered the kitchen and set them on the table. "Blanche, sweetheart, who is that?"

Blanche looked from Chloe to Almeda who was sitting beside her and back. "That's Garfield Steele. He's from back in Ohio. He was my husband's doctor and..." Blanche took a big breath then let it out slowly. "And Nancy and John's father."

"Oh, Blanche. Did you know he was here?" Chloe asked.

"No. I never would have moved here if I'd known."

"He's Doc Steele's father," Almeda said. "He and his wife come out to visit, they did. Let me think. Just about the time Dottie Preston was borned. They was wanting to get Doc Eli to move back to Ohio. He wouldn't go. So they left on the train that exploded. His wife was killed and he lost his foot. Blamed Doc Eli for taking it off.

"He lives in the hotel now. Leah says Doc's sisters might come out to take him back, but they haven't yet."

Blanche brought a shaky hand holding a handkerchief up and wiped her eyes. "It started when Garfield would come to tend my husband, Oswald. He was ill for so long. Garfield was so sweet and kind. He'd come so often and well… He'd comfort me as I fretted over Oswald's illness. One thing led to another. Nancy was born several months after my husband's death. I don't think he knew I was expecting. I never told him.

"Garfield was such a help during those months. He'd bring me supplies, food, coal. It just kept going on. Then I told him I was expecting again. He changed. Became angry. He told me I'd either need him to fix it or leave town. He wasn't going to have a bastard child living in the same town he was."

Chloe realized that since Nancy had been conceived while Oswald Basking was still alive she would be considered his daughter. John, Blanche's five-year-old son didn't have that protection.

"So, I left town. Garfield gave me money to take the children and move. I didn't have a clue where we were going. I just took a train west. Ozzie and Will, who were seven and five at the time, found this fancy rail car and met Nugget Nate and Penny. They helped me get to Sanctuary Place. John was born there." Blanche laid her head on the table. "I so wanted to make a new start. What do I tell the children? Where do we go?"

Chloe and Almeda patted Blanche on the back. Chloe couldn't think what to say. Blanche was her best friend. It wasn't what she'd told them of her past that distressed Chloe. It was that they'd just opened the cafe and the future had looked so bright. What a blow. How could God have let this happen? Why bring Blanche out here to make this new start and have her past show up like this?

Not only was the man the father of two of Blanche's children, but he was dealing with so much loss and grief in his own life. To top it off, Doc Steele was half brother to Nancy and John. Oh my. What a mess.

"Blanche," Chloe took her by the chin and looked straight in her eyes. "Nothing needs to be done this minute. We can keep you out of his path until you decide what needs to be done. Maybe his daughters will come get him before long and you won't need to say anything. Or maybe it'd be better to take this head on. I don't know. I do know who does, though. God. Let's take this to Him and ask for His will. He already knows all the details. We just need to ask how He wants you to proceed."

"That be right, Blanche," Almeda said. "We go to God who has all the answers."

The three ladies clasped hands, bowed their heads and asked for divine guidance.

~~~~~

Two days later, Blanche knocked on Chloe's door. It was after the supper chores were all done and the younger children put down for the night. Chloe opened the door then stepped out into the hall. Lil-Pen was asleep in the room.

"Would you take a walk with me, please?" Blanche asked.

"Of course. Let me tell Ruth that Lil-Pen's asleep."

"John is, too."

Soon the two ladies were walking slowly down the street in front on Sanctuary House toward the train tracks. They wouldn't walk on Main Street as they didn't want to chance Garfield Steele seeing Blanche from the hotel. He'd been in to eat at the cafe one other time, but they'd kept her in the kitchen so he wouldn't see her.

"I've decided I need to speak with Doc Eli. I want to tell him about his siblings. I think he has a right to know."

Chloe kept silent. It wasn't her place to do more than support.

"It won't be easy, confessing my sin to a stranger. It may blow up in my face. He may reject them and me, but if I want to stay in Stones Creek, it's what I need to do. Nancy looks so much like him. I knew Garfield's daughters. Nancy is going to look like them. The same eyes and hair. Doc Eli might be able to help me with Garfield."

"What do you want from Garfield?"

"Nothing really. Just to leave us alone and let us live a normal life. I don't want money or a relationship, especially if he's bitter and resentful of what happened to him."

They had reached the railroad tracks and turned to head back up the street.

"I'll go with you if you want." Chloe knew it would be very difficult for her friend to talk with her lover's son, telling him of siblings he had no clue about, but she would support Blanche in whatever way she could.

"I'd appreciate that."

CHAPTER TEN

Myra sat in the workroom of the dress shop sewing buttons on a jacket. An unexpected knock on the window startled her so badly she pricked her finger. Sticking it into her mouth, she glimpsed a dark haired woman with large brown eyes signaling her to come out. Then the woman ducked down below the sill out of sight.

Not sure what this was about Myra set the jacket down and went out the door, through the back room of the general store, then out into the street behind. The woman stood there, slim with a face painted to attract men.

"May I help you?" Myra asked.

"You're one of those women who come to town lately, right?"

"Yes."

"Can you get me out of town and to that place you come from?"

Myra grabbed the woman by the arm, pulling her into the back room of the store and through to the workroom. "Does Curtis Fain know you're here? What's your name?" Curtis Fain was the saloon owner and managed the brothel upstairs.

"I'm Rosa Lazaro. No, he doesn't and can't. I told them I was going to the store. I can't stay long and have to buy something, maybe some soap."

"I'll see what I can do. You really want out of the life?" Myra knew the desperation of wanting to escape prostitution. She didn't know why or how Rosa got into the business, but would do whatever she could to help her escape. "Do you have any money? Anything that would help with train fare?"

"I've been saving for a long time. I don't know how much a ticket would cost. I'll bring what I have next time I can get away from the saloon."

"Are you able to leave even for a bit. Maybe for some fresh air in the alley behind?"

"Some. Not often. He doesn't let us out of his sight much."

"Which room is yours?"

"Second from the left, back side of the building, second floor."

"See if you can get out next Monday morning, early. Say around seven. I could either meet you in the alley or you could drop it to me from your window. I'll have talked with the other ladies by then and hopefully they'll help. One way or another I'll help you leave town."

Rosa's eyes filled with tears. "Thank you so much. I hate what I'm doing. You ladies are getting a new life. A chance for a normal, decent life. I want that."

"It's more than just a normal life, Rosa. It's a life with God, knowing that Jesus died for my sins and your sins and accepting that. You can have that, too."

"He wouldn't want me."

"That's the best part. He does want you. He loves you. There ain't time to talk about this now. Fain will be looking for you. Just pray. Talk to God about how you want to learn about Him and Jesus. He'll make it happen. He doesn't want anyone to die without Him. That's a promise in the Bible."

Rosa looked skeptical, but nodded. "I have to go."

Myra grabbed a packet of pins. Several were missing as it wasn't brand new. "Here, take this. Save your money for train fare."

Slowly, Rosa took the pins and then hugged Myra. "Thank you. I'll try to be outside next Monday morning about seven. If not I'll be at my window." Then she left, heading out the way they had come into the workroom.

~~~~~

"Can I talk with you ladies?" Myra asked that evening. All eight of the women who'd come to Sanctuary House were gathered in the sitting room. Some were sewing, several were knitting or crocheting. With the number of children something was always needing to be mended. Sweaters, mittens and socks would be needed to keep warm come winter.

Murmurs of agreement bolstered Myra's courage. She was nervous about bringing Rosa's request up, even though she felt positive the ladies would be willing to help.

"I had a visitor at the dress shop today. One of the saloon girls, Rosa Lazaro. She wants out of the life and would like help in getting to Sanctuary Place. I told her I would. Are any of you willing to help her?"

Everyone voiced their support. Questions and ideas were thrown around as to how to help Rosa leave town before Curtis Fain found out one of his girls had run away.

"Seems to me the major problem will be getting the train ticket. If one of us buys it ahead it'll be reported to either the pastor or sheriff," Chloe said.

"Maybe we should talk to one of them about this. They might be willing to help. Maybe even buy the ticket."

Myra grimaced. She'd had a run-in with Sheriff Riverby and really didn't want to involve him. She would if necessary, but would rather avoid him.

"Let me meet and talk with Rosa before we bring either of them into the mix," Myra said. "Do we have any clue how much a train ticket costs?"

The tickets for them to come to Stones Creek had been purchased as a group so none of them had a clue. The conversation then centered around what Rosa would need to take with her and whether she had any proper clothing. The dress Rosa had worn when she met with Myra had been street worthy but rather more revealing than would be acceptable on a train.

~~~~~

Monday dawned dreary with drizzle that threatened to turn into a true rain. Myra wrapped an oil cloth sheet around her shoulders and hurried into the alley behind the saloon. The other side of the alley was composed of the backs of McIlroy's blacksmithery and the jail. Myra prayed Sheriff Riverby didn't frequent the alley as she really didn't want him to spot her chatting with Rosa. Who knew what he'd think and Myra didn't want to find out.

Huddled beside the wood pile was Rosa. Myra ran on tiptoe and crouched beside her. "Is he asleep?" she asked, referring to the saloon owner, Curtis Fain. She kept her voice low not wanting anyone who might be awake in the saloon to overhear their conversation.

"Yes, I think. I can't stay long. Here's the money I've saved." Rosa handed a handkerchief tied around some coins to Myra. "That's all I have."

Myra really had no clue by the weight if the coins would be anywhere near enough. What she was sure of was that she would help Rosa leave Stones Creek. She had been in pretty much the same position as Rosa. Worse actually. At least Rosa wasn't pregnant and being forced into an abortion. Myra was determined to help Rosa have the same second chance she had had.

"Have you got any clothes you can wear on the train? It cain't be anything that'd attract a man's attention. If not, we can help find something or alter something you have. The ladies all want to help."

"You told the other women?" Panic tinged Rosa's words.

"Had to. I cain't do this by myself. We may need help from a man, too. We cain't buy the train ticket. Maybe the preacher or the sheriff."

Rosa frowned but nodded. "I've got a couple of dresses that may work. I'll bring them to you. I'd need to get them to you ahead anyway. No way I can take a suitcase out, even if I had one."

They spoke a few more minutes, setting up the next time they would try to meet, then hugged. Rosa quietly snuck back through the alley door of the saloon leaving Myra hunkered down beside the wood pile.

It was raining in earnest now and she didn't relish the trip back through town to Sanctuary House. She silently repeated her prayer that no one noticed her. As she stood up to leave the clearing of a throat made her jump swinging around to face whoever had made the sound.

"Why don't you and I move into the jailhouse for our discussion, Miss Hope?" Since the voice belonged to Sheriff

Riverby Myra knew God's answer to her prayer had been a resounding, "No."

Following the tall lawman into the building, Myra frantically tried to figure out what to tell him. She decided on the truth. Maybe this was God's way of working out the details of how to buy the needed train ticket. She opened her mouth to begin her explanation when Riverby rounded on her.

"You wanting back in the life?" he snarled. "You come out here claiming to be wanting a fresh start. Possibly marrying a man wanting a fine Christian woman. Then here I find you talking in the back alley with one of the brothel's best. So just what do I tell Pastor Noah and Nugget Nate? Huh? Not even here a month and one of his flock of soiled doves is abandoning the pursuit of purity, heading back into the den of iniquity. What about your son? He's what? Four, five? You going to abandon him or taking him with you into that life?"

Myra's mouth dropped open when he began railing at her. Then, as his words penetrated, her anger rose. Finally, at the mention of her son, her anger turned to fury and she saw red. She stepped up to him, her head barely level with his armpit, and punched him as hard as she could in the stomach. His breath chuffed out but he didn't bend from the blow.

"You listen here, you big oaf. How dare you assume I'm wantin' back in the life? You done thought nothin' but the worst 'bout me since you first seen me. You may be bigger 'an me, smarter an' can talk better, an' have that fancy star on your chest, but you know what?"

Myra poked him in the chest with her index finger. "You know what?" She poked him three more times. "There ain't nothin' in God's green earth, in heaven or hell that's gonna separate me from His love 'cause I gots me a whole heap of Jesus. He rescued me and cleaned up my past, present and future. I'm wrapped up in His arms and nothin' can take me away from Him. I'm sealed."

Myra poked him again. "Sealed. You hear me? You're just as much a sinner as me. All have sinned and fall short God's glory. That means you, too, so don't you be a judging' me especially when," her voice rose until she was nearly yelling at him. "You ain't got no idea what's goin' on." She poked him one more time for good measure then stepped back, turning away from him.

Myra took a deep breath trying to catch hers. It seemed like she never could escape what she'd been before. Christians could be the worst at not accepting that when a body accepted Christ they were new. The old was gone and forgotten. She'd hoped moving to Stones Creek would change the way others looked at her, but obviously, it hadn't. Tears burned in her eyes.

Why couldn't he see her the way she was now? She'd left that life behind over six years ago. She'd accepted that Jesus had paid for her sins. Once for all. Once for all time. Except it wasn't enough for people. She'd never live down her past. She'd never be good enough, clean enough for people, especially the stupid sheriff, to see her as she was now. Forgiven. Living her life like Jesus wanted her to. Okay, she failed some, but didn't everybody?

The feeling of continual failure overwhelmed her. Myra collapsed in a heap on the floor.

~~~~~

Newt Riverby looked at the small young woman curled in a ball sobbing. Shame washed over him like a flash flood wave. 'Judge not lest ye be judged.' The verse pounded in his head as if trying to jump out.

She was right. He was judging her as if she was still working in a brothel. He was one of the men entrusted by Nugget Nate to understand the suffering these women had gone through. To know how much they had overcome in their lives. Entrusted to help them achieved the new, fresh start they all wanted. To make sure that whoever wanted to marry them looked beyond their past to see them for the God honoring women they were now.

Newt knelt beside her. "Miss Hope, Myra. You're right. I'm sorry. I was looking at you not through the eyes of forgiveness but judgement. I hope you can forgive me."

Myra just kept sobbing. The sound of her grief broke his heart. He wanted to help Myra calm down. Hopefully she'd be willing to tell him why she was meeting with Rosa Lazaro.

Bending down, Newt scooped Myra up into his arms and carried her into a cell. She was such a little bit of a thing. He sat down on the cot, placing her next to him. The movement had the desired effect. She gulped, slowly getting control of her emotions. He pulled a bandana handkerchief from his pocket and handed it to her. Taking it, Myra blew her nose that was red and running. Her eyes were red also, rimmed with dark circles.

Newt was unsure what to say but decided to find out if she was willing to open up about Rosa. "Miss Hope, will you please," he figured being polite was a good step, "tell me what you and Rosa were talking about? I can't think why you'd want to meet with her. It colored my thoughts leading to my jumping to poor conclusions."

Myra silently took his measure. He tried not to squirm under her scrutiny and hoped he hadn't alienated her totally.

"Rosa wants out of the life. She wants to go to Sanctuary Place in Iowa. She came to me asking for help. All the ladies want to. Rosa gave me the money she's saved. We don't know how much a train ticket is, but we're gonna help her leave town."

Newt was stunned. He hadn't given a thought to saloon girls wanting out of the life. Here they were just across the alley from him, from help if only they'd seek it out.

"Why didn't she come to me? I'd have helped her, helped any of them get away."

"Right, and that would o' worked so well. You'd a what? Bought a train ticket to someplace and stuck Rosa on it? She ain't even got the right clothes to wear on the train. Rosa would look like what she is and without a safe place to go she'd end up right back making a living on her back."

Chagrinned, Newt realized it was true. He would have only been able to spirit her onto a train and away from Stones Creek. With the ladies of Sanctuary House there was now a connection to a safe, secure destination and support for Rosa's escape without Fain's knowledge.

"You're right. We need to do some planning. Show me see how much money she gave you."

Myra handed over the knotted handkerchief and waited quietly as he counted it.

"There's not quite enough here, but I can make up the rest. If you ladies will make sure she has whatever she needs to take with her, we should be able to get her away within the next couple of weeks."

"You won't be tellin' no one, will you?"

"No, the fewer who know about this the better. You make sure the ladies don't go spreading it around."

"You ain't needin' to be worrying 'bout us spillin' the beans. We know what'd happen to Rosa if Curtis Fain found out afore hand."

CHAPTER ELEVEN

McIlroy pounded the nail a last time. He was working on a side of the school building the town's people were constructing. The goal was to frame and raise the sides of the building during the morning and the roof and siding in the afternoon.

"Would you like a donut and coffee?" It was the voice that caused his chest to ache.

Straightening from his crouch, McIlroy stood and looked at her. "Thank you."

She was tall and thin. Thinner than he thought she should be. Her hair was shiny black, piled up in that way women did. Her oval face framed large dark eyes. So dark he couldn't tell if they were a deep blue or brown. She lifted the tray of donuts urging him to take one.

"McIlroy," Leah's voice broke through his paralysis. "This is Mrs. Chloe Ashburn. She's new in town."

McIlroy wiped his sweaty hand on his britches and carefully picked up one donut between two fingers and his thumb. Leah poured a mug of coffee and handed it to him.

"Pleased to meet you, ma'am." He glanced down at his hands wondering how he could offer one for her to shake. He lifted the coffee mug as a sort of salute.

"Likewise."

McIlroy didn't have a clue what to say so he took a bite of his donut, getting sugar around his mouth and down his shirt. Not able to brush it off because his hands were full, he licked around his mouth.

Chloe cleared her throat and looked at the ground. McIlroy hoped he didn't look as dumb as he felt. It was as if he was sixteen again. This wasn't good. He wasn't interested in her. He'd had a woman before and he didn't think he wanted one again. But she sure was pretty.

"Mama, can I have a donut?" It was a little girl asking. She was cute. Black hair like her mother, but with big bright blue eyes. A tightness came around his heart.

"May I have a donut?" Chloe corrected.

"Okay, may I have one?"

Chloe leaned down so the girl could take one from the tray. "Here you go. Mr. McIlroy, this is my daughter Lil-Pen. Lil-Pen this is Mr. McIlroy."

Lil-Pen gave a small curtsy. "Pleased to make your quaintness."

McIlroy smiled at the pretty little thing. His heart hurt but he kept his smile clear. "Pleased to meet you, too. So you like donuts, huh?"

"Yes sir. Mrs. Almeda makes the bestest donuts."

Several other men came up at the moment. Their intent was donuts and an introduction to the pretty Mrs. Ashburn. McIlroy backed away and turned to look over the crowd milling around the school yard. They'd been working for a couple of hours and were taking a break.

Not only was the day's purpose to raise the school building but also to introduce the ladies living in Sanctuary House to more of the community. That's the way Pastor Preston had explained it anyway. McIlroy took that to mean for the women to meet the men of Stones Creek and the surrounding area.

Everyone knew the reason the women and children were here was to provide wives for the men. This event was a perfect way to begin that process.

McIlroy set his coffee mug down on a pile of boards and brushed the sugar off his shirt. He'd do well to stay away from all the women. Mrs. Chloe Ashburn especially. She reminded him too much of his past. Not that she was similar in looks or physical form, but how that form made him feel.

"Pretty good donuts, huh?" asked Dak Levine, one of the cowboys from the Chasing R Ranch.

"Yeah, they're Almeda's. You don't want to miss them. Coffee's good, too." McIlroy looked around and saw several other cowboys from the ranch.

"Mr. McIlroy, Mama told me to ask if you wanted another donut." Lil-Pen was holding up a plate with several donuts on it. Dak already had one in his hand. The plate was tipped dangerously with the donuts sliding to the edge.

He took one then decided he needed to be more polite. He gently lifted the plate to be more level. "Thank you. So, Lil-Pen, how are you liking Stones Creek?" It was a question he thought she could answer. He figured she was around five years old.

"It's fun. At least, so far. Dunc isn't bothering me much. He sure did when we were on the train. He bossed me around something fierce. Mama finally made him stop."

"Dunc?" McIlroy asked.

"My brother. He's thirteen and thinks he knows everything. That's him over there." She pointed to a skinny youth just on the verge of puberty. He stood with a few other boys who all looked as if they wanted to be doing something like the rest of the men, but didn't know quite how to start.

McIlroy took pity on them. He remembered being too old and too young at the same time. Maybe he could help them out.

"Lil-Pen, how about you go get another plate full of donuts and meet me over where your brother is?"

"Why?"

"Cause those boys need energy for what I'm going to set them to doing."

"Okay."

McIlroy went over to Massot and caught his attention. "Massot, how about we set those boys to laying out the boards for the roof struts?" He tipped his head toward the group. "Gives them something constructive to do, and it's a very important job." The last words were said in an exaggerated manner.

Massot looked over at the boys and rubbed the stubble on his chin. "McIlroy, you're smarter than you look. Come on, you can help me explain their job and help lay out the first one so they understand how to do it."

Lil-Pen and Mrs. Ashburn met him and Massot as they

approached the boys. They handed out the donuts as Massot explained what he wanted done.

McIlroy was impressed with the boys' eagerness to do the job and how they listened carefully to the instructions. Soon the boys were moving the planks into position. They stood watching for a few moments then Lil-Pen pulled on McIlroy's pant leg. He looked down into the upturned face.

"How come you talk funny?"

"Lil-Pen, that's rude. Mr. McIlroy doesn't talk funny. He speaks with an accent. Remember how Uncle Nate speaks with an accent." Mrs. Ashburn's cheeks had turned bright red with embarrassment over her daughter's question.

"Tis fine. Lil-Pen, I come from a different country. I'm from Scotland. I came over to America nye onto fifteen years ago. We speak a wee bit differently over there." McIlroy strengthened his brogue for emphasis.

"I like it. Can you teach me to talk like that?" Lil-Pen was jumping with excitement.

"Well, I ken try, but you'll be a needin' ta ken 'at most will na be understood."

"What did you say?" Lil-Pen looked confused and McIlroy laughed. So did Mrs. Ashburn. Ach, but she was a pretty thing.

"I said I can try to teach you to talk that way but you'll need to understand that people won't be able to understand you."

"Oh." Lil-Pen drooped, dejected. "I don't think I want to learn then. Mama, there's Nancy. Can I go see what she's helping with?"

"Yes, but be sure to mind the other ladies."

"Yes, ma'am."

McIlroy watched the little girl run across the yard. He wasn't sure how to keep the conversation going. He just knew he wanted to.

"Mr. McIlroy, thank you for getting the boys involved. I heard you speak with Massot about giving them a job to do."

"Just McIlroy. No mister. It was no problem, Mrs. Ashburn. They looked like they wanted to help but didn't know how to ask."

"It's just Chloe. You don't need to call me Mrs. Ashburn.

Thank you anyway. The boys are good workers and helpful, but they are boys and tend to fall into mischief if not kept busy."

McIlroy smiled. "Ach, don't I just know it. I was a boy meself once."

Just then there was a shrill whistle. Linc Pierce, foreman of the Chasing R Ranch, stood on an upturned crate and hollered that the brake was over and it was time to get back to work.

"Thank ya for the donuts and coffee, Mrs. Ashburn. They were mighty good."

"You're welcome. I'll tell Almeda and Blanche. She made the coffee. I just served."

McIlroy's gaze followed Chloe's slim form as she walked away. Sensations he hadn't had in years began slipping through his mind and body. He shuddered to shake them off. He didn't want desire again. Didn't want the chance for the pain and guilt.

"She's a lovely lady, isn't she?" Doc Eli had come to walk with McIlroy back to their work area.

"She is at that, but she's not for me. I'm not in the market for a wife."

Eli clapped McIlroy on the shoulder. "Neither was I. Then I met Leah."

~~~~~

Blanche and Myra cornered Chloe near the huge cauldron set up to heat water for washing the dishes. She had tried to avoid them but they'd approached from both sides making escape impossible.

"So, is he nice?"

"What did you talk about?"

"Are you interested?"

"Is he interested?"

They fired questions at her one after the other not allowing her to answer. Chloe laughed.

"He's nice. A bit nervous, but nice. Lil-Pen dominated the conversation. She wanted to learn how to speak with a Scottish accent until she found out it was hard to understand."

Blanche and Myra laughed with Chloe.

"He had Massot set the boys to laying out boards in a pattern. I think it has something to do with the roof. It was thoughtful of him."

"Yes, Ozzie came and told us. He was pretty excited at having such an important task."

Chloe dipped hot water from the cauldron into a dishpan and began shaving soap into it. "I noticed Cora speaking to a cowboy and Massot seems to be asking Ruth questions on a fairly regular basis."

Myra giggled. "Yep, I had me a couple of cowboys introduce themselves. This courting thing might be fun for a while. I ain't in a to hurry to get hitched right soon. I got a job making pretty dresses so I can take my time in deciding."

"You're right, Myra," Blanche said. "We need to be in prayer asking for His guidance in choosing a husband. Getting married to the wrong one will not only effect us but our children as well."

"Right. You think all of us ladies need to talk 'bout that?"

"Probably. Might be wise to ask the pastor to come and talk with us. I think several of us may be overly excited with the possibility of a man in their lives. Especially after all the attention today."

Chloe dunked a dish into the water. The conversation had taken an uncomfortable turn. Not about being cautious in choosing a husband. That was most important. No, having Pastor Preston, her long lost brother, come to Sanctuary House to speak with the ladies. The thought that he might recognize her as his sister made her stomach into a hard knot.

CHAPTER TWELVE

Myra entered the sheriff's office biting her lip as she went. She didn't like having to come to the jail, but she needed his help in getting Rosa out of town. Someone needed to purchase the train ticket and none of the Sanctuary House ladies could. The town was small and gossip would have its way.

"Afternoon, Miss Hope. What can I do for you?" Sheriff Riverby asked. He was sitting with his feet on his desk. He moved them to the floor but didn't rise. Just as well since he'd tower over Myra if he did.

"I, er, we need some help in getting Rosa out of town. You said you'd pay for the ticket, but with what she had and what the ladies put together we think we got enough. Trouble is we ain't got a way to purchase it. Cain't be at the last minute 'cause Curtis Fain can see the station from his saloon. He might see Rosa and come after her."

Riverby nodded.

"I, er, we was wondering if you'd be willing to buy the ticket for her." Myra held out the little pouch with the money inside. She was too far away from the desk so took a couple of steps closer.

"When is she wanting to leave?"

"Um, as soon as possible. You be a buyin' the ticket and Rosa will get out of the brothel. Then, when the train's arriving we'll move her to the station and on the train."

"Just how're you planning on doing that?"

Myra was uncomfortable with Riverby's intense scrutiny. His

eyes seemed to pierce through any little bit of confidence she had. "If you can buy the eastbound ticket for a Tuesday. That's Rosa's day off. She can sneak out of the saloon after closing that morning. She'll come to Sanctuary House and we'll hide her until time to catch the train."

"You don't think it would be better for her to hide out here? As sheriff, I can keep her safe."

"Rosa don't trust the law. She was used by lawmen and none tried to help her escape. A couple even told she'd asked. She got a beatin'. No, she won't want to stay here even for a few hours."

Riverby nodded. Myra still held out the pouch. She didn't know why he wouldn't take it.

"How much money is in the pouch?"

Myra named the amount. Rosa had saved for several years to gather almost all the cost. The ladies had added from their earnings from the past few weeks to complete what was needed and supply a bit more so Rosa had a few dollars extra. At least they thought there was enough. They couldn't very well go and ask how much a train ticket to Dubuque, Iowa cost.

Riverby nodded, leaned forward and took the pouch. "We'll plan on next Tuesday, then. I'll purchase it the day before so there's less chance of the agent's slipping up and saying something. I'll warn him not to talk." Riverby grinned. "I can be rather intimidating when I want to be."

"I'll say," Myra murmured. Then she swallowed. Riverby must have heard because his eyebrow lifted. "Well, I think that 'bout covers everything for right now." She took a step back and bumped into a chair causing it to scrape across the wooden floor. She turned around and fled out the door.

~~~~~

Newt Riverby held in his laughter. He really shouldn't be so hard on her. She was such a plucky little thing. He'd been unfair to her and felt guilty for his thoughts and words. Now she was trying to help another woman trapped in the life of a prostitute get out.

Newt had to hand it to her. Myra was brave to attempt this. If Fain figured out what was going on he'd not only beat Rosa, but he might send his thugs after the ladies of Sanctuary House.

Newt went to the stove to pour himself another cup of coffee.

The jailhouse door opened again and Dak Levine walked in. The man wasn't overly tall but was built solid and strong. He had a good reputation as a hand on the Chasing R Ranch. Dak came to church every Sunday and was reputed to be a firm believer in Christ.

"Afternoon Dak, what can I do for you?"

Dak took his Stetson off and circled it around in his hands. "I was wonderin', Sheriff, if you could use a deputy?"

Newt was surprised. Dak seemed satisfied as a ranch hand. "You interested? Stupid question. You wouldn't be asking if you weren't."

"I'm thinking that being a ranch hand doesn't have much possibility for settling down. You know. For having a family." The young man's face turned bright red under his dark brown hair.

Something caught in Newt's chest. "Want a cup of coffee? Have a seat." He took a mug down from a small shelf build above the stove.

"Thanks."

When they were settled in their chairs, blowing on the steaming brew Newt looked at Dak. "You interested in one of the Sanctuary ladies?"

Dak cleared his throat and shifted uneasily in his seat. "Thinkin' I might be."

"Mind if I ask which one?"

"Cora Sepal, she's got Susan who is two. She's taken over the upkeep of the House while the others work. That's how she's earning her keep. She's only nineteen and when she told her parents she was expecting she got kicked out. Nugget Nate found her and took her to Sanctuary Place. Now she's here. She's a real sweet thing. So is Susan."

While Dak babbled on about Cora the tightness in Newt's chest loosened. He'd been so afraid the man would say a different name. The name of the little lady who had so recently left his office. Who would have thought that? Not himself but now that Newt thought about it he was more interested in Myra than any of the other ladies so recently arrived in Stones Creek.

"Well, Sheriff, would there be any possibility of a job?"

"Might just be. I hadn't thought about needing a deputy, but with the town growing having at least one more on the payroll to cover the hours I don't is probably a good idea. Let me talk with some of the others on the council and I'll get back to you. Say on Sunday, after church?"

Dak's whole body shifted with relief. It was obvious the man had it bad for Cora. Not only would Newt be talking with the council about at least one deputy position, he'd also be talking with Pastor Noah about one of the ladies being courted. Or maybe he'd talk to him about two ladies being courted.

~~~~~

Newt left the jailhouse shortly after Dak headed back to the Chasing R. First, he spoke with Ben, head of the town council, about hiring a deputy or two. Ben was agreeable and said he'd speak with the others members. Next, he headed to the gunsmith's shop to speak with Pastor Noah.

To protect the women from being wed to abusers each man who wanted to marry a woman had to be approved by Preston, Ben Cutler, Eli Steele and Sheriff Riverby. If Newt was truly interested in Myra it would put him in an awkward position. He'd have to excuse himself from the approval process. He was the only unmarried man in the group of men chosen to safeguard the women who'd come to find new lives in Stones Creek.

As Newt was passing Leah Steele's dress shop the door opened and Myra Hope came barreling out and right into him. He managed to catch her as she bounced off his tall frame, keeping her from tumbling down.

"Oh, Sheriff, excuse me." She bent down and picked up the paper wrapped parcel she had dropped. "I'll just get out of your way." She sidestepped him and ran down the steps of the boardwalk and across the street to the hotel.

Newt kept his gaze on her, admiring the subtle sway of her backside. She was petite but she seemed to fit pretty well against him. Yes, he just might have to think more about doing a little courting of his own.

Newt started walking again once she entered the hotel and was out of sight. He went into the gun shop and found Noah behind his counter with four boys lined up watching him put a Colt revolver back together after cleaning.

They were the oldest of the boys who lived in Sanctuary House. He estimated them to be from about ten to twelve. Soon he hoped they'd begin to integrate with the boys from town. Once the school was open that would happen naturally. At the moment these boys had built in playmates.

"Afternoon, Sheriff," Noah said. "What can I do for you?"

"Needing to talk some business with you."

"Okay, boys. I've got real work here so you'll have to skedaddle."

"Okay, Pastor," the tallest boy said. "Come on, guys."

"Hold on a minute," Newt said. "Pastor, how about you introduce me? I'd like to know who these fine lads are." He smiled looking at each boy.

"This one is Ozzie Basking and his brother Will. Their mother is Mrs. Basking. She and Mrs. Ashburn run the cafe with Almeda. This is Duncan Ashburn. The short stuff there," Noah pointed to the smallest and obviously youngest boy. "Is Eddie Duffle. His mother is starting the laundry business."

"I know her. She does a fine job washing my things. I appreciate having clean clothes more often."

The boys gave polite greetings then ran out of the shop. Newt watched them go with a smile. "They certainly have been raising those children well. The ladies, I mean. Every time I see any of them they're polite and well mannered. Puts the Fugard and Brook children to shame. Fine upstanding families that they are."

Noah chuckled. "He who has been forgiven much appreciates it more. I think the ladies understand the concept more than some others might."

Newt nodded.

"So, what business do you need to talk about, Sheriff?"

"I had a visit from Dak Levine today. He's interested in becoming a deputy. Wants a job with a bit more advancement power and in town. He's interested in one of the ladies. Cora Sepal. I thought I'd give you a heads up. He'll most likely be coming to speak with you once he gets word about the job."

"He's a good steady man. Works hard. A believer. He'd make a good husband and father."

"I think so, too. He'll make a good deputy."

They chatted on about Dak and his qualities, then Newt shuffled his feet.

"Anything else you want to talk about?" Noah wiped excess oil off the Colt with a cloth.

Newt cleared his throat. "I may be thinking about asking if I could court one of the ladies."

"Oh?" Noah laid the revolver back in the case.

"Just in the thinking stage right now. Not sure if I'll pursue it or not."

"Might want to think pretty fast, Sheriff. There was a lot of interest at the school raising. I expect there'll be several inquiries in the next few weeks."

Riverby nodded then left the shop. He headed on down the street deciding to make the rounds of the town. The walk would give him time to think. It was mid-afternoon so the cafe was closed. He turned at the corner and headed toward Sanctuary House.

Several children were playing in the dirt yard next to the house. Whoops and hollers filled the air as they ran around. One boy pushed another down and was promptly scolded by one of the women sitting on the porch watching them.

He knew Myra had a child, but wasn't sure which one it might be. Some possible suitor he was, not even knowing such basic information about her life.

"Sheriff Riverby. Good afternoon," said Chloe Ashburn. She was hanging some laundry on a line extending along the side of the house.

"Mrs. Ashburn." Newt tipped his hat to her. "I believe I met your son today. He and some of the other boys were visiting Pastor Noah in his gun shop. I must say, the boys were very well behaved and polite."

"Thank you. We try to instill manners in the children. It's good to hear we've had some success."

A little girl and boy came to stand next to Chloe. They held on to her skirts peeking out from behind.

"Who are these two cuties?" Newt asked.

"This is my daughter, Lil-Pen, and Myra's son, Troy. They are both four."

"I'm going to turn five in Septlember," Lil-Pen said.

"My birsday's in August. I'm older." Troy stuck his thumb in his mouth then looked up at Chloe and pulled it out, wiping it on his pant leg.

He was a cute boy. His hair was darker than Myra's but he had her blue eyes fringed with thick lashes. The girls would be envious of them when he grew older.

Newt touched the brim of his hat and walked on. He'd thought about mentioning Myra talking to him about Rosa but thought better of it. Who knew who might be listening although there didn't seem to be anyone else around.

As he passed the front of Sanctuary House, Newt thought about courting Myra. Yes, he was attracted to her. She was small, quite short actually, but extremely pretty. Eyes nearly too large for her face. Blond hair that looked soft to the touch. Small, rosebud lips. Had he actually thought rosebud lips? He cleared his throat to get rid of the image.

She had a son. If he courted her, he had to intend to marry her. That would make him a father to a five-year-old. Of course they wouldn't marry until after the August 'birsday'.

Did he want to take that on? He'd not really ever given fatherhood a thought. He supposed he just assumed it would happen once he found a wife. Seemed the way things went.

Taking on an older child, if you could think of a five-year-old as older, brought more challenges. Developing a relationship with the boy. Learning about him and being willing to truly be a father to someone else's son. Would the man who had fathered Troy ever be around or realize he had a son if he was?

Was Newt ready to accept that responsibility? The boy was cute. Seemed well behaved in the brief time he'd interacted with him. Time would tell. Being around him more, too.

That was the problem. Newt didn't want to commit to courting Myra unless he was willing to truly be a father to the boy. If he married her, he would want to adopt Troy. Being illegitimate would hinder the boy all his life. Adopting him would be the right thing to do. That would make the relationship more solid. Unbreakable.

Huh, sort of like what Jesus made possible for us. We could have a relationship with the Father because of what Jesus did on the cross. Not that Newt was, in any way, thinking he'd be anything like God.

No, the analogy was that our heavenly Father adopted us and that bond could never be broken. It took Jesus being willing to die on the cross to accomplish that, because he loved us. He set his own needs and wants aside to make a way for us to be legitimate children of God. Newt would have to set aside any reservations about being a father to a child not his own to marry Myra and adopt her son.

It seemed right. Just… right. The peace that settled on his shoulders pushed aside any doubts he had. Yes, Newt would pursue a relationship with Myra intending to marry her and adopt Troy as his son.

Newt frowned. He'd messed up pretty badly in how he'd handled Myra. First, he'd accused her of frivolous spending, then of wanting to go back to work at the brothel. Today, he'd made it difficult for her to ask for his help in getting Rosa out of town. He had some crow to eat. A lot of crow. Maybe if he got that ticket bought and Rosa onto the train next week it would help him get into Myra's good graces. At least it couldn't hurt.

CHAPTER THIRTEEN

On Friday evening, after the children were upstairs in bed there came a knock on Sanctuary House's door. Chloe answered it and found Pastor Preston, Ben Cutler, Sheriff Riverby and Dr. Steele standing on the porch.

"May I help you?"

"We've come, as the committee who has approval over any suitors, to discuss with you ladies about you being courted. There was quite a bit of interest at the school raising. We'd like to set some plans and options in place before too many men make inquiries."

Chloe was tongue-tied. Knowing Pastor Preston was her brother and he didn't realize it made her extremely nervous. The topic he and the others had come to discuss only added to her distress. She simply stared at the men.

"Come in, gentlemen." It was Blanche who spoke. She had come up behind Chloe and gently pressed her out of the way. "Chloe, why don't you go make some coffee and heat water for tea? We've got that sponge cake left from supper. Slice some and bring everything to the parlor. I'll gather the ladies."

Chloe fled to the kitchen. Her hands shook as she filled the coffee pot with fresh water. Filling the teapot didn't go any smoother. She wasn't sure she'd be able to cut slices of the cake without making it disintegrate into crumbs.

"Are you all right, Chloe?" Myra asked. She took the long knife from Chloe.

"I'll be okay. It's just…" she waved a hand indicating she

couldn't speak.

Myra sliced the cake into even pieces and began placing them on dessert plates. Chloe was grateful that she didn't talk simply to fill the silence. It gave her time to gather herself.

"Thanks. It's just hard. I'm so scared he'll find out about my past. That I've born and buried children without the benefit of marriage. That my two precious babies don't have a right to their last names."

Myra laid the knife down and pulled Chloe into a hug. "They got God's right to that last name. You told me Lloyd was looking to find a justice of the peace to make you all legal when he got hisself killed. Just cause you ain't got a paper sayin' it don't matter. 'Sides, if you get married maybe you can get the man to adopt your kids. I'm gonna make that part of the deal for my hand. I won't marry any man what won't make Troy his legal like."

Chloe hadn't thought of that. She'd been so afraid Noah would find out about her that she hadn't given any thought about a man courting her and how it would affect her children. Myra was right. Any man who wanted to court her would have to be willing to give his name to her children as well as her. It would mean telling him more of her background than she'd like but supposed she should reveal all anyway.

That gave her pause. If Chloe was going to tell some man she might marry about her past she really should be willing to tell Noah. Shouldn't she?

He was her brother. He was also a pastor, one who preached forgiveness and acceptance. Surely he'd be able to understand and forgive her. She'd repented of her past. She'd been washed clean of the sin that stained her so thoroughly. The question was, did Noah actually practice what he preached? There was only one way to find out.

Chloe had let nervousness and fear nearly paralyze her. Those were not of the Lord. Now they fell away as she let His peace fill her.

Decision made, Chloe began setting cups and saucers on a tray making it ready to take into the parlor. She would ask Noah if she could meet with him the next afternoon, after the cafe closed.

After they had served the cake and beverages Pastor Noah explained that several men had expressed interest in possibly courting the ladies. Nugget Nate had given instructions to safe guard the women. He knew they had all come from difficult, untenable lives. His goal was for them to find Godly husbands who would overlook their pasts, take their children as their own and give the ladies a good life. That the women would be valued as the much loved children of God that they were.

Nate chose Noah and the other men and gave them the task of approving all suitors. If a lady didn't want a certain man to court her he would not be allowed to. If the four men tasked with vetting the suitors didn't approve of the man a lady was interested in she would have to defer to their greater knowledge of him.

This was all familiar to the ladies. It had been explained to them back at Sanctuary Place in Iowa. Each lady had to agree to the conditions before they were funded to move to Stones Creek.

"We all understand, don't we ladies?" Blanche surveyed the faces focused on her. "We all seem to have worked out how to support ourselves. We came out here to find husbands and appreciate that you men have our best interests at heart. While a few of us," Blanche shot a look at two of the women. "Have a bit of an issue with letting you possibly nix a potential suitor, we do understand that you know the men around here better than we do."

"I appreciate your compliance," Noah said. "Now, I have had several inquiries as to the process from some of the men. Only one has made it clear who he's interested in. The others were more general inquiries."

Chloe looked at Blanche who shrugged. The other ladies looked interested but perplexed. None of the women seemed to have been approached by a man directly.

"I'm not going to mention who it is or who he's interested in tonight. There're a couple of issues he needs to have cleared up before he wants to reveal himself. Nothing of any concern. He's a fine upstanding believer who wants to make sure of some things before he makes his interest known. I commend him for his forethought and planning."

"Can we have a clue?" Birdie's eyes twinkled with merriment. The other ladies giggled.

"Well, I suppose saying he's interested in one of you younger ladies. He's in his mid-twenties, if that helps." Noah grinned. Myra, Birdie and Cora looked at each other. Myra was twenty-three, Birdie, twenty-one and Cora was nineteen. They all would mix with a mid-twenties man.

"Shucks," said Esther, who was a thirty-four-year-old ex-prostitute. "I were hopin' I'd be the first to marry. I'll jest have ta go out an' find me a man. I don't care what he does or how rough he be or what he does for a livin'. I just want me a God fearing man who'll be treatin' me right."

The other ladies laughed.

Ruth, sitting on the settee next to Esther, leaned over and gave her a hug. "Don't you worry none. God's got a man picked out for you who'll do just that. He does for each of us. We just have to be willing to wait for God to reveal him to us."

"Amen to that, I suppose," Esther said.

When the men got up to leave Chloe took a deep breath and released it slowly. She walked up to Noah and cleared her throat. "Excuse me, Pastor."

Noah turned to her and his eyes, so like their father's, looked at her. Chloe dropped her eyes afraid he might recognize her. It nearly took her breath away how like her memory of her father Noah was. Except, except there was a kindness and love within the blue depths of Noah's eyes that had been lacking in their father's.

"What can I help you with, Mrs. Ashburn?"

"Um, I was wondering, um, if I could take a bit of your time tomorrow or someday real soon. I'd like to talk with you and your wife about something." Chloe twisted her hands together. Realizing it, she dropped them to her sides.

"Of course. I normally have Vernie there when I speak with a lady. No need to worry. She knows how to keep a confidence. When would you like to meet?"

"I work until after two. So would three work or would some other time be better?"

"Three will work well. If it's convenient for you, would meeting in our apartment be all right? The baby is napping then and it would make it convenient for Vernie."

Chloe nodded, relieved they wouldn't be someplace, like the church or Noah's shop, where someone might walk in at any moment.

Noah placed his Stetson on his head and touched the brim. "Until tomorrow then. Goodnight."

Once the men had all left Myra and Blanche trailed Chloe up the stairs. The other ladies were taking care of the dishes.

"So what's going on with you tomorrow speaking with Pastor Noah?" Blanche asked.

Chloe stopped just past the top of the stairs. "I realized I've been letting panic keep me from having faith that God brought me to Stones Creek to reconnect with my brother. Fear is not of the Lord. So, I'm meeting with him and his wife tomorrow to tell them who I am." Fear suddenly overwhelmed Chloe again. "Pray for me. I'm afraid."

The ladies hustled Chloe into the sitting room by the stairs and closed the door.

"We'll pray right now." Blanche wrapped her arm around Chloe and drew Myra into the hug, too. Then she began to pray asking for the peace of the Holy Spirit to chase away all fear. Myra added her prayers and Chloe felt her anxiety drain as if washed by a gentle rain.

~~~~~

The next afternoon Chloe locked the cafe door as she exited. The day was hot, normal for August in the Colorado mountain foothills. She walked up the boardwalk, meeting Noah as he exited and locked his shop.

"I'm sorry to make you close your shop. We could wait until a different time. I have duties later today at Sanctuary House but if this isn't convenient for you…"

"Pastoring will always come before my other work, Mrs. Ashburn. Let's go meet with Vernie."

They crossed the street and climbed the steps on the side of the building that housed Doc Eli's clinic on the first floor and Noah's apartment on the second. He opened the door and stepped aside allowing Chloe to enter first.

"Welcome," Vernie said. "I just checked on Dottie. She's sleeping peacefully."

Soon they were settled in the parlor, Vernie serving tea. A plate of cookies sat on a table.

Chloe stirred her tea trying to settle the butterflies in her stomach. *Please, help me find the right words to say. Please, let him understand.*

"So, Mrs. Ashburn, how can I help you?" Noah was sitting across from her, relaxed but attentive.

"Please call me Chloe. Or maybe," Chloe hesitated. This would be the moment he realized who she was. "Call me Coco."

Noah went stock still. His eyes widened. He slowly rose and turned away, walking to the windows overlooking the street. Chloe's heart sank. Tears welled in her eyes. He hated her. She knew he'd reject her. She was so dirty and worthless. How could such a good man ever want to claim her as his sister?

She got up, preparing to leave. Vernie gasped causing Chloe to look at her. She read concern in the woman's eyes. "It's okay. I'll just go."

"No!" Noah yelled the word. Dotty cried out at the sound. Vernie went into the other room to comfort her. "No, Coco, my God, how I've prayed for you. Every night of my life I've prayed for you to be returned to me." He rushed across the room and wrapped his arms around her like he was afraid she'd disappear. He held her, crying into her hair as he laid his head on hers. "I prayed and prayed, all the time. Papa wouldn't let us even say your name. He said you were dead to us."

Noah pulled back and looked down at her, searching her face. Then he pulled her close to his chest again. "He said you were being punished for your sin. That mama was, too. She cried and cried. She would tell me that God didn't think that way. That God loved me and her and you. That Papa was wrong not to try and protect us.

"When I learned to read I had to find out if God really didn't want us to fight. To fight evil. If we were just supposed to let the bad guys stomp all over us. I read the Bible as soon as I could. Over and over I found God saying he hated evil and injustice.

That we were supposed to fight against it."

Chloe was crying now, too. She clung to Noah, weeping for the little boy who tried to understand why God would allow such a thing to happen to his mother and sister. Vernie quietly entered the room and sat down in her chair.

"God didn't want you and Mama to be assaulted and you to be stolen away. He wanted Papa to take a stand against the evil men. I saw that as I got to know God more and more.

"I prayed for you, that you would somehow escape and find a way back to me. I prayed that you'd find out how much God loves you. That no matter what happened in your life he loves you so much he died for you. Praise the Lord Almighty. He answered my prayers"

They clung to each other, crying out the pain of years of separation. Finally, Noah loosened his hold and moved them to the settee. He didn't want to let her go, so held her hand while they each wiped their faces with handkerchiefs. Vernie was crying, too. He shot her a watery smile.

"Can you believe it, Vernie? It's Chloe. My big sister restored to me."

His wife smiled and waved a hand, too overcome to speak.

"Noah, I was so very scared to tell you who I was. I was afraid you'd hate me. Hate me because of how I had to live my life."

"Oh Chloe, I've wanted to find you for so long. Whatever you've gone through doesn't matter. You're here now. I love you."

"You don't understand. I'm not Mrs. Ashburn. I'm really just Chloe Preston. Lloyd, the leader of the gang that took me, never got around to marrying me. I took his name because of the children."

Noah could see that was Chloe's biggest fear. That he'd reject her because she'd born children outside of marriage. Now he had to reassure her. "Chloe, how long were you with this Lloyd Ashburn? Did you consider yourselves married?"

"Once I turned thirteen he stopped all the other men from using me. Later he started calling me his squaw." Chloe began crying again. "That was after Cindy died. She was my first baby. I was fourteen when I had her. Just turned. She died when she was three months old. I was fifteen when I had Duncan. After that I buried Jacob, Matthew, Tina and Caleb. I don't even know where anymore. My babies."

Chloe was crying in earnest now. Vernie got up, left the room, then came back with a stack of handkerchiefs. She placed one gently in Chloe's hand and the rest on the settee next to her.

"I was expecting Lil-Pen when Lloyd got killed in a robbery. He was the gang leader. The other men all wanted his place. Dunc and I were just liabilities then. We slowed them all down. They left us in southern Minnesota. Dunc was just eight. That's where I met Nugget Nate." With a trembling hand Chloe took a drink of the now tepid tea.

Noah hated hearing of his sister's suffering but knew she needed to tell him everything.

"I was in labor. I figured the baby would die. I couldn't take care of Duncan and myself in the broken down shack. We had maybe three days of food left. How was I going to keep a baby alive? Dunc spent the time I was in labor with Nate looking for a place to bury the baby. He'd done that before."

Noah just wrapped his arms around her again and cried. He hurt so badly for his big sister. She didn't deserve the life she'd had to lead. He thanked God for Nugget Nate and his Callin's. The mountain man was a legend for his obedience to God and his slightly skewed sense of justice. But he and Penny had found Noah's sister and made it possible for her to be reunited with him.

CHAPTER FOURTEEN

Chloe walked back to Sanctuary House exhausted, but felt lighter than she had since she'd first arrived in Stones Creek. The emotions of the afternoon had drained her. Myra and Blanche would want to learn all the details. That she could handle today. The other pressing issue was the need to tell Dunc and Lil-Pen about their uncle and aunt. She'd not mentioned her brother to either of them.

As she walked Chloe thought about what Noah had told her after their tears had dried.

"Both Mama and Papa are dead. Mama just grieved herself to death. At least, that's what I think. After you were kidnapped Papa never slept with her again. He blamed her for the attack. She began sleeping in your bed in the loft with me. I'd hear crying when she thought I was asleep.

"She simply kept getting weaker and when I was eleven she just gave up and died. Papa was a bitter man even before she passed. He didn't accept the struggles he had in life.

"When I was sixteen I'd had enough of the bitterness and anger towards God Papa exhibited and I left. I moved into town and took a job at the livery stable. I'd mucked out stalls, living in a small room at the end of the building for two years. I questioned why God would allow such evil and why innocent victims would be to blame. The town's pastor helped me understand God's love, grace and mercy along with His desire for justice. I studied with him for two years.

"The war was going on when I turned eighteen. I joined the

one hundred-twenty-ninth Illinois Infantry and spent the next two and a half years fighting in the War of the Rebellion. That's where I learned gunsmithing.

"I got news that Papa died in 1864. I wouldn't have gone to the funeral even if I could have gotten from Mississippi to Illinois in time.

"After the war I moved west, met and married Vernie. Last December we moved to Stones Creek. Since the congregation can't pay me a full time wage I opened the gun shop."

"How do you reconcile being a pastor and a gunsmith?" Chloe asked.

"Simple," Noah said. "God wants justice and the protection of the weak. Evil men didn't care about that. By protecting, with force when necessary, I do what I can. I prefer to use Scripture and God's message of love and forgiveness, but that's not always an option.

"Papa was wrong in not fighting the evil men who had kidnapped you and assaulted Mama. Papa was too much a pacifist. I understood, even as a six-year-old, that something was dreadfully wrong with that viewpoint.

"It's not the gun that does evil. It's the man who holds it. Not fighting back against evil is just as wrong as standing by and doing nothing. I will stand and fight evil whenever and however it rears its ugly head."

Chloe had seen the steal of conviction in his eyes and in his words as he spoke them. He had a wife and daughter. The terrible crimes that had happened to his mother and sister would not happen to them.

By now Chloe had a massive headache coupled with her exhaustion. Ruth saw her come in and immediately inquired about her.

Ruth hustled Chloe upstairs and helped her settle in for a nap. She said to not worry about any chores she might have that evening. The rest of the ladies would handle them. Ruth would make a plate for her to eat whenever she woke up. She would also have Lil-Pen sleep with her daughter Kathryn that night.

Again, Chloe began to cry. God was so good. He'd given her back her brother. Now she was being coddled and cared for. She couldn't remember the last time anyone had done that for her. Ruth had hugged her and tucked her in. Chloe was asleep before the door to her room was quietly closed.

~~~~~

Duncan Ashburn wandered down the street looking in the windows of the shops. His usual companions, Ozzie and Will Basking, had gotten into trouble with their mother by sassing about doing a chore she had asked of them. Now they were stuck in their room the rest of the afternoon copying pages out of the primers they'd brought from Iowa. Eddie was playing wth his little brother, leaving Dunc alone.

He heard a rhythmic banging and crossed the street. The sign on the building read McIlroy, Master Blacksmith. A large doorway open to the street allowed Dunc to watch what the man was doing.

There was a huge hearth filled with flaming coal. The man, who Dunc figured was McIlroy, pulled a glowing, yellow-orange piece of metal from the fire and, placing it on an anvil, began pounding it with a large hammer. Dunc had seen blacksmithing before. Everyone had, he supposed. They were as common as a saloon.

They made horseshoes, of course. They also made hinges, latches, locks, tools, rings for saddles and bridles and sign hangers. Some, the very best, made fancy decorations for rich people's houses and businesses. Seemed McIlroy was one of the best as he was pounding the metal into some scrolling design.

Duncan inched closer to the building, fascinated as McIlroy gripped the metal with his long tongs and stuck it back into the fire. Sweat beaded on the blacksmith's forehead. He pulled a large bandana from his back pocket and wiped his brow.

"You gonna be staying out there all afternoon or come in an' meet me like a man?"

Dunc nearly jumped. He hadn't realized he'd been noticed. He straightened and walked into the building. The forge added to the heat of the day. He could even smell the fire blazing hot enough to melt metal.

"I met you at the school raising. You're Dunc Ashburn. I'm McIlroy, if you've forgotten. You interested in smithing?"

Dunc thought for a moment. "Might be. I never been this close before. How'd you make that fancy scroll work?"

McIlroy smiled. "Practice, son, practice."

Several hours later Dunc had a much better idea of the work it took to become a simple blacksmith, let alone one as proficient as McIlroy. The smith had taken time explaining the craft and how he heated the iron to the proper temperature so it could be bent and shaped without breaking or weakening.

Duncan had even helped make a horseshoe. It would never be used on a horse as its shape was uneven and the thickness varied. Instead, he carried the shoe with him as he headed back to Sanctuary House.

He knew he was later than he should have been, so he ran down the street. His ma might skin him alive for not getting his chore done on time. He was to draw the water to put in the tank on the stove to heat for washing dishes after supper.

Dunc stuck the shoe in his back pocket. It was too big so one end hung on the outside. He'd have to remember to take it out before he sat on a chair.

"Where've you been, Dunc?" Ruth Naylor asked. "You should have been back a half hour ago, at least."

"I'm sorry. I lost track of time. Look at what I made." He'd thought to show his mother first, but he just couldn't wait to show someone.

Ruth took the slightly lopsided horseshoe. "My word, you weren't just loafing and ignoring your chore. That's a mighty fine first effort, I'd say."

"I'm going to ask Mama if I can learn from McIlroy, he told me not to call him Mr. McIlroy, how to be a blacksmith. He said I could apprentice with him, if that was okay with her. Do you know where she is?" Dunc put the pail into the sink and began pumping the water. When it was filled he would pour it into the tank connected to the stove.

"She came home a while ago and said she was real tired and had a headache. She went up to take a nap. You don't go disturbing her."

"She's not getting sick is she?" Dunc was always a little scared something would happen to her and leave him and Lil-Pen without their mother.

"I don't think so. I think she's just tired and needs a bit of extra rest."

~~~~~

McIlroy had enjoyed his afternoon. The boy, Dunc, was bright and showed a talent for blacksmithing. He smiled remembering the horseshoe they'd made. When they had finished he reached up to the corner of the room and took down the very first shoe he had made. It looked quite similar to Dunc's. That brought a smile to the boy's lips.

"If this is how you started then there's hope for me," he'd said. McIlroy was impressed with his attitude.

The offer of teaching Dunc blacksmithery had surprised him. He hadn't planned on doing so, but as the afternoon had worn on the enthusiasm the young teen had displayed brought the idea to the forefront of McIlroy's mind. He'd hesitated to offer. Maybe he should have asked his mother first. But his mother was Chloe Ashburn. That opened a whole other bucket of worms.

McIlroy couldn't keep her out of his thoughts. She was lovely with a low soothing voice. She carried herself with a grace that belied her rough past. He wasn't sure what her previous life had been, just that she had ended up at Sanctuary Place about five years ago.

Banking the fire in the forge, McIlroy shook his head. He needed to stop thinking about Chloe Ashburn. No, to be honest, he wanted to stop thinking about her. It brought up memories he wanted to keep buried. They wouldn't though. Not if he was going to teach Duncan to be a blacksmith. That would bring the pain to the surface. Would he be able to deal with that now after so many years?

Rather than think about it, McIlroy climbed the stairs to his apartment. He'd heat up the leftovers of the stew he'd made the night before. He was sure tired of stew. It was just about the only thing he cooked well. It was easy and made enough for several days. He missed having a larger variety of meals.

Occasionally he ate at the restaurant in the hotel, but that got expensive. Sometimes he would be invited to Ben's or Eli's for supper. He felt guilty not being able to reciprocate, but he went anyway. He made sure to do something to give back to show his appreciation for their thoughtfulness.

Maybe he'd go to the cafe some for breakfast or lunch. It would be more within his budget and he liked the idea of supporting the ladies in their endeavor. That brought thoughts of Chloe Ashburn back into his mind. *Lord, please quit bringing her to my attention. Ye ken I canna be thinking o' taking another wife, let alone being a father to her two bairns. I failed before and na be able ta handle failing agin.*

He realized he'd slipped back into a more Scottish dialect in his thought and pulled them back. It made his pain all the more.

No one else in Stones Creek was from Scotland. That suited him just fine. When he'd received that last letter from home he'd severed his homeland from his thoughts and speech as much as he was able. When he was upset the speech patterns would slip through, even in his thoughts.

McIlroy dished up his stew. He looked at the shelf with a bottle half filled. He fisted his hand. No, he wouldn't reach for it. Nothing good came from having even a wee sip. He'd tried that before and found it only made this thoughts more maudlin. More depressed.

Sitting down at the small table tucked into a corner of the one room he lived in, McIlroy spooned the meal into his mouth. It tasted like sawdust. He really needed to get out. If he stayed inside this evening he'd take that bottle down and pull the cork.

Once he'd finished his stew, he set the dish and spoon in a pan of water. The summer evening was long and he didn't relish sitting in his room until the light faded. Grabbing his Stetson, he descended the stairs and left the smithy by the back door.

McIlroy walked first toward the train station then up the main street past Ben Cutler's general store. In the next block Hank Johnson sat in a chair in front of his barber shop.

"Hey, McIlroy, when are you going to darken the door and make use of my services? You're getting more and more grizzly. There won't be a woman who'll want you looking as scruffy as you do."

McIlroy forced a grin. He was glad he did have as much hair on his face as he did. It would mask his true expression. "Not looking to court a woman, Hank. Just trying to keep my money in my pocket as long as I can before I give it to you to waste."

Hank laughed loud and long. "Well, you'll miss out on having a warm woman beside you this winter."

"You looking to court one of the ladies?" McIlroy's chest tightened. He hadn't thought one of the other men might be wanting to court Chloe Ashburn. The thought of her with another man made the stew in his stomach curdle. What was he to do about it? He waved to Hank and went on his way.

At the end of the block he debated which way to turn. He decided to cross the street and head toward the hotel rather than past Sanctuary House. With his mixed up feeling of attraction and guilt he just couldn't walk that way.

As he headed back up the street past the front of the clinic McIlroy found himself turning and walking up the stairs along side the building. He hadn't planned to do so. His feet just took him there.

There were several minutes of just standing on the landing before he knocked on Noah's door. It still took him by surprise when the pastor opened the door and greeted him.

"McIlroy, what a pleasure. Would you like to come in?"

"Um, Pastor, could we go for a bit of a stroll?"

"Of course. Let me tell Vernie I'm heading out for a bit."

McIlroy waited at the bottom of the staircase for Noah to join him.

The two men walked down the street. McIlroy realized Noah was allowing him to set the pace and direction.

When they reached the train station McIlroy turned east and walked along the tracks. They stretched across the plains and into the darkness creeping up at the horizon. There would still be time before night swallowed all the light but even if they talked long, by staying near the tracks they could easily get back to town.

"Pastor, you don't know much about me. My past. It's been buried for a long time and now everything's coming up and eating me up from the inside. It's not something I talk about. I don't even want to think about it. It's a grievous failure and I'm needing some guidance on how not to repeat it."

Noah didn't say anything. He just kept walking beside McIlroy.

"I came from Scotland with my wife fifteen years ago. Annie was a beauty and I loved her deeply. Her kin didn't want us to immigrate. They didn't want to lose her. She was their only daughter. Her hair was red and she had a temper to match." He paused, then took a breath and continued. "We settled in Missouri. I had a spot of land. We were doing okay. Not getting rich but doing better than we would have in Scotland.

"We had three beautiful babes. Our son Angus and the girls, Bridget and Fiona. Angus would be fourteen now. He was born before we arrived in Missouri. Bridget would be eleven, nearly twelve and Fiona seven. There were three more we buried. Nearly broke my Annie's heart to do that."

McIlroy pulled his bandana from his back pocket and blew his nose.

"You lost them all? I'm so sorry." Noah placed a hand on McIlroy's shoulder.

"I failed them. Left them and they died. Tis a shame I'll carry forever."

"Whatever your shame, Jesus took it on himself on the cross."

"I left them and went to the war. I joined the Union army. Left them to fend without me. Missouri was such a mixed up state. Part Union, part Rebel. There were several really rabid Rebel families. I'd heard rumors they'd threatened any family with Union leanings. I dismissed them as just that."

He stopped walking. He didn't know if he'd be able to keep from collapsing from the grief and guilt.

"I went to fight. About three months later I got called into the colonel's tent. He'd gotten word from the sheriff from my county back in Missouri. They'd arrested the Baker clan for murder. They'd set my house on fire and my wife and three bairns were…" He did collapse then. Fell to his knees sobbing. Noah knelt beside him and pulled McIlroy against his chest.

He hadn't, in the five years since the murders had happened, given in to his grief. "My beloved Annie, Angus, Bridget, Fiona, my precious bairns. Dead, because of me."

McIlroy didn't know how long he sobbed, but they finally slowed and he started to catch his breath.

"It wasn't your fault. Evil men are to blame. Satan's servants who know no shame. *Our enemies have no reason to gloat over us. We have fallen, but we will rise again. We are in darkness now, but the Lord will give us light.* That's Micah seven, eight. They think they accomplish something when they do evil deeds. All they do is pile up judgment for the last day. Do you know what happened to the Bakers?"

"They were hung. I wasn't able to go for the funerals, or trials, or executions." McIlroy was on his hand and knees now. "I'm so guilty. I'm glad they are dead. Just like my sweet ones."

"McIlroy, their punishment is the just consequences of their actions. Their sin. There's no sin in wanting justice. That's what God wants. Justice for the innocent."

"But that didn't bring my beloveds back," McIlroy cried, his anguish spilling out filling the air.

"No, but remember David. He was the cause of his heartbreak. His actions set everything in place. But he understood God's forgiveness. He also knew the promise. He stated it in second Samuel twelve, *Someday I will go to him, but he cannot come back to me.* You will not see them for a while, but you will spend eternity with them."

McIlroy turned and sat on the ground, his arm resting on his raised knee. "I believe you're right, Preacher, but it doesn't help right now. My grief and fear are all twisted up. I'm afraid if I love again I'll mess up and fail them. That they'll be taken from me again. I can't seem to get past it."

Noah thought for a minute. "McIlroy, you're trusting in yourself, in your strength. You need to do as David did in Psalm twenty, seven and eight. *Some people trust in chariots, others in horses; but we praise the LORD's name. They will collapse and fall, but we will stand up straight and strong.*

"That is unless you're not man enough to trust Him to keep your loved ones safe."

McIlroy looked up with fire in his eyes. "Are you calling me yellow?"

"Not at all. I'm calling you weak just like us all."

~~~~~

Later that evening as he lay in bed curled around his wife, Noah wondered just which lady living in Sanctuary House McIlroy was interested in.

CHAPTER FIFTEEN

Sheriff Newt Riverby watched from the shadows as the black haired woman slipped out the back door of the saloon. She was dressed in as simple a dress as she probably had and carried a small cloth bag. Most likely a pillowcase. No doubt everything she owned was in that bag.

It was just before dawn. The shadows had yet to be chased away by the rising sun.

Rosa hurried down the alley then around the blacksmith shop into the street. Riverby followed, wanting to be sure she arrived at her destination safely. He prayed Curtis Fain was sound asleep and would stay that way until Rosa was at least at the House, or better yet, on the train moving away from Stones Creek.

Newt had, in his pocket, the ticket that would take her to Dubuque, Iowa. Someone from Nugget Nate's woman's shelter would pick her up and take her to the facility. At the mission she would learn many of the life skills never taught to her. More importantly, she would learn of the love of the Lord. The main goal of Sanctuary Place was to have the women, and their children if they had them, come to a saving knowledge of Jesus Christ. With that, healing from the abuses and mistakes from the past could begin.

Rosa disappeared between the row of shops along the main street and the large house where the ladies lived. Newt followed to the end of the alley. Once she had entered the back door Newt turned away and walked back to the jail. It was still a few hours before he needed to escort Rosa to the station and made sure she got safely on the train.

~~~~~

Myra hugged Rosa once the young woman was cloistered within the kitchen of Sanctuary House. "You made it. I'm so glad. Are you hungry? Tired? We have food and a bed if you want."

"I'd take both, if it ain't too much trouble. I ain't had nothing since mid-afternoon. It was a busy night."

"Come, sit. Have some coffee. I'll fix up some food for you real quick." Myra poured a cup of coffee and set it on the table in front of Rosa. She kept up a stream of talk knowing the woman was nervous and scared Fain would figure out she was gone and come to take her back to the saloon.

As soon as Rosa had eaten eggs, bacon and fried potatoes, Myra took her up the back stairs to her own room. "I've changed the sheets so you can sleep on clean ones. Here's a gown. Put it on and I'll wash up your other things. If they aren't dry when we need to leave I'll give you some of mine."

Rosa's eyes filled with tears. "Why are you being so good to me. I'm dirty and worthless. I understand you want to help me get away, but why do so much?"

Myra wrapped her arms around Rosa. "A couple of reasons. It's the right thing to do and what Jesus wants me to. Treat you like I'd want to be treated. I didn't have no one to help me when I got out of the business. I didn't have no one. I was expecting Troy and no one to help me. I were on the street. I found a job at a feed store. I hauled bags o' feed all day long. It was hard. More than I should a been doin', but I needed to eat and have a place to live.

"One day I were haulin' a bag across the way an' this tall man in really dirty buckskins grabs it and rips it outa my hands. He starts yellin' about takin' care o' God's precious gift to me. He throws the bag onto the wagon then grabs my wrist and takes me back into the store. He were Nugget Nate Ryder. He starts yellin' at the owner, callin' him a low down money hungry waste of a man, using a expectorating woman to do his work for him.

"Then he hustles me away and onto the fanciest train car I ever did see. Mrs. Penny were there, too. They treated me real nice. Made me rest. They talked to me 'bout how much God loves me, even with what I was. That He had a hooker in His family line, too.

"They told me everything I ever done wrong had been nailed to that cross they hung Jesus on. No matter what I thought, it'd all been paid for. All my debt of sin were gone if only I'd accept that Jesus were God and He died for my sins.

"I didn't understand. How could my wrong doing be taken on by someone else? Not anybody else, just Jesus, who never done nothing wrong. Why? Penny just smiled. Then she said, 'It's because He loves you. So do we.'

"That's all she said. It were at night and she'd just helped me into my soft bed in the rail car. Then she kissed my cheek and left the room. I laid there, heavy with my john fathered child, and cried that I wanted to be loved by someone. I wasn't good enough to be loved by anyone. I'd been a whore for several years. The only reason I quit was because my madame wanted me to get rid of my baby. How could God love me?

"But then I felt something I'd never felt before. A feeling of acceptance. It was almost as if I heard a voice. 'I love you. Believe in me and be forgiven and free.'

"I cried out, 'I want to, but I don't know how.' Then I knew. I don't know how but I did, I was forgiven and loved more than anything else in the whole world.

"Rosa, you can be, too. It just takes crying out to Him."

~~~~~

Myra nearly floated down the stairs. Rosa had cried out her need for a savior and been cleansed, made whiter than snow from the filth of her sin. Now she would be able to move forward to heal just as Myra had. It wouldn't be easy. It hadn't been for herself.

She found several of the ladies in the kitchen now. Breakfast was in the making and someone had thoughtfully done the dishes she had left in the sink. "Rosa's up stairs in my room trying to sleep. I hope God does another miracle and lets her." She grinned and twirled around in a circle. "Rosa accepted Jesus as her savior. She's forgiven and free from her burden of sin."

"Praise the Lord. She's started her new life with a whole lot more than just a change of address." It was Ruth who spoke and grabbed Myra into a hug.

The other ladies in the room expressed their joy, too. Then plans for the day were reviewed. Laura grabbed the garments Myra had planned to wash and went to do so saying she was experienced and had water heating already.

Esther sorted through the pillowcase Rosa had brought and outlined what all the woman would need that she didn't have. Each lady offered some of their own items and soon the table was filled with Rosa's things and the gifts from the ladies of Sanctuary House.

Myra went up to the storage room and brought down her own suitcase. It was a beat up carpetbag, but would be able to make at least one more trip across the plains to Iowa.

They packed the case, leaving room for the clothing being washed. They would also include food tucked into the pillowcase that was also being washed. Tied in a sock was three dollars and seventeen cents collected from the ladies pin money.

Chloe excused herself and ran out the door. About fifteen minutes later she returned with a smile. In her hand she clutched a Bible. "I know no one wanted to give up their Bible so I went to Noah and asked if there was a way we could get one. That a new believer needed the Word. He had this one. Said he always keeps a couple to give away when needed. Isn't he a great brother? He didn't even ask who it was for."

Breakfast was nearly ready and the children coming down ended the talk of Rosa. Her carpetbag was placed out of sight behind the copper tub used for Saturday baths. Not something the children inspected very closely.

The ladies tried to be casual about the day but they were all extremely excited. It wasn't every day they were involved in subterfuge.

It was just about eleven o'clock when Sheriff Riverby knocked on the front door. Myra rushed to answer it.

"Ma'am, is Rosa ready to go? We have about half an hour before the train arrives. I want to be sure to have her ready to board as soon as it stops."

Myra blushed. He was looking at her very intently it seemed. What was causing that? "I'll go get her."

When she and Rosa came down the stairs all the ladies who

weren't away at their various jobs were standing in the entry. The carpetbag was closed and ready to be taken, sitting on the floor by Sheriff Riverby.

Ruth stepped forward and hugged Rosa. "Many of us have been in your same place or similar. Others from the same circumstances will be at Sanctuary Place, too. You'll find acceptance there. Don't worry. No one will look down on you. You're a child of God now and that's a very lofty position indeed."

Laura, who had washed the clothing and ironed them dry, hugged Rosa next. "There's food in your pillowcase so you shouldn't have to be buying any on the way."

The other ladies each had a kind word and a hug. Rosa was crying by the time they were done. She kept saying she couldn't believe how kind they all were.

Myra had waited until the last. "Chloe got a Bible from Pastor Noah for you. He didn't know who it was for so don't worry. She couldn't be here as it's almost noon and the cafe will be busy, so this hug is from her." She hugged Rosa then pulled back. "We put in bookmarks with our favorite Scripture verses on them. Just bits of brown paper, but it'll help you begin to read and learn. Keep the papers in place so you can find them until you're familiar with them. The book's really long. Easy to lose your place."

"We need to leave now," Sheriff Riverby said. He picked up the carpetbag.

"I'm going along," Myra said. She linked arms with Rosa.

The sheriff's eyebrow lifted but he didn't protest, simply waved them ahead of him when he opened the door.

The trio took the back street route to the station. They didn't move out from behind the livery until the whistle of the approaching train sounded. Even then they stayed on the west end of the station building so as not to be seen from the street or the third floor of the saloon.

Noah Preston walked past on the street in front of the station. He looked up catching Riverby's eye and nodded then winked. Seems he was familiar with the events though Myra hadn't been aware he knew anything about the escape plan. The pastor's duster was unbuttoned and his twin Colts were seated in the holsters tied down on his legs.

Her heart was beating fast and she was in constant prayer that nothing would stop Rosa from getting on the train and leaving town. Rosa clutched Myra's hand in a tight grip. She was just as nervous if not more so. She had so much more to lose if Fain figured out she was leaving before she was on the train.

The train rattled into town and slowed to a stop, steam billowed out, creating a cloud obscuring the platform. Riverby took Rosa by the hand and led her into the fog. Myra scurried along after them.

No one disembarked, so just as the conductor set the step on the platform Rosa placed her foot on it and climbed into the train. Riverby handed her carpetbag to the conductor. They'd already decided she would take a seat on the far side so if Fain happened to look at the train he wouldn't see her through a window.

Myra saw Rosa turn just at the top step, smile and wave. Then the conductor yelled, "All aboard."

Riverby took Myra by the elbow and drew her back across the platform as the whistle blew and the train began moving east out of town. He didn't stop walking until they were behind the general store, past the livery.

"You did a great thing, Myra. I'm proud of you. Not only did you help Rosa leave town, but I heard you led her to the Lord."

Myra just looked at him. Up at him. He was so tall. In his eyes were approval and pride. She didn't think anyone had ever said they were proud of her before. Certainly not her parents. Heck, she wasn't even proud of herself for anything. She didn't realize how starved she'd been for it. To have someone tell her she'd done something right, something well.

Tears filled her eyes. "Thank you. I just wanted to help Rosa the way Nate helped me."

"You did a great job. I believe Nugget Nate would be proud of you, too."

CHAPTER SIXTEEN

"Chloe," Blanche said. "I've put it off long enough." She had just reentered the kitchen of the cafe. The two women were doing after hours cleaning and preparing food for the next morning.

The cafe had been a success and the three partners were overjoyed. Each day they served a good number of mostly men for breakfast and the tables were filled several times with men and women for lunch. The bakery also did a brisk business. If things continued the loans taken out would be paid off more quickly than planned.

Chloe looked up from the potato she was peeling. "You're sure?"

"Yes, Doc Eli has a right to learn he has a half sister and brother. Also, if Garfield's daughters come, I want him to be forewarned. I think John looks like Doc when he was little. His sisters are older. They may see the resemblance."

"What about Garfield Steele? Does he have a right to know?" Chloe placed the peeled potato in a bowl of water.

Blanche sat down across the table from where Chloe stood working. "That, I'm not so sure of. He didn't want for me to even carry John." Her eyes filled with tears. "He wanted to, well, do what we did but wasn't willing to deal, in a good way, with the consequences. I know what I did was wrong. I should never have let myself be tempted and never have succumbed to the temptation. I was so lonely and so scared. Garfield was so helpful and kind. His attitude wasn't anything like it is now."

"He's been through a traumatic experience. Losing his wife and his foot."

Blanche was thoughtful and silent for several minutes. Chloe kept peeling potatoes and waited for her friend to continue.

"Garfield was always prideful. He had the most influential and affluent families as his patients. He was very proud of that. If someone wasn't in the highest social status he was reluctant to take them on. My husband was a lawyer and well thought of. He was also a good friend of Garfield."

"I'm not saying anything about his late wife, just that she was never my favorite person."

Chloe set the bowl of potatoes soaking in water into the ice box, sat down at the end of the table and took Blanche's hand. "So what do you want to do? I'll be there for you, no matter what."

"I don't want to face Garfield without Doc Eli knowing the truth. I don't trust Garfield. He could have done much more for me. What I did was wrong. Very wrong. I not only betrayed my marriage vows, but continued in sin after I was widowed. How could I do that? Why?"

"We all make terrible mistakes. That's why what Jesus did for us is so very wonderful. He loves us enough to take those sins to the cross with Him."

"I just wish I had known Jesus at the time. I thought I was a believer but really I wasn't. Oh, I went to church every Sunday." She gave a sarcastic laugh. "We went to the same church as the Steele's. Sometimes we would even sit in the same pew. Even while Garfield and I were having our affair. I'd sit right beside Fidelia. Can you believe the hypocrisy? Sitting in church supposedly worshiping God, and sitting beside the wife of my lover.

"It took Garfield telling me to let him kill my unborn baby to make me see the evilness of my life." Blanche was crying now. "When he said he wanted me to let him…" She brought her hand to her mouth, biting the knuckle of her index finger. "I knew then that I had to leave. I told him I wasn't going to let him conveniently get rid of our 'little problem.' I was taking my family and leaving Ohio for good. I'm not proud of it, but I told him I needed money and if he wouldn't give me what I wanted I'd tell Fidelia all about us.

"He didn't want that, so he gave me money. I sold the house and most of our belongings. Within a month we were on a train heading west."

"How did you meet Nugget Nate? I don't think I've ever heard."

Blanche gave a watery grin. "There was this fancy Pullman car on the end of the train, just in front of the caboose. You know Ozzie and Will. Even at such a young age, barely seven and five, they were adventurous and oh so curious. At a water stop they got away from me. Just before the train was getting ready to start moving I realized they weren't in the car. I contacted the conductor and soon everyone was looking for the boys. Then this tall man in dirty buckskins came toting them, one under each arm.

"Nugget Nate walked up to me and said, 'Are these here varmints yours?' I was so embarrassed, relieved and angry at them. Then Nate laughed and said, 'I'd be most 'bliged iffen you'd let me an' my sweet Penny have the pleasure 'o yous company fer lunch. My Penny do love younguns.'

"Somehow, I ended up telling Nate and Penny all about my life, my mistakes. They told me about Sanctuary Place. We ended up staying with them in the Pullman and they took us right there."

"And that's where John was born?"

"Yes. Only Ozzie really has any memory of his father. Will was not quite three when he died. All of the younger children only know Sanctuary Place as their home. Now here in the House, too."

"You hadn't been at the Place very long before I arrived. John's about six months older than Lil-Pen."

"We moved there in January so about ten months before you. John was born in March."

Silence settled over them and they sat for several minutes reflecting on memories of the years they'd lived within the safety of Nugget Nate's sheltering care. He was truly an angel from God for all the ladies and children who lived at Sanctuary Place and House.

~~~~~

Blanche and Chloe entered the back door of the general store after supper that evening. Blanche had sent Ozzie that afternoon, to inquire if they could take some of Doc Eli's time that evening. They climbed the stairs and Chloe knocked on the door to the couple's apartment situated above Leah's dress shop.

Eli opened the door and greeted them, ushering them into the front parlor room. Leah joined them carrying a tray with tea, coffee and a plate of cookies.

"Welcome, ladies. To what do we owe the pleasure of your company?" Leah's smile confirmed her words. She seemed truly pleased they were visiting. She poured the cups and passed the cookies with ease and grace.

Blanche wondered if the feeling would be the same after she revealed her secret. She twisted the floral handkerchief between her hands, cleared her throat and sent a frantic glance at Chloe. Her friend nodded her encouragement.

Clearing her throat again, Blanche sent up a quick silent prayer that the Holy Spirit would give her the right words. She knew what she had to tell Doc would rip into his heart.

"I have some news you have a right to know, Dr. Steele. It's not news I ever thought I'd be telling you. I'm not proud of what I've done, but I wouldn't give up what I gained from my mistakes."

"Please, call me Doc or Doc Eli. Dr. Steele is my father." From his tone Blanche thought he must not have a very good relationship with his father.

"You may both call me Blanche." She glanced at Chloe.

"Please call me Chloe."

"Now that we have that settled, what do you need to tell me?" Eli had leaned forward resting his elbows on his knees and steepling his fingers below his chin.

Blanche swallowed. "Um, this is so very hard for me. It's difficult to tell a stranger about your sin. And it is or was sin. My sin and… Um, that of your father."

Eli sat back and stared at her. "My father?"

"I come from Ohio, originally. The same town you grew up in. My husband, Oswald Basking, and your father were friends. We were patients of your father." Blanche paused and took a deep breath.

This was so much harder than she thought it would be. Confessing such a sin would hurt both her in the telling and Eli in the hearing. She looked down at her hands, knuckles white, clenched in her lap. "My husband became ill. Terminally ill. Your father came often to treat Oswald. He, your father, was so kind and understanding of what I was going through. He gave me comfort." She swallowed then went on. "Comfort in all ways."

Blanche glanced up and saw Eli's face had drained of all color. She looked back down at her hands. "After Oswald died I gave birth to Nancy. Garfield delivered her. Everyone thought she was Oswald's. Garfield and I— continued our relationship. When I conceived again he wanted to 'fix' the issue. I refused and we left town. John was born at Sanctuary Place in Iowa." She couldn't look at him again.

"So, Blanche, you're telling me Nancy and John are my half-siblings."

"By the law, Nancy is Oswald Basking's daughter. John doesn't, technically, have a father."

~~~~~

Eli stood up and walked slowly to the window, pulling the floral drapery aside and looked out across the street at the hotel. It was where his father was staying. After the explosion of the locomotive engine that killed his mother and caused his father to have his lower leg amputated, Garfield had been nursing his bitterness.

Several times Eli and Leah had reached out to try and help him. Each time was rebuffed most vehemently. They had stopped making any effort.

The father-son relationship hadn't been close to start with. Proud that his son had followed in his footsteps, Garfield had looked forward to Eli finishing medical school and joining him in practice. The War of the Rebellion had intervened. When Eli had returned it was with a scarred face and damaged hand. Garfield hadn't been welcoming of the 'cripple'. The result was Eli moving to Stone Creek.

Early in the year Garfield and his wife, Fidelia, had come to town in hopes of persuading Eli to return to Ohio and set up a practice specifically for war veterans. Though it sounded altruistic the real reason was that the social elite didn't want to go to the same doctor's office with disfigured veterans who were missing limbs or ears or jaws. Eli had refused.

Now Garfield was stuck in Stones Creek as it would be difficult for him to travel alone on the train back to Ohio. Just today Eli had received a letter from his sisters. They were coming to take their father home.

Now Eli had even more reason to be glad to see the back of his father. Hearing that his father had committed adultery had been a shock. But as he thought about it he wasn't really surprised. His mother hadn't been the most loving person in the world. But she still deserved a faithful husband.

What disgusted him even more was that his father, a man he should be able to look up to as a person of sterling character, had wanted to kill his own child before it was even born. The thought turned his stomach.

Eli turned around. "Blanche, why did you tell me this?"

"You deserved to know you have a sister and brother. Also, I worried that John might look like you did as a boy. If your sisters come to get your father they may recognize that. I wanted to tell you rather than have it come out in a public accusation.

"I realize you might not want to have anything to do with me or your half siblings. I understand and will accept that. I just ask that you don't hold it against them. That you just pretend you don't know. Don't hurt them. People might call John names. Bad names. I don't want that. Please." Blanche's entire demeanor was one of begging, pleading.

Eli sagged and walked back, sitting down in his chair. "I'll tell you the truth, Blanche. I won't ever do anything that would hurt you or Nancy or John or your other children. I'm in shock, though. I don't have a clue whether I can have a relationship with them. I'm confused and need time. I have anger towards my father for many reasons. This just added another layer onto it. I need time to pray and ask God to sort out my feelings in the way He wants. Can you give me that?"

He saw tears in Blanche's eyes. But they weren't hopeless tears. They were tears of understanding and of hope.

"You take all the time you need. I understand how awkward this is. Sin alway has consequences and those ripple out over others like waves when you throw a stone in a pond. My sin has rippled into your life. I'm sorry for that.

"If I could go back I'd never accept the first bit of comfort Garfield extended to me. But I can't. All I can do is lay my burden of sin at the foot of the cross. I did that years ago and have been forgiven. I just wish the consequences were only mine and didn't spill over onto you and Nancy and John. Not to mention Ozzie and Will."

CHAPTER SEVENTEEN

McIlroy stepped up to Chloe after church on Sunday. He'd thought about Dunc's request to be taught blacksmithing. He figured he had to ask his mother. The boy was only thirteen after all.

"Ma'am," McIlroy said as he stood behind her. She was with a group of ladies. Vernie Preston was in the middle of the group. The rest were cooing and ah-ing over the baby who was passing out wide toothless grins.

"Yes?"

"Might I speak with you a moment?" He watched Chloe's face turn red with embarrassment. Maybe he should have approached her in a less crowded place.

"Of course. Is there a problem, Mr. McIlroy?"

"Just McIlroy, ma'am, and no, no problem." He took a few steps away, then paused and waited for her to follow. They walked to the side of the church building nearer to the school. "I had a visitor at my shop the other day, your boy, Dunc. He was real interested in my work. Did he show you the horseshoe he made?"

"Yes, he was very proud of himself. He said it wasn't fit for a horse to use, but that you had the first one you made and it wasn't either."

Chloe was smiling when he glanced up at her. He'd been looking at the ground as he spoke. She was just too pretty to look at.

"I appreciate you showing it to him. It was encouraging to him to see where you started."

"My master did the same for me. Showed me some of his first work. Made me think I could do it. Get better that is. That's what I want to talk with you about. Teaching the boy smithery. He's interested and got a talent for smithing."

"You'd be willing?" Chloe asked.

"Wouldn't have mentioned it if I weren't. He'd have to come everyday for a few hours. I don't have the time for him to be there all day. Besides, school will start in a few weeks. He needs to finish his book learning, too."

"I'm glad you said that, mister, er, McIlroy. That's something I'm insisting he do."

McIlroy was pleased with the conversation so far. He'd gotten her permission to teach the boy. Now came the hard part. He knew she couldn't pay him for his tutelage, but he really couldn't do the teaching for free. The time he took to teach the boy would eat into his profits because he wouldn't be working on orders. He needed to negotiate how the lessons would be paid for.

"Ma'am, back in the old country I was apprenticed to a master smith. There was an agreement between my family and him. I worked and learned in his shop and he was paid. Now, I'm not looking for an apprentice. I'm willing to teach the boy and I know you can't really be paying me in cash. I'm willing to do a barter. He works and does what I tell him, chores and such around the smith. Hour for hour, but my teaching is worth more than the work he can do. For my pay I'd like meals. Every day he gets a lesson I'd like a meal in return, either lunch at the cafe or supper supplied by you. Doesn't have to be fancy. Just not my cooking."

Chloe's eyes lit up and so did her smile. "McIlroy, you've got yourself a deal. My son is getting the better part. As part of the whole thing, I want you to call me Chloe."

She stuck her hand toward him and he gave it a gentle shake. Her hand looked so small in his. His hands were large and strong, developed because of the work he did.

"Dunc was hoping you'd talk with me. He wants to learn smithing very much." Her eyes took on a pensive look. "No man has ever really taken a real interest in him. I think you'll be good for him. A good man's influence."

McIlroy was stunned at her comment. That she thought him a good man and wanted his influence for her son. The responsibility settled on his shoulders like a cape. He thought about his little boy and girls in the graves in Missouri. He swallowed the lump clogging his throat. "I look forward to teaching him, ma'am."

As if she realized she'd affected him emotionally, Chloe patted his arm. "Let's go find Duncan and tell him. You can come for lunch tomorrow at the cafe as your first payment."

Duncan's excitement the next morning was palpable. He hurried through his chores at the House and nearly ran out the door without saying goodbye. Chloe called him back and gave him a hug.

"You be good and listen, and do everything McIlroy tells you. Come to the cafe with him for lunch. I want to hear all about it."

"Okay, Ma."

"Hey." She grabbed him by the back of the neck. "You plan to spend the afternoon with Ozzie and Will. They look a little lost this morning."

Duncan looked at his friends. He hadn't thought how they'd feel about him spending so much time with McIlroy. "I will, Ma. I need to do this though. I want to learn to be a blacksmith. It's important. I need to be able to make a living. A real one. Not robbing other people like Pa did. That's wrong."

"I'm proud of you, Duncan. It takes a real man to understand that."

The joy in Duncan's face told Chloe she had said words he needed. She vowed she'd pay more attention to that need. Daily life could be so hard and Lil-Pen needed more of her attention than Dunc. He was at an age when he could so easily be pulled from the right path and head down the one to destruction. Saying a few words of encouragement might make all the difference.

"Go now, my man, and learn all you can. Be good." She ruffled his hair and let him go. She smiled when he stopped and said a few words to Ozzie and Will.

~~~~~

McIlroy stoked the forge. He had several new orders and the time he would need to instruct Duncan would delay their start. He'd never taught anyone before and a young teenager wasn't something he was familiar with.

If he showed Dunc the different types of metal he used that would enable the boy to sort and fetch and carry for him. That would help. McIlroy continued planning the types of things he needed to teach the boy. He got a scrap of brown paper and a stub of pencil and made a list. Then he numbered them in order of importance.

"Morning, Mr. McIlroy." Dunc came into the smithy nearly bouncing. "I'm ready." He was grinning from ear to ear.

"Morning. First and most important," McIlroy growled. "Just McIlroy, no mister." He fought to keep from grinning when Dunc swallowed, his smile fading. Then he smiled at the lad.

Dunc smiled back. "I get it. No mister. I'll bet no Mac either."

McIlroy laughed. "Right, no Mac either. Glad to have you here, Dunc. I'm looking forward to us working together. Now let's get started."

McIlroy went over safety first. He told Dunc they'd go over that every day until he was sure the lesson was ingrained. Dunc looked at him speculatively. "What's your question? Spit it out."

"You're over getting treated at Doc Eli's a lot. Maybe you need to learn the lesson, too."

McIlroy let out a loud guffaw. "Insolent pup. You may be right though. It just goes to show you need to be real mindful of what you do. It's one thing if I hurt myself. Quite another if you're injured. Your ma might skin me alive if you do."

"Maybe. She might skin me, too. I wouldn't want to find out."

They spent the morning getting acquainted with one another and Dunc learning about the tools and metals of the trade. They decided to head to the cafe more toward one o'clock so as to miss the noon crowd. Chloe would be busy before then, but would want to talk with them about their morning.

As they were cleaning up in cold water from a bucket Dunc said, "McIlroy, thanks for taking me on to teach. I appreciate it. If you ever need to tell me to leave so you can work just say so. I know I'm taking up lots of your time."

"Son, I've enjoyed every minute of the morning. I wondered. Didn't know what I was getting myself in to. But I think we'll do fine. Just keep minding. I'll be a bear if you don't."

"Yes, sir."

~~~~~

Chloe glanced out the window of the cafe as she wiped a table. McIlroy and Dunc were walking up the middle of the dusty street. Dunc was looking up at the tall scruffy man in rapt attention. Oh, how she hoped this mentoring worked out. Duncan desperately needed a male influence in his life.

Lloyd hadn't been very interested in his son, then died just before Dunc had turned eight. Since then he'd lived in the mostly female community of Sanctuary Place and now Sanctuary House. This move to Stones Creek could open opportunities for all the sons of the women living in the House.

Dunc burst in the door and came straight to her. "Ma, it was great. I learned about all the tools and how to stoke the forge and…" He went on talking, bursting with excitement. Chloe glanced at McIlroy. The man had a proud indulgent smile as he listened to the garbled explanation of what they had done that morning.

Finally, Dunc ran out of words. Except two. "I'm hungry."

Chloe and McIlroy both chuckled. "I've got meatloaf, mashed potatoes, gravy, peas and carrots, slaw, rolls and either apple pie or chocolate cake for desert. I hope that's okay with you, McIlroy. It was the special and we have plenty."

It worried her that he would want to order off the menu. Blanche and Almeda had agreed to allow Chloe to feed McIlroy at a discounted price if he ate the special. They hadn't wanted to charge her at all but Chloe insisted. The children could always eat for free.

"Ma'am, that's so much better than what I can cook for myself I'm pleased to eat whatever you place before me."

Duncan had headed to the kitchen as soon as his mother began listing the offering. He came back with two plates filled with food. "There's another plate with less food on it, Blanche said was for you, Ma. I'll bring it."

Chloe was surprised at Dunc's consideration. While the

residents of the House made everyone wait until all were served and grace said before they ate, she didn't think he'd offer to fetch her plate. One more thing to be proud of and mention to her son, but later, after McIlroy left. He didn't need to know she was surprised at Dunc's action.

"Sit, please, McIlroy. I'll bring water and coffee." She thanked Dunc as she passed him on the way to the kitchen for their drinks.

Soon they were all eating and Duncan was once again talking all about his morning. Chloe glanced up and smiled at McIlroy. The man had definitely made an impression on Dunc.

Once they were enjoying their desserts McIlroy said, "I'm planning on having Dunc come every morning. Once school starts it will be after school he'll be coming. If he can't keep up with his grades the teaching will stop until summer comes again."

"I'll study hard, I promise. And I'll make sure I keep up with all my chores, too."

"You see that you do. If I hear you be slacking off I'll not keep you on. A man does what's needed to fulfill all his responsibilities. The one who doesn't isn't much of a man." McIlroy gave Dunc a look that said he meant every word. The teenager nodded. Chloe thought her son understood that McIlroy held high standards as to what a man was. Lloyd, nor any of his gang, never could measure up to that standard.

CHAPTER EIGHTEEN

Eli and Leah stood on the platform at the train station waiting for the westbound train to arrive. They'd just heard the whistle. Eli's sisters were arriving to take their father back to Ohio, hopefully. How long they would be staying hadn't been decided. Lord forgive him, but he didn't want it to be long.

"Have you decided whether to tell your family about Blanche, Nancy and John," Leah asked.

"No, I still can't decide what would be best. He will never acknowledge John as his own even though he looks enough like I must have as a boy."

"Your're right. That daguerreotype you have of your family when you were small shows that. I hope our child is as cute as John is." Leah was about three months pregnant.

"I hope she's as pretty as you." Eli placed an arm around her waist and a quick kiss on her cheek as the locomotive moved past belching steam from the breaks.

They stood side by side and waited for the conductor to lower the step. Two well-dressed women stepped down and one hurried across to them.

"Eli, it's so good to see you. This must be your wife. I'm Katherine Winthrop. I'm so pleased to meet you. I was so excited when I got the news he had married. Shocked, as he hadn't written he was seeing anyone."

Eli hugged his sister but didn't give any details of how he and Leah got together. Though they loved each other deeply, their marriage hadn't been a result of love. That was another story, one he wasn't going to share with his sisters, or their father for that matter.

The other sister came over and gave Eli a cursory hug. "Leah," Eli said. "This is my oldest sister, Louisa Stross. Louisa, my wife, Leah."

"Welcome to Stones Creek, Louisa." Leah held out her hand for the woman to shake. Louisa looked past her to where the luggage was being off loaded.

"Eli, will you please make sure our trunks are taken to the hotel?"

Eli glanced at Leah and gave a small shrug. "I've made arrangements. Just point out the ones which are yours."

"I'll do it," Katherine said. As she turned away she poked Louisa in the side. "You be nice."

Eli took Leah's arm and looked at his sister. "Leah and I need to go back to work. See that building there, at the end of the street? That's the hotel. Garfield is there. Don't expect me to visit him. He's been nothing but ill-tempered and rude since he and Mother arrived. Since the accident and his injury he's been worse." He led Leah over to where Katherine was speaking with the baggage handler. "Katherine, if you'd like to join us for supper you are more than welcome. Please, just come by yourself. I don't want Leah upset by another rude member of our family."

Louisa harrumphed and began walking toward the street, leaving Katherine to deal with the luggage.

"Eli," Leah said softly. "How did you get to be so nice with the majority of your family the way they are?"

"God's grace, Leah. When you have that, you have the capability to rise above the poor influences in your life."

"Amen, brother. Amen," Katherine said.

~~~~~

Blanche watched as two women walked into the hotel. One looked friendly. The other gazed at the town with disdain. She knew both of them from back in Ohio. Eli's sisters, Garfield's daughters. Kathrine Winthrop was sweet, caring and much like Eli. Louisa Stross was so much like her mother and father, judgmental, arrogant and prideful. Blanche wasn't looking forward to seeing either of them.

Eli had stopped by just as the cafe was closing the other day and asked to speak with her. She'd served him a piece of pie with a mug of coffee and sat down across the table from him.

"Blanche, I want to thank you for your honesty in coming and talking to me. It took more bravery than most people have to confess any sin let alone one that had such lasting consequences."

Blanche simply nodded. She couldn't speak. Her throat was clogged with a huge lump.

"I want to meet the children. I'm still not sure about what to tell them. My father will never accept them."

"I wouldn't expect him to. And to be truthful, I don't really want him to have anything to do with them. I've repented and been forgiven. I'm not sure him knowing they are here would benefit them in any way."

"I think that might be best. My father is not the most— forgiving, accepting."

Blanche chuckled a bit. "No, he's not. I am sad to see how bitter he has become."

"Yes." Eli stirred his coffee. "It doesn't show much faith in God. We're supposed to turn to Him when we face trials. Instead my father has turned away and blames Him."

"A couple of verses come to mind, Doc. *Count it all joy, my brothers, when you face many trials, knowing that the testing of your faith produces endurance. Let endurance have its perfect work, that you may be perfect and complete, lacking in nothing.* Also, this verse; *'My grace is sufficient for you, for power is made perfect in weakness.' So, I will boast all the more gladly of my weaknesses, so that the power of Christ may dwell in me.*"

"James and Corinthians. Both so lacking in my father. I wish it were different, but only God can answer my prayers for him."

Blanche reached across the table and squeezed Eli's hand. "I know."

They sat silently, each lost in thoughts of the man who was so different from the one now living in the hotel. He hadn't been perfect by any means, but there was forgiveness and peace just waiting to be grasped.

Now, Blanche needed to decide whether to tell Garfield she and the children were in town. He would be leaving Stones

Creek shortly, likely never to return. There didn't seem to be any benefit to revealing it to him or them. She had left the past behind was pressing forward in this new life.

No one had ever really questioned either Nancy's or John's parentage. She'd just stated that John was born after her husband's death and let people assume what they would. She operated under Proverbs twenty-nine eleven: *A fool utters all his mind: but a wise man keeps silent.*

"Eli, do you think it is okay to just not tell Garfield we are here? Just let him leave with your sisters without making any contact. It's worked so far. I've been very careful not to let him see me. He might have seen the children, but if he has, he hasn't made any connection."

Eli was silent for a while looking down at his coffee. "If we can manage that, I think it would be for the best. I don't think there's any up side to telling him. Or my sisters when they arrive. I'm sorry, but that's the way I see it."

Blanche gave a small wry smile. "Me, too."

Now they only had a few more days. Eli's sisters had arrived and would be leaving on the Tuesday eastbound train. Four days. Surely they could avoid detection for four days. She'd just have Nancy and John stay close to the House. Their resemblance to Eli probably wouldn't be noticed by those here in Stones Creek, but Garfield and his daughters had known Eli as a child. Both of Blanche's youngest looked enough like she remembered him that they might figure something wasn't quite right.

CHAPTER NINETEEN

McIlroy and Dunc came into the cafe Saturday for lunch. As usual, it was shortly before closing. Dunc ran into the kitchen and hugged his mother around the waist. McIlroy stood just outside the swinging shudders that hung in the doorway between the two rooms.

"Thanks, Ma, for letting me work with McIlroy. I'm learning a lot and I like the work. Where's our lunch?" He let her go and turned around searching the kitchen for the plates ready and waiting for them. He grabbed them and raced back out into the dining room.

McIlroy looked at Chloe and smiled. "Um, can ya come sit with us whilst we eat, Ma'am? I've a feeling Dunc would like to tell you of his morning."

Chloe looked a bit ill at ease and glanced at Blanche who was washing dishes but nodded. "Let me get myself a plate. I haven't eaten yet."

McIlroy made Duncan wait until his mother joined them and said grace before he could begin eating. For several moments there was silence. Out of the corner of his eye McIlroy watched Chloe, drinking her in.

She was so beautiful. Her hair was coal black with shiny highlights. Brown eyes that had a depth he could fall into and not reach the bottom quickly. They remind him of someone else's eyes, but he couldn't think who. Chloe was tall. Taller than his Annie.

He pressed the memory away, then realized it wasn't as painful as before. He pictured her and his bairns. The stabbing ache was duller. Maybe he was finally getting past his grief. He would always miss her and the children, but it didn't need to define his future. He took another look at Chloe. Hum.

"Ma, I made a horseshoe and we used it on a horse. Sheriff Riverby came by and needed his horse shoed. I'd made one early this morning and McIlroy showed it to the sheriff. They both inspected it and said it was good enough to use. I even got to pound some of the nails in."

McIlroy smiled at the pride and enthusiasm exuding from Dunc. He really liked the boy. He worked hard and took instruction well. He'd miss him being there every morning once school started. Dunc had tried to convince him that school was an unnecessary waste of time, but McIlroy had reminded him of their agreement. Dunc had to go to school and if his grades were not good enough the lessons would stop.

Another thing McIlroy would miss once school started was the meals he was getting as pay for teaching Chloe's son. Getting one meal complete with dessert and something to take home with him for later was more than enough recompense for his mentorship. He didn't look forward to going back to stew everyday.

"McIlroy, I want to thank you again for taking Duncan on. He's really enjoying the lessons." Chloe speaking brought him out of his revery. Dunc had gone into the kitchen presumably to find dessert, though he might also have been wanting a second helping. "The work's helped him focus on getting his chores done well the first time, too." She grinned showing her pretty white teeth.

"I enjoy having him around. I'm not much looking forward to school commencing. It'll be lonely in the mornings." He winked at her. "Will miss the lunches, too." Her blush made him grin.

Duncan came back. "Blanche says there's plenty more ham loaf and sweet taters if you want some. Also, we have a choice of peach or cherry pie for dessert."

McIlroy declined the seconds but chose the peach pie. Duncan returned to the kitchen to bring both his and McIlroy's taking the dirty dishes with him.

"He's been raised well," McIlroy said. "Most boys his age wouldn't take the dishes with him."

"He knows he'll be sent back to fetch them if he doesn't. Adds more steps and time to the chore."

"Ah. Smart."

"McIlroy, as long as Duncan is taking lessons from you, whether school is going on or not, I want you to come and eat lunch here. I know I can't pay you what you're worth, but this I can do."

"You don't need to do that, but I'm mighty appreciative of the offer."

Dunc returned with two pieces of pie and a plate filled with more ham loaf.

"Please. Blanche, Almeda and I have talked about it and they are fine with it." Then she smiled a sly grin. "Besides we have need of a few shelf braces we'd like made. We'd like to do some bartering of smithy services for meals."

McIlroy smiled back then opened his mouth to receive a forkful of peach pie.

~~~~~

Chloe tried to decide if she was hoping McIlroy was interested in her for more than meals or not. It had been over five year since she'd been with a man. To be honest, she seldom missed it. Lloyd hadn't been a particularly giving lover, nor a very giving person in general. She didn't really know any different and it made her wary of any type of relationship with a man.

It was why she and the other women had come to Stones Creek, to seek marriage in a woman-starved part of the country. Still, her past didn't lend itself to trusting a man. She'd been hauled around and made to be a woman when she was just a child. No quarter had been given to her size and youth, or later when she'd been pregnant. When the gang had to hightail it away from an area they had been robbing, she was yanked along.

In her heart Chloe knew Lloyd had been relieved whenever one of her babies had died. She'd cried each time they left a tiny grave. The last grave, a much larger one containing the shot up body of Lloyd, had been left with fewer tears. What tears she'd shed were more from fear of what the future would bring. She was expecting again and had seven-year-old Duncan. What would the now leaderless gang do with them?

The answer had been to leave them in an abandoned cabin in southern Minnesota just days before Chloe gave birth to Lil-Pen. Nugget Nate and Penny had answered one of his Callin's and come just in time to help the girl be born. Then they'd offered her the opportunity to move into Sanctuary Place and taken her and the children there. It had been life changing for Chloe.

Not only was she settled in one place for the first time in fifteen years, but Chloe was able to attend school as well as learn the skills needed to live in a civilized environment. More importantly, she had been introduced to a loving, forgiving, protective God who wanted a relationship with her. No matter what her past was. She was more than grateful.

Now though, Chloe was again at a crossroads. She'd made the choice to go to Sanctuary Place, then move here to Stones Creek. McIlroy or some other man would be looking to her as a possible wife, a helpmate, a lover. She was coming face to face with resuming a relationship with a man. It scared her, but at the same time her body hummed with anticipation. Especially when she thought about McIlroy.

~~~~~

McIlroy, once again found himself at the top of the staircase outside of Pastor Preston's apartment above the clinic. This evening his hands sweat for a different reason. What if the Pastor didn't think he was worthy? What if he'd mustered up the courage to ask then was told no? Well, then… McIlroy would simply have to accept he'd not paid enough penance for the deaths of his family.

No, wait. That's not how God worked. Forgiveness was a free gift to all who believe. Noah had assured him of this over and over from the pulpit. We didn't have to work to have our pasts forgiven and forgotten as far as the East is from the West. He pushed the thought aside.

Raising his hand, McIlroy hesitated. Then he dropped his fist against the wood a couple of times. Within moments the door opened and Noah's tall form blocked the light from inside.

"McIlroy, would you like to come in or shall we take a walk?"

The question flummoxed him. He stood there and stared at the pastor who laughed.

"Let's take a walk. I'll go tell Vernie." Within moments Noah was back with his Stetson and a jacket. "Come on." He led the way down the stairs. "Which way?"

McIlroy decided to meet the topic head on. "Well, I suppose if you're agreeable we might want to make several stops along the way."

Noah gave him a quizzical look. "Who else are you wanting to speak with?"

"Um, Ben, Doc Eli and the sheriff."

The pastor's smile shone like the dawn. "I'm agreeable. I think you'd make a lady a fine husband. Well, if you'd pay a visit to Hank Johnson that is."

McIlroy couldn't believe the relief he felt. With the pastor approving of him paying court to one of the ladies, he hadn't even asked which one, the rest would take his lead, hopefully.

"Come on, let's go see Ben and Eli. We can talk with them at the same time. Then I happen to know this is Newt's evening at the jail so we can see him there. Which of the ladies are you interested in courting?"

McIlroy cleared his throat. He hadn't said it to anyone. "Chloe Ashburn."

Noah's long stride stopped. Then he began walking again. "That's fine. Once we talk with the other men I want to talk with you in private."

Now McIlroy was worried. If it was fine why did the pastor want to speak with him in private? Was there some issue with Chloe or one of her children? He hoped Dunc and Lil-Pen were all right. He wouldn't want anything to happen to either of them.

They arrived at the back door to the general store building, entered and climbed the stairs. Two apartments comprised the second floor housing the Cutlers and Steeles. Noah knocked on Ben's door and McIlroy on Eli's.

"You injure yourself, McIlroy?" Eli asked when he opened the door. "I charge double for after hours calls."

Ben had opened his door also and all four men laughed.

McIlroy was renowned for his injuries.

"Not this time, Eli," Noah said. "Let's go down to your back room, may we, Ben?"

"Of course." They trooped down the steps and settled in chairs around a table that sat next to a potbellied stove. "I'd offer coffee but don't have any made and the stove is cold."

"None needed," Noah said. "I suppose you can guess why we're here. Newt can't be here since he's working, but we'll go over there once we're done here."

"So who's the lucky lady, McIlroy?" Eli lifted an eyebrow.

"You're okay with me courting one?"

"Sure," Ben said. "When Nate came up with this plan the four of us bandied around the men we hoped would find a lady. You're name was one of the first."

McIlroy found his mouth open in shock. "Me? Why?"

"Well, let me think." Eli had a twinkle in his eye. "You work hard, are a believer, supply most of my income, and still manage to pay your other bills."

"Yeah, you pay up your account every month," Ben said. "Seems like you'd make a woman a right noble husband."

"Well, thank you, gentlemen, for your vote of confidence. I appreciate it."

"So, who are you planning on courting?" Eli repeated his question.

"Chloe Ashburn."

"Good choice. She's a real fine lady."

Ben looked him over with a critical eye. "You might want to go visit Hank Johnson before you go speak with her. Just a thought."

Noah laughed. "That's what I said."

When they were done laughing at him, McIlroy and Noah headed over to the jail. Newt Riverby was seated with his feet up on the desk.

"What can I do for you, gentlemen? His thumb pointed to the stove. "Coffee's fresh." Once they each had a steaming cup and were sitting around the desk Noah came to the point.

"McIlroy wants to court one of the ladies of Sanctuary House. We've just met with Ben and Eli. Since we all agree he's a good candidate you've already been outvoted if you disagree."

Newt eyed McIlroy and leaned forward. "My answer depends on who you're interested in courting."

"Why's that, Newt?" Noah glanced at the sheriff.

He leaned back and cleared his throat. "Um, well, I've been thinking of courting one of the ladies myself."

"You said that before. Why haven't you approached me and asked?"

"McIlroy probably can answer that. I'm sure he feels the same."

Nodding, McIlroy said, "It's nerveracking to come for permission to court a lady. Doesn't seem right to ask a bunch of men who aren't related."

"He hit the nail right on the head. I know why and agree with Nugget Nate's position on this. Still, it's awkward." Newt sipped his coffee.

"That's part of the point. If the man isn't willing to get that permission he isn't worthy to court one of these ladies. Each one has been abused in some way. They will need to be treated especially well. By submitting to the process we can make sure they are, at least to the best of our ability," Noah said.

Both McIlroy and Sheriff Riverby nodded.

"So, McIlroy, which lady are you interested in courting?" There was a bit of a challenge in Newt's tone.

"Chloe Ashburn."

Riverby's shoulders relaxed. He smiled. "I think she'd make you a fine wife. And you'd make fine husband."

McIlroy smiled, then looked Newt in the eye. "So who're you wanting to court?"

Newt turned a bright shade of red. "Myra Hope."

Noah and McIlroy both burst out laughing.

"You've got a long uphill climb to win her over. I've seen you two fratch like two cats with their tails tied together," McIlroy said.

"I'm sure you have, but I've mended my fence and plan on mending hers as well."

"Well, I hope you succeed. She's a sweet little thing who could do worse than you."

Newt smiled then. "McIlroy, a bit of advice. Before you go

making your suit to the lovely Mrs. Ashburn, you might want to have Hank Johnson clean you up just a bit. I don't think she could see you for all the hair on your face and sticking out all over your head."

Noah, who had just taken a sip of coffee, snorted it out his nose.

~~~~~

McIlroy and Noah crossed the alley between the jail and the smithy. "You wanted to talk with me about something having to do with Chloe?" McIlroy said.

"Yes. Do you mind if we talk in the smithy?"

"Don't mind if you don't. I don't have much in the way of seating even in my room. Just one chair and the bed."

"That's fine."

They entered through the back door and McIlroy led the way up the stairs into his small living space.

"You're right. You don't have much. I hope you plan to see about a different place to live if Chloe and you marry. You two and the children can't very well live here."

That was an understatement, but McIlroy hadn't really thought about it. The idea of having a family again was a new one. If he was intending to marry Chloe and take her children as his own he needed to start thinking about living arrangements.

Massot had a string of houses needing to be built. Ben Cutler's was framed and the interior was being plastered. Eli Steele had also hired Massot to build him and Leah a house. They didn't hope to have it done before their baby came, but that was the next one the carpenter was planning to build.

Maybe he'd talk with Ben about renting his apartment until Massot could build one for him. The Cutler's living space above the general store had three bedrooms.

"McIlroy, I need to tell you a few things about Chloe." Noah's voice was serious. "It might not be my place, but in a way it is. You see, she's my older sister."

To say he was stunned would be an understatement. He didn't know what to say so he just looked at Noah.

"We haven't said anything to anyone else yet. Chloe is rather sensitive about it. She didn't even tell me until a couple of weeks ago."

"What? You didn't know?" Again, McIlroy was stunned.

"When I was six my mother and sister, Chloe, who was ten at the time were…" Noah had to stop.

McIlroy could tell he was struggling with strong emotion. He waited until the pastor could go on.

"My father was a pacifist. Totally. He didn't believe in any form of violence. The farm was attacked. They raped my mother and sister and took Chloe away. Kidnapped her. My father stood by and allowed it to happen."

Noah talked about all he had gone through growing up and some of what Chloe had lived through. "I'm telling you this in confidence."

"I won't tell a soul even if she doesn't want me. I figured all the ladies would have backgrounds that weren't the best but… poor child."

"I prayed for her every day. McIlroy, some days the burden for her had me weeping, prostrate on the floor. I thank the Lord now every day that she's been restored to me. I love her and her children and want the best for them. I'm going to be praying that you are that best.

"But I warn you. You do anything to hurt her and you will answer to me. She may not have had a protector in the man who fathered her, but she definitely has one now in me."

"You don't need to worry, Noah. I'm hoping she'll let me take care of her the rest of her life. I care for her already and think I can grow to love her easily. Duncan already feels like my son. I'm loving teaching him smithing. Not really had many dealings with Lil-Pen, but she seems to be a precious little girl.

"Pastor, I failed to protect my family once. I won't again. If she'll have me anyway. You have my solemn promise on that."

Noah took the hand McIlroy extended to him and shook it. Then he smiled.

"You better head over to Hank's. I can't have a brother-in-law who looks like he's spent the winter running trap lines."

CHAPTER TWENTY

Blanche stepped down from the church stairs onto the grass of the yard around the building. The service had been a good one. They sang some of her favorites hymns that would be running through her head the rest of the day. Loving others as you want to be loved had been the message. She looked across the yard trying to find her children who had bolted out of the building without waiting to greet the pastor standing at the door.

One, two, three, four. They were all there talking and playing with their friends, both ones they'd come to town with and others they had met.

Just as Blanche was turning to speak with Vernie Preston, she saw Louisa Stross march across the church yard. The woman grabbed John by the arm and began hauling him away from his friends. Her mouth was moving but Blanche couldn't tell what she was saying. John began to cry. He was scared.

Blanche yelled at Louisa to let him go and ran over. She knew everyone was watching and hated what was going to happen next. Everyone was going to be privy to her sin. Her and her children's future in Stones Creek now stood in the balance as to how the citizens would react to hearing all about her past.

Eli passed her as she ran. He grabbed John up in his arms and told Louisa to be quiet. That there was nothing to talk about here in the church yard. When she opened her mouth again Katherine was there telling her the same thing.

Then Noah was there by Blanche's side.

"Stand strong. We'll deal with whatever it is. But not here. Eli, can we use your clinic to talk?"

"Yes, come on Louisa. We won't have a scene." Eli began walking away, John still in his arms.

"But…"

"No, Louisa. Keep your lips shut. You have caused enough gossip." Katherine Winthrop gave her sister a slight shove getting her started walking, or rather, stumbling down the street.

"Blanche, I'll take the children home." It was Chloe who spoke. "Eli, hand me John." She took the crying boy and held him close, kissing his cheek and murmuring softly as she went to round up the other children, both her own and Blanche's. They were all standing watching the confrontation of the adults. Everyone else was, too.

Eli and Leah, Blanche, Noah, Louisa and Katherine walked up the street. Eli unlocked his clinic and allowed the ladies to enter first. He looked at Noah with a grim expression.

Eli and Noah gathered chairs and placed them in Eli's office. They sat down and looked at each other. Then Louisa opened her mouth.

"Blanche Basking, how could you corrupt my brother and have his child. That boy is obviously his. He looks just like Eli did as a boy."

"What?" Eli yelled. "You think I fathered John? I thought you were a bit more intelligent than that, Louisa. Just where was I five years ago?"

Louisa looked shocked that Eli would speak to her in such a tone. For that matter so did Katherine. Blanche realized they didn't, even now, look on their brother as the capable adult he was.

"You were away at war," Katherine said. "You weren't home for all those years."

Blanche didn't say anything. It would all come out now. She didn't need to speak her sin. She'd been forgiven, but that didn't make it any easier to talk about.

"Well, the boy still looks like you, so who?" Louisa said with disdain. "This woman certainly sinned with someone."

"You who are without sin, cast the first stone," Noah said quietly.

"But she had to have…"

Katherine slashed her hand through the air."Shut up, Louisa. You are just showing how judgmental you are. It is not attractive." Katherine pulled her handkerchief out and wiped the sweat from her forehead. "I think it's pretty obvious who else was involved in this."

"Well, then who?"

"Our, oh so perfect, father."

"What? You are slandering a saint. He'd never do such a thing."

"Louisa." Blanche finally had to enter the conversation. "Would you be interested in hearing what happened, at least my side of the story?"

"I don't want to hear anything. I don't want it to be true. I don't want that little boy to even be." She sniffed in annoyance.

That touched a spot in Blanche's heart. "Neither did your father. Not only did he father John, but he also fathered Nancy two years earlier. She would be considered Oswald's. You remember my husband. You flirted with him enough." That had always annoyed Blanche. Louisa, though a number of years younger, had flirted shamelessly with her husband. Oswald had liked the attention and hadn't discouraged it as he should have.

Louisa snorted again.

"When I told Garfield I was expecting again he was livid. He told me he'd take care of it. I would come to his office after hours and he's do a procedure. Then I wouldn't be expecting anymore."

Both Louisa and Katherine gasped.

"I told him no, in no uncertain terms, and left town with my children. I never contacted him again. Never expected to see him or any of you again.

"When I found out Eli was living in Stones Creek I wanted to move away, but that wasn't an option. Instead I met with him and Leah and told them about his half-sister and half-brother."

"They are no siblings of mine." Louisa put her nose in the air.

"That's fine." Blanche said. " I wouldn't want them to have you as a sibling."

Eli grunted a laugh.

Louisa snorted. "That's not funny, Eli. This woman corrupted our father and had two children by him."

"So you don't think Father had any responsibility in this?" Katherine looked at her sister in dismay. "Mrs. Basking was in a stressful situation. One neither of us has been in. She was vulnerable to the attentions of someone she trusted. Mr. Basking was a friend of our parents for years."

"That doesn't make what they did right," Louisa crossed her arms over her chest.

"No, it doesn't," Noah said, "But remember, it takes two to make a child. No matter who influenced the other, it takes two people. We are also not to look at others and judge. Beware of the log in your eye before you look at the speck in another's."

"This isn't just a speck, Pastor." Louisa shot him a haughty look.

"No, but the concept is the same no matter how big." Noah's tone was sympathetic. "I understand how difficult this is. Sin always is. The repercussions can travel far and effect many people. But forgiveness is the gift God extends to us and that we need to extend to others.

"This is not your business really." Noah continued, his tone calm but serious. "This is only Mrs. Basking's and Dr. Steele's. They dealt with it. Made what peace they could over it. At least in Mrs. Basking's case, she has repented and been forgiven by the only one who matters, God. Her sin is covered by the blood of the Lamb. What right have you to say differently or treat any of them as anything other than someone loved by God?"

Louisa didn't say anything. Tears slipped down her cheeks. Finally she took a deep breath and let it out slowly. "How could he do something like that?"

"Louisa, he's human, just like the rest of us. You've placed him on a pedestal so high he was bound to teeter and come crashing down." Katherine had moved to kneel beside her sister's chair, taking her hand and squeezing it in comfort.

"Louisa, Katherine," Eli said. He waited until they looked at him. "It's up to you, but I don't think we need to say anything to Father about this. He washed his hands of it years ago. There is nothing to be gained by telling him we know and that they are here in Stones Creek."

"You're right. He wouldn't appreciate it being brought to his attention," Louisa said.

Katherine snorted. "Definitely not. He never liked when Mother mentioned his shortcomings."

"Okay, good. One more thing. I'm going to develop a relationship with Blanche and all her children. I want to help them grow up. Two of them are siblings and the others are fine boys themselves. They've not had much in the way of male role models. If I can be one for them, I will."

Louisa and Katherine simply nodded.

Blanche began crying. Knowing she had Eli's support meant a lot. Also knowing she wouldn't have to speak with or confront Garfield took a burden from her shoulders she hadn't realized she was carrying.

She found herself in Katherine's arms being comforted.

"Write me, Mrs. Basking. Keep me posted on you and your children's progress, all of them. Please."

Katherine's words made Blanche cry all the more.

~~~~~

Tuesday, about eleven-thirty, even though it was a very inconvenient time, Blanche asked Almeda and Chloe if she could take a few minutes to herself. Both her friends nodded saying for her to take all the time she needed.

Blanche slipped out the kitchen door into the alley and walked behind the general store and livery. She bit her lip to keep her emotions in. Before slipping across the street she looked to be sure those she was looking for were not within sight.

She climbed up the railroad station steps and went over to the end of the building. Peeking around the corner she saw Eli, Louisa, Katherine and Garfield. He was seated on a bench they'd pulled from under the wide eve to be nearer the tracks. His crutches lay on the platform next to him.

It wasn't that she wanted him. No, he'd hurt her too badly when he'd wanted her to abort John. He'd shown the depth of his lack of character then. Not that she'd been much better. She had broken her vows to her husband as he had to his wife.

What she did want was to see the threat to her and her

children leave town. Blanche wasn't sure Louisa would keep the promise not to mention that she was living in Stones Creek along with the children Garfield had fathered. Until they were on the train she didn't feel confident of that. Not that Louisa couldn't tell him at any time but having them heading East would give Blanche a measure of peace.

She gave a small intake of breath when Louisa and Eli stepped away from the others. The woman pulled her taller brother down and spoke softly into his ear. Eli nodded and hugged her. The whistle of the approaching train sounded and they moved back to the others.

With a clamor and a whoosh of steam, the train pulled into the station and stopped. Within moments Garfield was helped onto the train followed by his daughters. As soon as the baggage was loaded the conductor called out and the train began moving.

Blanche waited until the caboose passed the end of the platform then stepped out and crossed to Eli. He placed an arm around her shoulder.

"How are you doing?" he asked.

"I could ask the same of you."

Eli gave a wry grin. "I suppose that's true. Having him here hasn't been easy. Even before the train wreck. I just hope he finds peace."

"That only comes from knowing Jesus."

"You're right."

He dropped his arm and they turned and began walking toward the street. "Louisa spoke to me before they boarded. She said if you ever need anything to let me know and she'd make sure you got it."

Blanche was shocked. "How? Why?"

"I'm not sure, but it was the right thing for her to offer. Difficult, too. She idolized our father. He's fallen far in her eyes. I'm praying that God will help her to see Himself as the perfect loving father He is, rather than think ours is."

"That's a worthy prayer, Eli. None of us are that good."

"Just as Scripture says."

"Only Jesus."

CHAPTER TWENTY-ONE

Newt Riverby dressed in his best shirt, pants and vest. He'd even gotten a new string tie. It was his evening off. Dak had been hired as a deputy and the council was looking into hiring another.

Newt now needed for Myra to go out walking with him so he could approach the topic of courting her. As he'd thought before, he had a lot of crow to eat. He figured he'd acquire a taste for it before she accepted his suit.

The evening was warm in mid-August. He figured Troy's birthday was coming up soon. The boy had mentioned it was during the month but not the date. Maybe he'd whittle the boy something as a gift. A whistle. No, that might annoy Myra with its noise. A horse or maybe a locomotive. Making the wheels turn would be a challenge. Newt liked challenges. Maybe that was one reason he liked Myra. She was a spitfire for sure.

Several of the ladies were sitting on the porch enjoying the sunset. Children were playing in the yard or sat with their mothers. Myra sat with sewing in her lap, her hands busy making stitches. It looked like she was sewing britches. Small ones. Probably for Troy. All the ladies looked at him. Just what he needed, an audience.

Newt walked up the path to the porch steps. "Evening, ladies."

They all greeted him, and stared.

Newt swallowed. "Miss Hope, would you be pleased to take a turn around the block with me?"

That Myra was shocked was quite obvious. Her mouth dropped open and the sewing fell to the porch floor.

"We'll watch Troy for you. Go ahead." It was Chloe who spoke. Several of the other ladies giggled.

Myra got to her feet and stood for a moment. "Let me get a shawl. I'll be right back."

"There's one in the parlor you can use," Birdie said while Cora giggled.

It wasn't long before Myra returned. She tucked her arms around her waist and her hands clenched the shawl.

It looked like she had wrapped herself in a protective cocoon. He'd made her feel that way with his critical words and actions. The thought made him ashamed. Well, the first bites of crow were being tasted.

They walked side by side down the street toward the church and school on the south side of town. The evening was cool with the smell of hay in the air. Myra didn't say anything and Newt was quiet until they were well out of earshot of the people who lived in the House.

"Miss Hope, um, can I call you Myra? We've been through some things and I hope they've made us, well, friends enough to use first names."

"Um, sure, I guess."

"Thanks. Myra, first I want to again apologize to you. I made some assumptions I shouldn't have. I assumed some motivations and attributed some actions to you that weren't correct. I was projecting the assumptions and it wasn't right or Christian to be doing so." He let out a breath. He'd gotten the apology out.

"Huh? I understood that you want my forgiveness, but the rest, I ain't sure what you said. I don't know some of them words."

"I…I'm sorry. I just was explaining that I thought some wrong things about what you were doing and thinking. It was wrong for me to do and I said somethings I shouldn't have, especially being a believer and follower of Christ."

"Oh, thank you. I forgive you." Her tone was gentle. Then it stiffened a bit. "Just don't be doin' it again."

Newt chuckled. "I'll try not to."

"Don't try, just do."

He chuckled again at her order and tone. "Well…" He stretched the word out. This might be the best opening he'd have. "Maybe you'd consider helping me do that."

They had been walking side by side both looking where they were going. Now, Myra turned a bit and looked up at him.

"Myra, I'm asking if you'd consider allowing me to court you. That may be why I was so hard on you. I was attracted to you, but afraid you wouldn't be interested. I let my fear put stupid thoughts into my head."

"You ain't stupid, Sheriff. You're one of the most smart people I ever met, 'cept for Doc Eli, maybe. He's right smart. Then there's Pastor Noah. He's smart, too."

Her comparing him to Eli and Noah was flattering, but a bit disconcerting, too. They were married so weren't competition for her hand but still… No man liked to be compared to another.

"There's a difference between being smart and stupid. Smart is what a person is. Stupid is how they act. My actions toward you were stupid. That's what I'm saying and asking you to forgive."

"I done that." She was a bit miffed at him. He could tell by her tone. He wasn't going to assume he knew what she was thinking. He'd let it go and press on towards his goal.

"Like I said. I'm attracted to you and would like to court you and see if we'd suit. I'd like to get to know Troy better. You, too. I don't know much about what you like and don't." He stopped so he wouldn't just babble a bunch of nonsense.

Myra was silent for longer than he liked. They had continued walking and looking where they were going rather than at each other. He glanced at her from the corner of his eye and was pleased she wasn't hugging her middle any more. She seemed more relaxed.

"I'm willing… But if you go and hurt me again saying those kind o' things I'll sock you in the stomach and leave you in the dust."

Newt laughed at her ferocity. "Fair enough." He took courage and reached out and took her hand in his. He held it as they turned around to head back up the street.

Myra fumbled with the corners of her shawl. "Hum, we're having a birthday party for Troy next Wednesday night at supper. If you'd like to come…"

"I would. I was hoping you'd want to include me. What time?"

"Five-thirty for supper and the party after."

"Good, that gives me six days to figure out a gift." Newt decided to whittle a locomotive.

"You don't need to give him a gift. Just come and be with us."

"I want to, Myra. He may be my son soon. It's something I want to do."

The look on her face as he spoke made his heart constrict. It definitely gave him hope. She liked that he wanted Troy to be his son.

~~~~~

Myra was stunned, excited, scared to death. Who would have thought Sheriff Newt Riverby would want to court her? Certainly not her. He hadn't exactly been the most welcoming person in town. No, that wasn't fair. He'd welcomed all of the ladies of Sanctuary House. He'd just seemed to be critical of all she'd done.

But, to be fair he'd adjusted his opinion and attitude once he understood what she was doing. Still, his asking if he could court her had taken her completely by surprise.

They walked back to the House in silence, her hand held in his. She thought he might release it when they came into view, but he didn't. If anything he held it just a bit tighter.

Troy came running down the steps to her as they went up the walk. "Hi Mama. Aunt Chloe let me have another cookie."

"Actually, we let all the children have another cookie," Chloe said from the porch. Myra saw her eyes twinkle. "Did you have a nice walk?"

"It was fine, indeed," Newt said before she could open her mouth. "Myra, here, has allowed me the privilege of coming to court her, so you'll be seeing a lot of me around here." He was grinning from ear to ear.

Myra felt her cheeks flush. She knew she'd be teased by all the ladies. Oh well. If things went as intended more of them would have suitors soon.

"Mama, what does that mean?" Troy pulled on her skirt wanting her attention.

Myra knelt down and looked him in the face. "It means the

sheriff and I want to see if we like each other."

Troy's forehead wrinkled. "Why?"

"You remember before we came to Stones Creek, we talked about findin' someone to be part of our family? Someone just for you and me?"

"Yeah."

"Well, Sheriff Riverby asked if we want to consider him. So him and me are gonna get to know each other better by spendin' time together. You'll come with us some, too. He wants to learn all about what you like to do."

Troy looked up at the tall sheriff. "He's not gonna 'rrest me, is he?"

All the adults and the older children listening to the conversation laughed.

"No, son. I'm not going to arrest you. I want to get to know you and your ma better. Spending time together is part of that."

"Oh, you wanna come to my birsday party? It's gonna be on Wednesday."

"Your mama already invited me."

"You gonna bring me a present?"

"Troy!" his mother scolded. "That's not polite."

Newt laughed. "Maybe not polite, but to be expected in a five-year-old." He moved his gaze from Troy and addressed all those gathered in the yard and on the porch. "Ladies, I want to ask you to be cautious for a while. More cautious than usual. There've been reports of a new outlaw gang in the area. It's the King gang. They've been known to attack wherever and whomever they want.

"We've got the state marshals out looking for them and hope to catch them soon, but I wanted to let you know so you can be vigilant in your movements. Stay in town, you're safer there. Let myself, Deputy Dak Levine or any of the other men in town know if you think you may have seen something suspicious. I'm not trying to scare you. Just be aware."

Myra pulled Troy against her legs and looked at Chloe. She'd gone white. Myra remembered her telling them one of the men of Lloyd's gang was named Buster King. He'd been the one seeming to take control after Lloyd had died. He was also the one who had abandoned Chloe just before she gave birth to Lil-Pen.

Newt said his good-byes, more to the group in general than to Myra in specific. She was glad for that. The ladies were buzzing with excitement that there was actually a suitor for any of them.

It was time to put the children to bed and once that was accomplished Myra went back down to the parlor. Might as well satisfy the curiosity of the others. As she expected most of the ladies were there. Waiting.

"He apologized for how he'd treated me an' asked if he could court me. That's the long an' the short of it."

That made the ladies laugh.

"You mean the tall and the short of it, don't you Myra?" That was Ruth Naylor. She loved to tease in a friendly way.

The comment made Myra laugh, too. That did describe her and Newt as a couple. Myra only came up to about his armpit. She was sure she would be able to walk under his arm if he held it out straight. "Yeah, you got that right."

She fielded a few more questions then the topic turned to Newt's warning. Myra looked at Chloe who seemed to have shrunk a bit with the mention of the King gang. She was stirring her tea and looking off into space.

"Chloe, are you all right?" Myra asked.

Chloe looked up, startled at the sound of her name. "Yes. Well… no. Not really. I don't want to think about that gang. I spent too many years with them."

The rest of the women in the room were all paying attention. Chloe's past was no secret and none of them wanted to have it catch up with her. Nor with themselves.

~~~~~

Duncan opened the door to his mother and sister's room. She kept the gun his father had used in the drawer of the small nightstand by her bed. He looked at Lil-Pen sleeping so soundly in the trundle. He wasn't going to let what happened to his ma happen to his sister. He'd protect them both.

Dunc lifted the gun from the drawer and then the small wooden box of bullets. He'd ask McIlroy to teach him how to shoot. The man had been a soldier in the war, after all.

He wasn't going to let what happened to his ma happen to his sister. He'd kill them all first.

CHAPTER TWENTY-TWO

Chloe couldn't believe her eyes. She blinked and looked again. McIlroy stood before her. She'd just finished cleaning up in the cafe. It was after closing and she was alone. Blanche and Almeda had gone home. Chloe had about another hour to work getting things prepared for tomorrow.

McIlroy had come with Duncan for lunch looking just as shaggy as always. Now his black hair was neat, trimmed, as was his beard. His lips were actually visible between his mustache and beard.

He had tapped on the window to catch her attention. Now he stood awkwardly in the doorway between the kitchen and dining room. The swinging doors pressed open and back against the wall.

"You look good. Less shaggy." Chloe rolled her eyes in her mind. Pretty stupid thing to say. She went back to peeling potatoes.

"Uh, yeah. Hank did a good job."

"Can I help you with something?"

It seemed to Chloe that he hemmed and hawed. He shuffled from one foot to the other. Just as she was about to ask if Duncan had been a problem, McIlroy stepped into the kitchen and took her hand in his.

"Mrs. Ashburn, Chloe, I spoke with the men making up the council and they gave me permission to ask if I could court ye. I'm wanting tae see if we'd make a match. Aa'm attracted tae ye and like Dunc as well. Ah dunnae kinn Lil-Pen much yit but swatch forward tae gettin' tae ken 'er tay.'"

As he spoke his brogue got thicker and thicker until she was hardly able to understand him. Her lips twitched but she was able to keep from laughing. Instead Chloe managed a subdued, "Excuse me?"

"Awk, tis that nervous I be." McIlroy cleared his throat. "Chloe, would ye be willing tae… to have me come a courting? I'm not worthy of your affections but I'm willing to try to be."

His words deserved her full attention. She drew him to the table where they sat down.

"McIlroy, it's I who are not worthy of you. You are such a good, caring, respectable man. All of you have some inkling of each of our backgrounds, but you need to know of mine if you are wanting to court me."

McIlroy gently squeezed her hand. "First, it doesn't matter. Nothing in the past has any bearing on the future. Paul says to leave the past and press forward toward the goal. I have my own past I want left behind. It's not something I want to remember. Yours can be placed next to mine, and we can journey on together, if you are willing.

"Second, Noah told me about you being his sister and what happened. Knowing didn't change my mind about courting you. If anything, I like the idea of having a preacher for a brother-in-law." He gave an awkward grin. "He's a mighty fine man just like his sister is a mighty accomplished woman. One I'd be glad to have on my arm.

"Third, you've raised one son to be a worthy young man, one I'd be proud to have as a son. Like I said, I don't know Lil-Pen very well, but if she's anything like her mother she'll grow up into an admirable young woman."

Chloe was blushing. Now she understood how Myra felt when Newt asked her to allow him to court her. Flustered, excited, scared whitless.

"Well, Chloe," McIlroy said. "Will you let me court you? Find out if we fit and could make a life together?"

Chloe hesitated looking down and lifting up a prayer asking for guidance. Her heart fluttered then a peace settled across her. She raised her head and looked at him. "Yes, I'm willing to find out if we suit. I don't want the children told yet. Dunc will be too excited and want us to decide right now. Lil-Pen won't understand and both will be very disappointed if it doesn't work out."

McIlroy gave her a quizzical grin. "If we can't tell them how are we supposed to court, and how am I supposed to get to know Lil-Pen?"

"Oh, that does cause a problem."

"How about you and I just sit down and talk with them?" McIlroy asked. "Dunc understands about you ladies coming and looking for husbands. He's talked about it while we work. He's a bit afraid he won't like who you pick. I think he was trying to make me interested in you. I already was, but he doesn't need to know that."

Chloe smiled back, mischief in her eyes. "Let him think you took his idea to heart. But if we don't work out we'll make sure he doesn't blame himself."

"Chloe," McIlroy's tone turned serious. "I'm not going to let it not work out."

Heat flamed her face again at the determination and desire in his eyes. It traveled down into the core of her body making her flustered. "You need to go back to work. If you're thinking of impressing me you need to be responsible at your job. Besides, I have potatoes to peel."

McIlroy chuckled and stood, then held her chair as she got up. "Will you let me sit with you and the children during Sunday service?"

"It'll cause talk."

"So will Myra and Newt sitting together. We can spread the talk around a bit."

"You know about them?"

"Yes, Newt mentioned he and Myra were walking out most evenings and he was going to sit with them starting this Sunday."

Chloe hadn't blushed so much in years and another one moved up her cheeks. "Yes, you can sit with us. Also, come Saturday afternoon and spend some time with Lil-Pen and me. Dunc might want to be there or he may go off with his friends. School starts in a couple of weeks and with him working in the smithy they don't have much time to play and explore."

"I will, thank you for the chance to get to know Lil-Pen. I appreciate it."

Chloe smiled and led the way to the cafe door. "Now, you get out of here. We both have work to do."

"Yes, ma'am." He walked passed her out the door she held open.

"McIlroy?"

He turned back to look at her. "Yes."

"You clean up real good."

~~~~~

Elated, McIlroy walked up the boardwalk. He took a left into the gunsmith shop. Noah sat behind the counter reading his Bible.

"Afternoon, Preacher."

"Afternoon, McIlroy."

"I just came from the cafe. Had a talk with Chloe." He couldn't keep the smile off his face. "She agreed to let me court her. I'll be spending some time getting to know Lil-Pen on Saturday afternoon and sitting with the family during Sunday service."

"Glad to hear it."

"She told me I cleaned up good, too."

Noah laughed. "See, we gave you good advice."

McIlroy headed back out into the sunshine. "Yep, you did."

Next he headed to the general store. He had a bit of business to discuss with Ben. A couple of things actually.

Ben was helping a customer when McIlroy entered so he wandered to the case with jewelry displayed. It was premature but he wanted to look about a ring. Even as little as he truly knew of Chloe he understood she wouldn't expect to have a wedding ring. Many couples didn't. They simply couldn't afford one. McIlroy wanted one for her though. He'd look over the selection Ben had and save for one if he didn't have the amount in his account at the bank. He believed in being prepared.

There were several there and he was relieved that they weren't outrageously priced. He'd be able to pick one when the time came.

"Can I help you, McIlroy?" Ben asked from behind.

"Maybe. I've got something to ask." He turned around.

"Well, you took my advice and got yourself a haircut and trim. You look mighty dignified, especially for a blacksmith." Ben's chuckle and slap on the shoulder confirmed the friendly teasing of his tone.

"Yeah, and Chloe was impressed, too." McIlroy couldn't keep the smile off his face. "That's what I want to talk with you about."

"Chloe?"

"Well, sort of. She is willing to let me court her. I'm one who likes all the ducks waddling in a row. If we decide to… well, get married we'll need someplace to live. Massot is pretty busy building your house and lined up with Doc's next. I'm sure we, if it comes to that point, won't want to wait until he can build one for us. Tis early days yet, but I want to have things ready."

McIlroy was jabbering and it was evident Ben realized it, too. He was smiling broadly, leaning back with his arms crossed over his chest.

"I was wondering if you planned to rent out the apartment above the store once you move into your house? If so, I'd like to put my name in for it. With Dunc and Lil-Pen, we'd need the bedrooms you have."

Ben rubbed his hand across his chin. "Well, I don't know. Scruffy, irresponsible man that you are, I'm not sure you'd be an asset to have around here." Then he chucked McIlroy on the shoulder again and said, "The place is yours for as long as you need it. We're hoping to be moved in by Thanksgiving, Christmas at the latest. I'll try to light a fire under Massot. I have a feeling he's going to be pretty busy during the next few seasons. We had another man come asking to court one of the ladies just yesterday."

"Oh?"

"Can't be telling. Wouldn't want it to get back to the lady involved before he came up with the courage to speak with her." Ben moved over next to McIlroy then and looked at the display case. "You interested in a ring already?"

"No, just another of those waddling ducks. Checking out the prices."

"Well, these are fine but I have some in the safe that are just a bit nicer. Want to look?"

McIlroy was intrigued but said, "Not today, I've got to head back to work. If I'm going to be acquiring a family I need to make a living. Looking at expensive jewelry doesn't get that done."

~~~~~

Chloe had Dunc and Lil-Pen come to her room once she'd finished at the cafe and returned to the House. She had decided they needed to be told she was being courted and might be considering marrying. They all climbed onto her bed and leaned against the headboard. It was a familiar, comfortable position they had used many times before. Whenever Chloe needed to speak to her children about something important they'd gather on her bed like that.

"Remember Sheriff Riverby coming by and walked with Myra, and asked if he could court her?"

"Uh huh," said Lil-Pen who was seated on her lap.

"Well, today I had a man come to the cafe and ask if he could court me." Duncan stiffen beside her. "I told him he could."

"Who was it, Ma?" Dunc asked.

"McIlroy."

Dunc immediately relaxed and from the corner of her eye she saw him smile.

"That's the man who talks funny. The one who's teaching Dunc how to make horseshoes," Lil-Pen said.

"Yes. He's a very good man. He wants to see if we like each other enough to get married. He wants to get to know you better, too, Lil-Pen. He already knows Dunc." Chloe gave her daughter a hug.

"Okay, but will I have to make horseshoes, too?"

Dunc and Chloe laughed, then she tickled Lil-Pen. "No, silly, that's just for Dunc."

~~~~~

The next morning Chloe left the house earlier than normal. She wanted to talk with Noah before going to the cafe for work. Hoping he was in the gun shop she headed that direction rather than to the cafe/bakery.

Noah was there and came around the counter to give her a hug. "Good morning, what brings you here? Not that I'm not glad to see you."

"I think you already know. You're smiling too big."

"McIlroy was in to see me yesterday." Noah hugged her again, then turned more serious. "He's an admirable man, Chloe. He'd make you a fine husband and the children an exceptional role model and father."

"I'm glad to hear you say that. You've known him longer than I have."

"He's steady, a hard worker, a firm believer. He had a family before, but he'll tell you about it in his time. He'll take care of you better than you've ever been before. Much better."

"So you think I should marry him?"

"Only if you think you should and you've prayed about it and gotten a firm answer. Also, if you do, you need to be willing to do whatever it takes to be the best wife you can be. You've not had good examples to base how to be a helpmate. None of you ladies have, except maybe Blanche, and she didn't succeed totally in it.

"Just be aware and come to me or Vernie if you need to talk. She wants to get to know you and the children."

Biting her lip, Chloe hesitated. "I, um, haven't told them about you being my brother yet. I'm not sure how they will take it."

"Don't you want them to know?"

"I do, of course I do. It's just… I don't want to talk about it all again. Dunc knows most of it. He lived it after all. Lil-Pen knows I was stolen from my family and that I had a brother but not all the details. She's so small yet to hear them."

"You don't have to tell all the details to her. Just be joyful that we've found each other again. I think you'll find out she isn't interested in the past but rather the future and how it pertains to her. She is only five after all." Noah said.

That sounded reasonable to Chloe so she smiled back and nodded.

Noah gave her a hug. "How about coming for supper on Sunday? It would be a chance for us all to be together as a family."

Chloe smiled. "I'd like that. Thank you." Then she blushed.

"Could I invite McIlroy to come, too? It would be good for us all to have time together."

"I was going to head over there and ask him myself."

"Oh, Noah," Chloe said as she headed out the door. "He does clean up well. Thank you for suggesting it."

"Me and every other man of the committee."

CHAPTER TWENTY-THREE

Myra answered the door with Troy at her heels. Newt Riverby stood there holding a brown paper wrapped package. It was lumpy and clumsily tied with twine. "Come in, welcome. We're just about to serve supper."

Newt stepped into the foyer and knelt down. "Hi, Troy. This is for you but you have to wait until after supper to open it." He handed the present to the excited now five-year-old.

"Thank you." Troy ran off and placed it on a small table with about five other packages. Then he raced over to where a couple of the other younger children were gathered.

"Come, let me show you where you can hang your hat." Myra led him into the parlor to a short rack of pegs. "I'm glad you could come. You didn't have to bring a gift for Troy though."

"I know. I wanted to." He grinned at her. "I had fun making it. I'd never attempted something that complicated. Don't ask me what it is because Troy needs to know first."

Myra grinned up at him. "Is that so? Maybe as his mother I should get to approve of what you're giving him."

"Too late. You should have said that when you invited me to the party."

She snorted a laugh. "Suppose you're right. I'll remember for next year."

Newt leaned down and whispered in her ear, "Next year I'll be his pa and have the final say."

Myra started at his words. "Is that so?"

"If I have my way it will be."

Just then eleven-year-old Kathryn Naylor stuck her head in the room. "Supper's ready to serve so come on. I'm hungry."

Myra and Newt exchanged amused glances and went into the dining room. Myra didn't have any duties this evening other than to manage the birthday celebration after the meal so she led Newt to the table they would share. Troy was already seated next to Lil-Pen, their typical arrangement. Chloe sat by Lil-Pen with Myra across from her. Normally Dunc sat beside Myra but tonight he left that seat open for Newt.

Esther Fuller said grace and the meal commenced.

"Sheriff," Chloe said. "Glad to have you with us for the party though it's made for a couple of very excited children." She eyed both the young ones sitting at the table. At the moment they were concentrating on their food.

"You don't say." Newt gave a mock stern look as the pair giggled.

After the meal the older children gathered up the dishes and took them to the kitchen. Myra had Troy and Lil-Pen bring the presents to their table. Then she had Troy climb on the table so everyone could remain seated and see as he opened the gifts.

He received a pair of pants and a shirt Myra had made. A top from several of the families pooling their pennies. A crocheted scarf from Chloe and matching mittens from Blanche. When Troy opened the gift from Newt he squealed and launched himself into the man's arms.

"Thank you. It's wonderful. See, Mama. It's a locomotive and the wheels go around."

Myra's eyes filled with tears. No man had ever given Troy a gift before. This man not only gave her son one, he'd whittled it himself. With wheels that turned. What could be better than that for a five-year-old boy? She decided right then that if Sheriff Newt Riverby asked her to marry him, she was going to say yes.

~~~~~

Newt realized he had made the right choice to take the time and effort to make the train engine for Troy. It was obvious the boy meant the world to his mother. Chalk one up for him.

He looked at Myra as she watched Troy eating his piece of chocolate birthday cake. She was smiling softly as he got the gooey icing all over his face. Fortunately she'd tied a large flour sack dish towel around his neck keeping the mess off his shirt and pants.

The woman was definitely beautiful. Blonde hair, blue eyes and a rosebud red mouth. That rosebud thought again flitted through his mind. Her face seemed that of an angel to him. Round but with such fine bones and large eyes. She was striking.

Newt knew he was falling hard and fast. He worried it was too soon to think about proposing. He figured if he pressured her, asked her too soon, she'd get scared and bolt. But then again, she was feisty and just might accept.

One thing for sure, Myra would be fun to live with. Right now she and several of the young girls were dancing around the tables singing Go Tell It On The Mountain. Everyone was laughing and several were singing along.

He looked over the group. Duncan Ashburn was the oldest of the children at thirteen and Susan Sepal the youngest at two. There was a whole passel in between. He'd have thought there would be fussing among them, but it didn't seem so, at the moment at least. Ozzie Basking was dancing in the corner with little Susan so she wouldn't be trampled. Duncan lifted Lil-Pen on his shoulders and joined Myra's group as they circled the many tables.

Who would have thought that the women who had lived such difficult lives would have so much joy in them? That's what loving the Lord and being loved so much by Him did to a life. It transformed sorrow and pain into love, laughter and hope.

A knock sounded on the front door and Birdie Pullman slipped out to answer it. She came back, grinning wide, with McIlroy following behind. When McIlroy saw Newt a blush rose up above his beard, which was trimmed and neat. The same sort of heat warmed his cheeks. He shrugged inwardly. Neither man had anything to be ashamed of.

"Come join the fun. We're celebrating Troy's birthday and the joy of the Lord." Newt waved a beckoning hand.

"Yes," Chloe said. "It's called making a joyful noise." She patted the seat Lil-Pen had been sitting in indicating he should sit. "Would you like a piece of cake? There's plenty." She stood up ready to head to the kitchen for another plate and fork.

"Don't mind if I do?"

With only the two men at the table silence fell between them. McIlroy picked up the locomotive and turned it over looking at it.

"Nice whittling."

"Thanks. Troy liked it."

"Making any headway?"

Newt knew exactly what McIlroy meant. "I think so. You?"

"I think so." McIlroy set the toy on the table.

They chuckled and went to watching the dancing that now had gathered most of the children. The women who weren't joining in with the dancing were gathering the dirty dishes as they sang.

"Here you go, McIlroy." Chloe set a large slice of cake in front of him and handed him a fork. "Did you come for any special reason or just for a visit?"

Now his face turned a bright red. "Well, to see you, Dunc and Lil-Pen mostly, but Dunc did just happened to mention a birthday celebration this evening."

Newt and Chloe both laughed.

"So the cake was more of a draw than our company, huh?" Chloe gave him a mocking glare.

"I didn't say that, and never would."

Chloe just slapped him lightly on the shoulder. "For that I'll just leave you with the sheriff." She turned and headed into the kitchen.

"Do you think she's upset with me?" McIlroy asked Newt, worry deep in his eyes.

Newt chuckled. "Nope." He pointed and McIlroy turned to look. Chloe was approaching with a mug and the large blue speckle ware coffee pot.

"Here." She poured him a cup then filled Newt's. She then went to the other tables offering to fill cups. When she finished the rounds Chloe took the pot back to the kitchen and came and sat next to McIlroy.

"Chore's done. Now I can sit and enjoy your company, even if the cake is more interesting." Her smile took any possible sting from her words.

The clamor of the singing ended. Children scattered either heading to the kitchen if they had a duty or outside via the front door. Myra came and sat down next to Newt, a bit out of breath.

"Hi McIlroy, what brings you here this evening?" When the other three adults at the table began laughing she looked confused. "What?" They laughed harder.

Newt patted the hand she had rested on the table. "Never mind. If we go over it again we might get McIlroy in trouble."

Myra looked from one to the other in confusion, then simply shrugged. "I guess you had to be here."

Troy and Lil-Pen came to the table. Lil-Pen climbed into Chloe's lap. Troy picked up his locomotive and then climbed into Newt's.

"Choo Choo. Here comes the twelve fifty-two. All aboard. Choo Choo." He ran the toy across Newt's chest, down his arm and onto the table.

A sudden tightness gripped Newt's chest. One he'd never felt before. His son. No matter that the boy wasn't of his blood. This small miracle, who could have been killed before he was even born, was his son.

Newt wrapped an arm around the small hips seated on his leg securing the boy in place. No matter how long it took, Myra was going to be his and this small child was, too. He'd be writing to a lawyer in Denver asking how to go about adopting a child with no legal status.

CHAPTER TWENTY-FOUR

McIlroy stoked the forge early Monday morning. The weekend had been good, productive in his courtship of Chloe. He and Newt had walked home together after the birthday party. He could tell Newt was just as enamored of Myra as he was of Chloe. He figured Newt would propose sooner than he would, mainly because the sheriff already had a house Myra and Troy could move into.

That made him wonder if he should talk to Chloe about his intentions and why they couldn't get married sooner. He didn't want her to think he was playing with her affections. Teasing her along with no plan to actually marry her.

Dunc came in just then chasing his thoughts away. The boy's expression was somber, worried.

"You got troubles, boy?"

"Did you see the wanted poster the sheriff posted? The King gang?"

"Yeah." McIlroy was afraid he knew what Duncan was going to say.

"That's the gang that used to be my pa's before he got himself killed."

Although Dunc tried not to let it show, it was evident he was scared. He reached out and pulled the boy into a hug. "Don't worry, we'll make sure you and your ma and sister are safe."

"You'll try, but I need to, too. I want to learn how to shoot a gun. I need to protect them. I don't want what happened to my ma to happen to Lil-Pen. I'm worried they're going to want my ma back. And… and me.

"They may want me to be part of the gang. I don't want that. I like my life here. I even liked living in Sanctuary Place in Iowa. I like you and working with you. School, I might not like that much.

"I want you to marry my ma and be my pa. I don't want to go back to the gang, robbing people. I've got Jesus now and I know it's wrong and I don't want to do it. I want to be a blacksmith and live in town and have friends and lots to eat and be safe.

"I never had that when we were with the gang and my pa was alive. I hated that my ma would have the babies and they'd die and she'd cry when we had to leave the graves. We were always hungry and cold."

McIlroy squeezed Duncan more tightly to his chest. The boy was crying. Wanting to give the comfort and support he needed as well as the time to recover and present a stronger front, McIlroy held him close not saying a word. He prayed for the ability to comfort and for God to give Dunc the security he needed.

Finally, Duncan pulled back. "Will you teach me to shoot, McIlroy, please? You were a soldier in the war so you can show me how."

McIlroy stepped back and rubbed his hand down his face. "I'd need your ma's approval for that, Dunc. I'll not be going behind her back with something that important."

The forge fire sputtered and popped. McIlroy turned to tend it.

"Please," Dunc begged, behind him. "I've got my pa's gun."

As McIlroy turned back Duncan pulled a revolver out of his pants pocket. Then a shot fired. Pain burst through him. His right leg collapsed tumbling him to the floor. The gun landed in front of his face. Duncan screamed and dropped down beside him.

"I'm sorry. I'm sorry. I'm sorry. I didn't mean to shoot you. I didn't know it was loaded. Please forgive me." Duncan was sobbing.

"Don't worry, Dunc. It's a flesh wound." McIlroy's hand was gripping his right butt cheek. Blood oozed between his fingers.

The wound hurt like the very dickens.

Running footsteps approached from both the back and front of the smithy. Then Doc Eli was kneeling beside him and trying to peel his hand away. Sheriff Riverby was lifting Duncan away asking what had happened.

"It went clear through. I'll need to clean it and put a couple of stitches into each end," Eli said. "Can you walk to the clinic?"

"Yeah, think so." Eli helped McIlroy to his feet. "Dunc, I'm gonna be fine so don't fratch yerself. Ae ken it t'were an accident. Go talk ta yer ma. She'll be a needin' ta ken aboot it. 'En coom back 'ere. Ae'll be a needin' soom aid for the day."

Duncan's eyes were bloodshot with tears as he nodded. "I'm sorry. I'm sorry."

McIlroy reached out and patted Duncan on the shoulder. "Ae ken. Ae forgive ye. Now scoot. An' take the sheriff with ye."

Duncan, head bowed, left with Newt's arm around his shoulders. McIlroy was sure the man would hear the entire story before they walked up the block to the cafe.

"Come on, Doc. Ae'm a needin' ta have ye do yer doctorin' so Ae can spend the rest o' the day lyin' on me bed."

~~~~~

The shot had been heard all over town and everyone in the cafe had crowded to the window and door. When nothing else happened the customers went back to their tables and Almeda, Blanche and Chloe back to the kitchen or waitressing. It was a small town. Someone would be in shortly with the news of what happened. Sheriff Riverby didn't tolerate bystanders around 'incidents,' as he called them.

A few minutes later the sheriff, Dunc and Noah entered. Chloe dropped the plates she held down on the table top. She felt the blood drain from her face. Her son's face was white and the pain on it was evident.

"What?" She couldn't get another word out.

"Chloe, he'll be fine. He's scared and upset." Noah had walked to her and taken her arm. "Come, we'll talk at the House."

They moved through the kitchen and out the back door. Soon they were seated in the parlor. Noah and Newt in chairs with

Chloe on the settee, her arms around her son.

"What happened?"

"I shot him. I shot McIlroy," Dunc wailed. He began to cry.

"What?" Chloe looked from Dunc to Newt to Noah.

"It was an accident," Newt explained. "From what I could understand Dunc took the gun from your nightstand. He told McIlroy about your past with the King gang. He asked McIlroy to teach him to shoot so he could protect you and Lil-Pen. He thought the gun was empty. As he was pulling it out of his pocket the thing went off."

Chloe gasped.

"McIlroy's going to be okay. Just a flesh wound. Eli is treating him now."

"Where was he shot?"

Newt looked at Noah who was pursing his lips to keep from grinning. "Um, at the forge."

"No. Where on his body?"

Newt looked at Noah again. Chloe looked at her brother.

"On his behind. Like Newt said, it's a flesh wound and he'll be fine."

Chloe turned her attention to her son. He had his head buried in her chest. She took his face between her hands and looked into his eyes. "I love that you want to protect us. You are such a wonderful son and brother. Thank you. How you went about it might have been different, but your intention was right."

"But I shot him, Ma."

"Not on purpose. He's going to be all right. Newt and Eli wouldn't have said so if he wasn't."

"But he'll hate me. He won't want to teach me anymore and won't want to court you and marry you and be my pa." Tears coursed down Duncan's face.

Chloe pulled him close and stroked his head. "If that's the case then I don't want to marry him."

"That's not what he said, Dunc." Newt reached over and patted him on the back. "He wasn't upset with you. He wants you to come back and help him today. He's not going to be able to move about much. He'll be in pain. You can help him a lot just fetching water, food, anything he's going to need. If he was mad he wouldn't want you around."

"You think so?" Hope laced Dunc's voice.

"Yes, I do." Then Newt grinned. "Well, I think so. His brogue got so thick it was hard to truly understand his words, but his intent was pretty clear to me."

Noah chuckled. Chloe felt Dunc relax in her arms. He pulled away.

"Ma, I know I shouldn't have taken your gun. I really thought it was empty. I didn't mean to shoot anybody. But I still want to learn to shoot. I need to know I can protect you and Lil-Pen and the others. It's real important to me."

"I know. It's time you learned, but not until McIlroy is healed. You're going to be busy taking care of him. He's your responsibility." She stood, as did the men.

Noah stepped over to Dunc and placed a hand on his shoulder. "I'll teach you, Dunc. I know exactly how you feel. Exactly."

"Thanks, Pastor Noah."

Chloe lifted an eyebrow and eyed her son. "Shot him in the behind did you? Can't say much for your aim."

~~~~~

McIlroy was lying on his stomach on the exam table. Eli had just finished stitching his wounds. It still hurt like the devil and he'd had to bite a piece of leather to keep from screaming words he normally didn't say. The whiskey that had been poured into the wounds had been the worst.

Eli making jokes about him being accident prone and that this was a place he hadn't treated on him before also didn't help matters. The doctor had left him there and gone to McIlroy's room above the smithy to get new drawers and pants for him.

The clinic door opened and the sound of footsteps indicating Newt and Dunc had returned. He closed his eyes. He wasn't ready to make conversation.

When he heard Chloe's voice he knew he really wasn't ready to see her. He didn't have any pants on. Thankfully he was covered with a sheet. Still, it wasn't the position one wanted to be in when he next saw the woman he hoped to propose to.

"McIlroy, how are you?" Chloe's soft voice sounded right next to his ear. He opened one eye. She was kneeling next to the exam table by his head.

"Been better. You?"

"Been better, but I'm better than you right now." Her lips twitched. She was fighting a smile. "I'm sorry you got shot. Especially sorry Dunc was the one who shot you."

"Me, too, but I'll be fine. It's just a flesh wound."

"So I hear."

"Is Dunc here?" He closed his eye. There was shuffling then a sniffle right by his face. He opened his eye again. "It's okay, Dunc, I'm not mad at you. I still like you and still want to teach you smithing."

"Do you still want to court my ma and be my pa?" The worry in Dunc's eyes touched McIlroy. Seemed the boy was very in favor of his interest in Chloe.

"Aye, Dunc, I do."

The boy nearly collapsed in relief. Tears filled his eyes. He blinked them away. "I'm glad."

The clinic door opened again and footsteps approached.

"Got a little crowded in here while I was gone," Eli said. "How about you all go to the waiting room. McIlroy and I will be out in a minute."

"Dunc, you stay and help me," McIlroy said. "You'll be helping me of the next few days. You might as well learn how."

"Yes, sir."

After Eli and Dunc had helped McIlroy into his drawers and trousers he gingerly walked out of the exam room to where the others were waiting.

"Don't be touching me," he said when each one reached out to try and help. "Just stay close in case I start to fall. Dunc, you're on my right. Noah, my left. Chloe open the door, please."

They scurried to their assigned positions and McIlroy made progress out the door and across the street at a snail's pace. There were a number of people standing around on the boardwalks and in the street watching. The tale would be around the county within a day, no doubt embellished until it was unrecognizable.

"Bank that, Duncan," McIlroy ordered as they passed the

forge. "Won't be getting anything done today. Maybe tomorrow either."

Dunc sniffled and moved to do as instructed. McIlroy paused to watch. All he wanted to do was go upstairs and lie on his bed, but he wanted to see whether the boy remembered what he'd been taught. He did.

"Well done, Dunc. I'm proud of you for remembering so well. Come on. Let's go upstairs. I need to lie down."

"I'll be leaving you here," Newt said. "I need to head back to the office. If you need anything send Dunc for me. Glad you weren't hurt any worse than you were."

"Thanks, Newt."

The sheriff left through the back door and McIlroy made his way painfully up the steps. The going was slow and he gritted his teeth every time he had to lift his right leg. He didn't groan. Didn't want to upset Dunc any more than he already was. The boy was racked with guilt. He'd have to talk with him about it. Maybe he'd have Noah stay to help with that.

When he reached his room he nearly groaned. Not because he was in pain, which he was, but because the place was a mess. Dirty clothes were piled and scattered on the floor. There were dirty dished from breakfast on the table and potbellied stove. Cobwebs hung in the corners. And Chloe was following him into the room.

She dodged passed him and pulled the sheet back. Then she grabbed the pillow and began fluffing it. The pillowcase was stained from his hair and the length of time between washings. She smoothed the sheet on the mattress and then stepped out of the way.

"Lie down. You have to be in pain," she said.

He followed her instructions and lay on his stomach. Dunc hurried to carefully remove his boots. McIlroy let out a relieved sigh as he settled. Eli had given him laudanum to take but he hadn't as of yet. He knew the medicine would put him to sleep, and he needed to talk with Dunc first.

"Dunc, go fetch a bucket of water." Chloe said. "Fill the one from downstairs. You'll need to be sure he drinks."

He looked and saw her picking up his dirty laundry and

stuffing the items in a burlap bag. Where she'd found that he didn't know. Noah was pouring water from a pitcher into a pot. He was obviously planning to wash the dishes.

"Sorry for the mess of the place. I'm not much for keeping things neat."

Chloe sniffed. "That's clear." Her tone betrayed her amusement.

Dunc came clattering up the stairs, splashing some of the water. He set the bucket on the table then took a mug from a hook and dipped it in. He held the dripping cup out to McIlroy.

"Want a drink?"

McIlroy leaned up on his elbow and took the mug. He wasn't going to not take a drink. The poor kid was so eager to do everything right after the fiasco of the morning. Besides, he was thirsty.

"Dunc, I need to get back to the cafe. I want you to come for your lunches at eleven-thirty. I'll have them boxed so you can carry them here. You'll need to bring the dishes back when you're done. You'll stay the rest of the day and overnight. So when you bring the dishes back go to the House and get a pallet and your pillow and blanket. Clothing for tomorrow, too."

"Yes, ma'am."

McIlroy started to protest that he could stay by himself. Chloe shot him a look with just about as much power as the bullet that had cut through his bottom. He closed his mouth, then took another sip of his water and placed the cup on the floor. He glanced at Noah who grinned at him.

Chloe continued giving orders to both her son and brother then came over to the bed. She knelt and took McIlroy's hand.

"I'm so glad you weren't hurt worse than you were. Make sure Dunc does as you ask. Send him for me if you need to. Don't hesitate."

"Yes, ma'am."

She touched his cheek then stood. She gave Dunc a hug, said good-bye to Noah, and headed down the stairs. As the sound of her steps faded Noah began to chuckle.

"You sure you want to have anything to do with the woman who just ordered us all around?"

CHAPTER TWENTY-FIVE

Chloe stepped back into the cafe and was immediately set upon by Blanche. The interest of the patrons was also quite evident.

"There was an accident with Duncan and a gun. My gun. McIlroy ended up injured but not terribly. He'll have a few uncomfortable days but that's about all."

Chloe moved toward the kitchen.

"What was your son doing with a gun?"

"He's only a child. He shouldn't have been handling one."

"Why do you have a gun?"

The customers who asked the questions were ones who weren't very friendly or welcoming to the women of Sanctuary House. Chloe didn't respond. She just continued on into the kitchen. Almeda and Blanche had carried her load of work as well as her own. She planned to let Almeda go home. She normally went home right after breakfast. The woman did more than her share and had an infant as well.

"Almeda, thank you for covering for me. You go home now and rest."

"You all right, Chloe?" Both she and Blanche had followed her into the kitchen.

Chloe laughed. "Yes, maybe. It's not every day your son shoots the man who's courting you in his behind."

"What?"

"Poor Dunc," said Blanche.

"Please don't spread this. What happened will be spread around town, but I don't want the why passed. Dunc took my gun, his pa's really. He asked McIlroy to teach him to shoot. The King gang is the same one we were with. He wants to learn to shoot so he can protect me and Lil-Pen, the rest of us, too."

"Oh my." Blanche sat down at the work table. "That poor boy, taking on that burden."

Almeda's eyes were wide in her dark face. "Guess I never gave his past a thought. Just thought of how it affected you. Gonna have to add this burden he carries to my prayers. Poor thing. He's too young to have such worries."

"Amen," Blanche echoed the sentiment.

Chloe took the pot of potatoes off the stove and poured them into the large colander. After the water drained she put them back in the pot and began to mash them.

"Almeda, you head home. You're looking tired. I don't want you over working yourself. Thank you for helping while I dealt with the situation."

"You're welcome, honey. Gonna go home and spend some time on my knees. It's what I can do since there ain't really nothing else I can."

"That's invaluable, Almeda. Thank you."

After Almeda left Blanche put her arms around Chloe. "Stop. Talk to me. How are you doing?"

Chloe stopped mashing and leaned against her friend. "I'm shaking on the inside. I hadn't realized Dunc was so scared for us. Then he was scared McIlroy wouldn't want to court me. Wouldn't want to be his pa." She went on to explain what had happened, what Dunc thought and his fears. Blanche listened and simply held her.

When Chloe finished, Blanche said, "You have a wonderful son. You know that. He wasn't thinking about himself. He wanted to protect you, Lil-Pen and the rest of us. That's a tall order for a short man. Be proud of that."

"I am. Noah has offered to teach him to shoot. Like he said, he understands exactly how Dunc feels. He'll be able to talk to him, help him work through it all."

Blanche nodded and released her. "Well, you ready to cook? We're a bit behind. Not much got done while we waited for news."

They were busy getting the preparations done for the noon meal when Lil-Pen came into the back door of the kitchen. She wasn't supposed to bother her mother during the morning but her daughter's worried look gave her pause. She knelt and wrapped her arms around her daughter.

"Mama, is Dunc okay?"

"Yes, Sweetie, he is. He's going to stay with McIlroy today and tonight."

"Is McIlroy okay?"

"He's got a pretty big owie."

"Did Dunc shoot him?"

"Sort of. It was an accident. He didn't mean to."

"Good. I like McIlroy. Dunc does, too."

"So do I."

Lil-Pen finally smiled a little. "Mama, can I have a piece of paper and a pencil?"

"Yes, why?"

"I want to draw a picture for McIlroy. To make him feel better."

Chloe rose, went to the storage shelf and took down a piece of brown paper and got a pencil from a cup sitting there.

"Here you go. I think that's a wonderful idea. I'm sure he'll appreciate it. Now you head back to the House. I'll come after work and we'll take your picture and their supper to McIlroy and Dunc later."

"Okay." Lil-Pen turned to go.

"Lil-Pen."

The girl turned back. Chloe knelt and gave her another hug. "I love you."

Lil-Pen smiled a big smile. "I love you too, Mama."

~~~~~

Dunc sat dejected in the lone chair in the room. Noah had gone down stairs to get another one for himself from the smithy. McIlroy lay prone on the bed.

"Don't fratch yourself so much, Dunc. I know you're ashamed and scared, but no permanent harm was done. My bum will heal in a few days." McIlroy couldn't think of what else to say that would help. He wasn't angry or upset with the boy other than what would be expected from such careless behavior with a gun, not checking to see if it was loaded. Even that he could understand. He'd done it himself. Nearly shot off his foot once.

Noah came back into the room and placed the chair across the small table from Dunc. He sat and reached over and patted the teenager on the shoulder.

"Chloe has raised you into a fine young man. I'm proud of you."

Dunc raised startled eyes. "I just shot McIlroy. How could you be proud of me?"

"God honors the intent, the motivation. He wants justice and mercy. You, no matter how the accident happened, have all those qualities. You want to protect your mother and sister. You want to protect the others you live with. That's much more important than…" Noah chuckled, "shooting McIlroy in the behind."

McIlroy chuckled, too. "Pastor's right. I'll take a bullet in the butt any day for you, your ma and sister. Heck, I'll take one for anyone to be protected from abuse and injustice. Scripture says pure love is being willing to lay down your life for a friend."

Dunc chuckled a little, but it didn't seem to take away his sorrow.

"Tell us what it was like living with the gang, Dunc," Noah said softly.

"It was all I knew until Lil-Pen was born. I was always cold and hungry. Well, not in the summer, cold that is. Ma kept me close. I wasn't to be loud or around the men. There were a couple of other ladies. They and ma stuck together. There weren't any other kids my age. There were some older, but the boys went some with the men.

"My pa was the leader so none of the other kids messed with me much. He didn't pay much attention to me. He'd tell me to get away when he wanted to spend time with my ma. He got real mad when she told him she was going to have another baby. He hit her one time in the stomach. Really hard. She had the baby really early that time. It was so small." Dunc lifted his hand. "It wasn't even as big as this. A little boy. Ma couldn't get up right then so I wrapped it in a rag and went out and buried it."

Tears were streaming down his face. "I helped bury three

other babies. One lived three months. She was so pretty. Tina.

"That's why I have to protect Ma and Lil-Pen. I don't want Ma to lose any more babies and don't want Lil-Pen to have to live like me and my ma did.

"I was so scared when my pa was killed. I thought the gang might kill us. Or make Ma be with each man. She was expecting Lil-Pen then. Then they left us at that cabin. I didn't know how to help ma. We didn't have much food and were so far from any town.

"Then Nugget Nate and Mrs. Penny showed up. Mrs. Penny helped Ma give birth to Lil-Pen. I looked for a pretty spot to bury her. I figured she'd die like the others did. Instead Nugget Nate and Mrs. Penny took us to Sanctuary Place." Dunc smiled.

"It was so much better. We had a real house to live in. Sure, there were other ladies and kids in it, just like here, but we had enough food and clothes. I got to go to school and learn to read and write and cipher. I could play with the other kids. We didn't have to move real fast, get away from wherever we were.

"Ma was really happy, too. Lil-Pen didn't die. She's a pest sometimes, but I love her and want her to have a good life. I don't want her to get kidnapped like my ma did. That's why I have to learn to shoot."

He'd been staring at the table most of the time he was talking. Now he looked at each man, his expression was firm, serious.

"I'll teach you. I promise," Noah said. "I'll make sure you know how to protect your family. That doesn't mean you can just shoot the men in the gang if you see them. That would be murder, but you can protect those you love and yourself."

Dunc nodded. McIlroy saw the resolve and determination settle on him like a mantle. At that moment the family resemblance between Noah and Dunc was evident. Noah would get that same expression on his face when he was pressed into defending either a person or a Biblical concept.

"Dunc, where did Lil-Pen get her name?" He asked.

"Oh, her real name is Penelope. She's named after Mrs. Penny, Nugget Nate's wife. They stayed at Sanctuary Place for the winter when we first moved there. Someone started calling the baby Lil-Pen and it just stuck. Can't remember who. She's been

Lil-Pen ever since."

Noah stood. "I need to get back to the shop." He pulled his pocket watch out and opened, looked at the time. "Or rather head home for an early lunch. It's about time for you to go to the cafe and get the meal your ma is packing for you two."

Dunc jumped up and said a quick good-bye. "I don't want to be late. I don't need any more trouble today." He dashed down the stairs, his steps sounding like a herd of stampeding cattle.

Noah and McIlroy chuckled, then Noah sobered and said, "Chloe hadn't given me quite that much detail of her life before Nate found her. I knew it was bad but…" He let the sentence hang.

"Don't worry, Noah. I'll treat her right. She doesn't ever need to worry about being mistreated again. Dunc either."

"I know, McIlroy. I'm more worried that if I see any of the King gang I'll pull my Colts and shoot them on the spot."

"I hear ya."

~~~~~

Chloe held on to Lil-Pen's hand with one of hers and a picnic basket with the other. They walked up the street heading to the smithy. They were taking supper for themselves, Duncan and McIlroy.

When they arrived Dunc was downstairs sorting through a pile of broken metal pieces. He stopped and smiled at them, taking the basket from Chloe.

"McIlroy took some of that medicine Doc gave him. He said it tasted terrible. He went to sleep. I've been down here cleaning and sorting. I hope I'm doing that right."

"I'm sure you are and if not, at least you've sorted it into some kind of order."

They went up the stairs and found McIlroy awake and obviously uncomfortable. Chloe went to the bed and helped him to stand.

"What do you need? Can I help?"

"No. I need Dunc to help me down the stairs."

"Why?"

"Woman, just let me go down with the boy. We'll be back in a few minutes."

Chloe realized what he was talking about and backed away. Dunc helped McIlroy down the stairs. She began removing the covered dishes from the basket.

"What are they doing, Mama? Why'd they have to go downstairs? I think McIlroy was hurting." Lil-Pen was looking at the stairs with concern.

"He needed to use the necessary. He didn't want to say it."

"Why not? Everybody has to go."

"It's just not something people want to talk about, especially between men and women."

"Well, that doesn't make much sense."

Chloe chuckled. "It just is, so don't."

They heard the men coming back up. When they came in McIlroy moved to stand leaning against the wall.

"You planning on eating standing up?" Chloe eyed him.

"Thought I might try it. I'm tired of lying on my stomach. Don't think I want to try sitting today."

Chloe ducked her head to hide her amused smile.

Lil-Pen reached into the basket and brought out a large piece of brown paper. She went to stand in front of McIlroy and tapped his knee. He looked down.

"I drawed this for you. To make you feel better."

McIlroy took it and glanced at Chloe. She fought hard to keep her lips from twitching. He looked at the paper and down at the face gazing up at him so hopeful for approval of her drawing.

"That's a mighty fine drawing Lil-Pen. Mighty fine."

"Will you hang it up on the wall so you can look at it every time you feel bad?"

This was a pivotal moment in her daughter's relationship with the man who would very likely be her pa.

"Sure, Lil-Pen. I'll be most proud to. See that box over there?" He pointed to it. "Get it for me, please."

Lil-Pen rushed across the small room and brought the box back to him. Taking the box, McIlroy opened it and picked out two sturdy pins. He turned and fastened the paper on the wall at about waist level. Lil-Pen's face burst into a huge smile. She hugged his legs.

Chloe looked at McIlroy and nodded. She knew that however

long it took, she'd wait for him to ask her to marry him. And her answer would be yes. She moved her gaze to the brown paper hanging on the wall. On it was a pencil drawing of a man with a shaggy beard and wild hair. His mouth was open, the expression one of pain. A line was through his bottom and circles that must represent drops of blood spread out over the rest of the paper. Yes, indeed. He was worth waiting for.

~~~~~

Dunc came home the following evening saying that McIlroy was up and moving well enough, if slow, and didn't need him to stay that night. He'd go back in the morning and help with whatever the man needed. Chloe, again, sat with the children on either side of her on the bed. She had decided they needed to know Noah was their uncle.

Waiting a few moments, Chloe cleared her throat and said, "There's something I want to tell you both. It's a good thing and has made me very, very happy."

Both children looked at her, questions in their eyes.

"I've told you about being stolen from my family when I was a girl. How I missed my mama and brother so very much?"

Dunc and Lil-Pen nodded.

"Well, God has been very good and He answered a prayer I had to learn what happened to them. Well," she took a deep breath. "I've found my brother. He lives here in Stones Creek. It's Pastor Preston. He's your uncle."

Silence met her words for several moments. Then Lil-Pen said, "He's nice and the baby is really cute. Mrs. Preston is nice too. I don't know her very much. Can I play with the baby?"

"That's all you care about, Lil-Pen?" Dunc laughed. "The baby?"

Lil-Pen harrumphed.

"It's fine, Dunc. Babies are cute and fun. What do you think of the news?" Chloe looked at him.

Dunc hugged her. "I think it's wonderful, Ma. When did you figure it out?"

"As soon as I saw him that first day we were here. He looks a lot like my pa."

"So, is he my uncle?" Lil-Pen asked.

"Yes, he is. Vernie is your aunt and Dottie is your cousin."

Letting out a deep breath, Dunc said, "Wow. I never had any family but you and Lil-Pen. Not real family. All the House people are family but this is blood family."

Lil-Pen sat up and looked across Chloe at her brother. "Yuck. I don't want any bloody family. It's messy."

CHAPTER TWENTY-SIX

Birdie Pullman walked up the boardwalk toward the front of Cutler's General Store. She'd taken on a job of cleaning the shelves of the mercantile, the train station and the jail, as well as doing the majority of cleaning on the House.

A buckboard sat tied to the hitching post. Three small children were wrestling in the back. The oldest didn't look to be about six years old. The youngest couldn't be more than two. They were dressed in clean but rumpled clothing. Just then the middle sized child tumbled out the open back falling onto the ground. The other two looked over the end but didn't try to get out of the wagon.

Birdie rushed over and scooped the little girl up. "Are you hurt, honey?"

She was crying and had a split lip. Birdie reached into her pocket and took out her handkerchief using it to blot the blood. She looked up at the oldest child who was kneeling on the edge of the buckboard bed.

"What're your names? I'm Miss Pullman."

"I'm Steven and I'm six, that's Mary, she's four and he's Jack. He just turned two. She gonna be okay?"

While Steven had been introducing himself and his siblings Birdie was inspecting the girl to determine if there were any serious injuries. Not finding any she hugged the child to her.

"It's okay. I know you're hurting but you'll be fine. It'll stop in a minute." She rocked Mary, who clung to her as she sobbed. She looked at the two in the wagon seeing Jack stick his dirty thumb in his mouth. "Where's your ma and pa?"

"Pa's in the store. Ma's in the cemetery. She done died last winter," the oldest one said. "Pa said she's with Jesus now. She got real sick. Even Doc Eli couldn't keep her alive and he worked hard trying to." Tears glistened in his eyes.

Birdie put Mary into the wagon then climbed up into it herself. She wasn't going to leave the children alone and chance that one would fall out again. How could any father leave such small ones alone out on the street like this?

She scooted to the far end of the wagon bed and leaned up against the boards of the frame. The children sat beside her with Jack climbing into her lap. He kept sucking his thumb but snuggled against her. She pulled his hand away from his mouth. Jack lifted his head then stuck his thumb back in and laid his head against her.

Birdie fell in love right then. She looked at the soiled faces and rumpled clothes. Mary's face had trails in the dust from her tears. She was leaning against Birdie's side. Steven leaned against her other side. Poor little guys. No ma and a pa who leaves them alone in a wagon on the street.

"What are you doing in my wagon?"

The wagon shook when several bundles were tossed in. Birdie looked up. A man in a black cowboy hat stood with his hands on his hips. His hair and eye color was shaded by his hat but he looked so tired. His clothing was rumpled like the children's. His canvas vest was stained but his pants and shirt looked clean, or fairly clean. He must have done chores before they came to town.

Birdie set Jack down and clambered to the end of the wagon and climbed out. "What are you doing leaving these children out here by themselves? Mary fell out of the wagon. She might have really hurt herself."

The man turned from looking at Birdie and jumped up into the wagon. She was surprised at his agility. He threw his hat to the bed of the wagon.

"Come here, baby doll. Where are you hurting? Let me kiss it better." He gathered his daughter into his arms and kissed her tear streaked face. Birdie watched him soothe his daughter and some of her anger left. The man truly cared about his children.

But still.

"Steven told me about their ma and I'm sorry for your loss. However, you shouldn't leave a six year old to mind his siblings. That's too much responsibility. You also shouldn't leave the endgate down. Mary fell out of it."

"Well, I can't watch them and get my trading done in the store at the same time. If you're so concerned about my children how about you marry me and become their ma?"

Birdie stared at him. She hadn't even learned his name but when she looked at the children all she saw was their need. She turned her gaze back to the man and saw his love for them and his fatigue at caring for his work, home and children.

"What's your name and where do you live?"

"Name's Harvey Hayes. I've got a spread about eight miles east. It's got water enough for several hundred head. I'm building to that. I've got a real house, not a soddy."

"Who's Jesus to you?"

"I could ask you the same but since you asked, He's my Lord and Savior."

Birdie looked him over once more. "I'm Birdie Pullman, one of the Sanctuary House Ladies. I can't marry without the men of the council's approval. We can go ask them and if they approve then, yes, I'll marry you and become their ma."

"And my wife."

Birdie understood what he was saying. She'd be a wife in every sense of the word. She swallowed. "Yes, your wife."

"Okay, then let's go talk with these men you need permission from. Come on, kids. You're going with us." Harvey helped his children down from the wagon. "So who do we need to talk with?"

Birdie was stunned at the turn her life was taking. She'd been passing the store after cleaning the train station. Now she was going to find out about getting permission to marry a total stranger. "Well, the committee's Ben Cutler, Doc Eli, Sheriff Riverby and Pastor Preston."

Harvey nodded. "Good men. They'd be the ones I'd choose to make sure the women weren't taken advantage of and married to those who'd abuse their trust. Come on, let's go talk to Ben first."

Harvey picked up Jack. Mary took Birdie's hand and Steven stuck his hands in his pants pockets. Birdie figured he thought himself too old to have his hand held. Harvey opened the door to the general store and allowed her and his older children to precede him inside.

"Harvey, what more can I help you with?" Ben asked as they walked up the center aisle to the counter he was standing behind.

"Miss Pullman here didn't appreciate my leaving my children alone in the wagon. Indicated it wasn't safe, and she was right. Mary fell out. Thank the Lord, she wasn't badly hurt. We spoke a bit and she's agreed to marry me and be their ma."

Ben's mouth dropped open. "But you just met. Not that I object to you courting her, but you don't know each other."

"We can get to know each other later," Birdie said. "God has placed a need before me. These children need a mother. Harvey's doing his best, I can tell from how the children's clothes are washed. That's just it. They are washed. Not ironed but washed. He's trying to do both his job and the job of a woman. Their mother. He's working himself to death trying to do all the work. What'll happen to the children if he does work himself to an early grave?"

Before Ben could answer the question Birdie went on. "I'm willing to become their mother and Harvey's wife. If you and the other men make us wait it'll just delay these children from getting the ma they need and Harvey'll just get more tired. That's going to wear him down even more, having to come to town and court me."

Ben looked at the exhausted Harvey and the rumpled clothing on him and the children. "Harvey, go find the sheriff, Doc and the preacher. We'll see what they have to say. I'm not going to encourage or discourage this. The rest of you come into the back room. There's a table and chairs as well as a few toys to keep the children occupied."

Birdie took Jack from Harvey's arms and led the way around the counter as Harvey went out the front door.

"Miss Pullman— Birdie," Ben said, drawing her away to the other side of the back room he had taken her and the children into once they were settled with some toys. "You only met

Harvey about fifteen minutes ago. How can you even think about marrying him?"

"Is he a man you'd approve of if he'd spent several weeks or months courting me?"

"Well, yes. I've known Harvey a long time. He's a good God fearing man who is raising his children in the Lord. He took it hard when Mabel died, but he stepped up and is taking as good a care of his children as he can.

"Several families asked if he wanted them to take in one or more of his kids but he wouldn't part with them. Said he loved them too much. He's been working the ranch and taking care of them, too."

"I understand that. He's doing the best he can and yet he'll kill himself if he doesn't have help soon. Then where will the children be?"

Just then Harvey, Newt, Eli and Noah came in from the front of the store.

"What's this we hear that Miss Pullman wants to marry Harvey and that they just met a short while ago?" Noah asked.

"That's right, Pastor. He's got a need I can satisfy." Birdie blushed, realizing what her words implied. "I mean that he needs someone to help him raise his children. They need a ma and therefore, he needs a wife. I'm willing to be that. I'm asking you all to approve it. Will you?"

Noah's eyebrow raised and looked straight at Harvey. "Don't you think that's a bit hasty?"

"Probably, Pastor, but unless I get some help with the children I'm not going to make it. I'm exhausted. My herd's small and I don't have a lot of hands. I can't pay for help with the children. A wife's the only way. My spread's far enough out of town that I can't come courting like the men who live here."

"Harvey, you're a decent man and you were a good husband to Mabel. We've been charged with the welfare of the Sanctuary House ladies. It's a big responsibility." Newt ran his hand over his chin. "I'm courting one myself so I understand the desire to make one your wife."

"I don't think you do, Sheriff. What you're thinking ain't my main thought here. I need a ma for my children. That's my priority. The other. It'll come later once we know each other better." Harvey bent down and picked up Jack. He'd been pulling on his father's leg ever since the men came in. "What ya need... Eeeewww. You stink."

Big tear drops came from Jacks eyes. "Need potty."

Birdie moved forward and took the boy in her arms. "It's okay, Jack. Let's go and clean you up." She looked at Harvey. "Do you have any other clothes for him?"

"That's part of the supplies I came to town for. I'll get them." Harvey went out to the wagon.

Birdie looked at the other two children who were seated at the table. They were watching the adults. They just looked sad and tired. She thought they hadn't had much to be happy about in a while. Harvey came back with a parcel and started to take Jack from her.

"No, I'll deal with this. You stay here and talk with Pastor and the others."

Birdie took Jack and went out the back door to the pump. As she stripped him down and cleaned him with a wet rag Ben had given her she prayed for guidance. She realized she'd not asked for the Lord's direction on this and it gave her a moment of panic.

Then, as she prayed, peace settled over her. Then Jack, now dressed in fresh clothes, wrapped his arms around her neck and hugged her. Birdie knew this family was God's will for her. She wouldn't have to fight for them because He would fight for her. But she did have an idea that would make things easier for today.

"I have an idea," she said when she carried Jack into the back room of the general store. "You've got to go back to the ranch. The children and I want to become better acquainted. We need to court a bit more to satisfy these men here." She waved her hand at the others gathered in the small room.

"How about you leave the children with me for a few nights? We have space at Sanctuary House for them to sleep. Would you be willing to come to town each day for a few hours until say Saturday? That's four days. By then we could spend some more time getting to know each other. We'd have time to become acquainted. You wouldn't have to tend the children so that's the time you take coming to town to see me and them."

Harvey nodded. "Might work."

Birdie looked at the men charged with safeguarding the women into good marriages. The expressions on their faces told her they approved of this plan better than allowing her to marry him that afternoon.

"I'll approve of that plan, at least to find out how you both still feel at the end of the week," Noah said.

"Will the other ladies mind having these three added to their numbers?" Eli asked.

"Shouldn't think so. We've all been in worse spots and needed help."

"I can pay for their upkeep," Harvey said.

"I don't think it'll be needed, but we can ask Blanche. She's sort of the head of the house."

Harvey took Jack from her and knelt beside the table where Steven and Mary sat. "Miss Pullman has offered for you to stay with her a few days while I work. I'll come into town every day to see you and her. Oh, baby." Mary's eyes had filled with tears. He gathered her to his chest with his other arm. "You'll have fun and be better taken care of. Then, on Saturday, if everything goes well, we'll take Miss Pullman home with us as your new ma."

Two sets of eyes shot to her. She smiled and hugged Jack just a bit closer. The boy and girl looked to their father again.

"You'll come every day?" Steven's voice held worry.

"Unless something happens on the ranch, I sure will. I need my hugs and kisses."

Birdie knew what the children were going through. She'd been left at a strange place among strangers, too. At eleven she'd been older, but her parents weren't coming back for her. They just left her at Sanctuary Place saying they had too many children and she was a girl.

"Let's get in the buckboard and ride over there." Harvey stood up and took Steven and Mary by the hand.

Birdie felt like she was the head of a parade with Harvey and the children, the men following behind. They piled the children into the back and Harvey helped Birdie up onto the seat.

"I'll come over after supper and help get the children settled if you think it would help, Birdie," Noah said.

"I'm coming for supper with Myra and Troy this evening so I'll see you, too." Newt tweaked Mary on the nose and smiled. Birdie was pleased that the little girl smiled back.

CHAPTER TWENTY-SEVEN

The front yard of the House was full of children, as usual. They all stopped what they were doing when the buckboard halted in front of them.

"Birdie, what's going on?" Blanche asked, coming out of the house and down the porch steps.

"We've got a few extras until Saturday. These are Steven, Mary and Jack. Their pa is Harvey Hayes. I'm most likely going to be marrying him on Saturday."

The women and children who had gathered around were vocal in their questions and surprise. Birdie didn't want to take the time to explain right now. She wanted to get the beds arranged and made so Harvey could see his children would be well cared for in his absence. She also wanted to make sure he had eaten a good meal and had some food to take home with him before he left.

"I'll tell you about it later. I need to make up beds with clean sheets for the children."

That was all it took. The ladies and older children trooped into the house and up to the third floor where Birdie's room was. They pushed her bed up next to the wall and moved a double bed in for Steven and Jack. There was a trundle under Birdie's bed for Mary to sleep in.

The room was crowded but would work. Birdie didn't want the children in a room by themselves. If they woke in the night in a strange place they might be scared. She wanted to be close if they needed her.

Harvey had purchased each of the children a new set of clothing so they would have clean clothes to wear tomorrow. At least if Birdie washed Jack's soiled ones. She would after supper. They'd hang in the washroom over night and be dry to put on in the morning.

Men weren't allowed upstairs in Sanctuary House so Harvey couldn't help with the arrangements on the third floor. He waited downstairs while Birdie took the children up to see where they would be sleeping. They came back down and Birdie was pleased to see they were excited to tell their father about their beds.

"Harvey," Birdie said. "I know you need to be getting back to your ranch. I want to make sure you eat before you go, or at least take something back with you. You don't need to be trying to cook tonight."

"I can get something at the bunkhouse. Cookie will feed me. He's been helping me some with meals since Mable died." He'd picked up Jack and was holding him close. She could tell it was going to be difficult for him to leave his children behind. It made her more certain he was a good father and cemented her thoughts that he had a positive character. He'd make her a good husband. She'd do what she was able to be a Proverbs thirty-one wife to him.

"How about you eat something here?" It was Blanche who invited him this time. "We've got leftovers from lunch. It'll tide you over and give you energy for the trip back to your place."

"Well, all right. You talked me into it."

Jack had laid his head on Harvey's shoulder. Mary looked tired, too. Birdie figured it was most likely their nap time. She didn't want to put them to bed alone on the third floor so hurried everyone into the dining room. Once Harvey left she would take the children upstairs and put the younger ones to bed.

"How about a snack?" She looked at each child individually. Steven nodded with a gap-toothed smile. Mary grinned and Jack nodded with his thumb in his mouth.

Harvey settled the children at a table while Blanche and Birdie got the food ready. Soon Harvey had a plate of pork roast, mashed potatoes and gravy along with carrots and applesauce in front of him and the children each had a ginger cookie and glass of milk.

Steven's eyes filled with tears as he took a bite.

"What's the matter, sweetie?" Birdie sat down next to him and wrapped an arm around his shoulders.

"Ma used to make these kind. I ain't had any since she got sick."

Birdie looked at Harvey. He had tears in his eyes, too. "I know how to make these. We'll call them Ma's cookies. How about that? It'll be a way for you to remember her by."

A tear slipped down Steven's cheek. He nodded and took another bite. Birdie hugged him then glanced at Mary across the table sitting next to Harvey. She looked so very sad.

Birdie realized the next four days would be hard for them. Especially for Steven and Mary. They remembered their mother and would be missing their father. Jack most likely didn't remember the woman who gave him birth but would be adjusting to not having his father around. She sent up a prayer for help, guidance and patience.

Jack had fallen asleep on Harvey's shoulder and didn't wake up when he was transferred into Birdie's arms. Mary cried when Harvey hugged and kissed her good-bye. Steven just looked sad. They watched the buckboard until it turned between the House and Cutler's store building, then Birdie took the children up to her room.

Jack snuggled right down onto the bed, sound asleep. Steven stood at the window looking out while Birdie tucked Mary in for her nap. She went to kneel next to him and murmured that they would wait until they were sure Mary was asleep before they went to find some toys or books. Birdie didn't want to leave them alone very long and risk having either child wake in a strange room without her there. Steven just nodded. She wrapped her arms around him and wasn't surprised when he started crying.

"It's hard having your pa leave you all here, isn't it?" She whispered.

"Uh huh."

"It's not for good. He'll be back tomorrow. Then there will only be three days before we can all go to the ranch."

In a few minutes they were certain Mary was sound asleep and they moved from the bedroom to the sitting room across the hall. They were close enough to hear but could speak in more normal tones. Also, there were toys as several of the boys stayed on this floor.

For a while Birdie asked Steven about the ranch and house. She was impressed with how much he knew about its workings. Blanche came upstairs with her son, John, who was five, and the boys began to play with the toy soldiers and wooden horses. She pulled Birdie to a set of chairs and they sat down.

"Well, I must say I'm surprised. You taking on this and planning to marry on Saturday."

Birdie grinned. "No more than I am. It just started happening and all of a sudden I'm agreeing to marry Harvey. Then I realized I hadn't prayed about it." She laughed. "Actually, I was cleaning Jack up from an accident he had and realized it. Then I started praying and such peace settled over me that I knew everything was of God."

Blanche reached out and took Birdie by the hand. "I'm so glad to hear you say that. I was afraid you were just letting your heart for the children lead you. Emotions can lie. Believe me when I say that." Birdie saw pain flash through Blanche's eyes. "I'm glad you took the time to ask God's will."

"I am, too. You can't believe how much peace I have over this entire thing. I know it won't be easy. I've got three very sad children and a grieving man in my life now. It'll take more patience than I have to deal with them and make them happy again." She grinned. "That's what I'm counting on the Holy Spirit to deal with. All I need to do is what I can. He'll do the rest."

~~~~~

Over the next three days Birdie had moments of doubt and hours of praise as she dealt with scared, sad children as well as hugs and laughter as she got to know the Hayes family. The first night was the most difficult. All three children woke several times frightened in the unfamiliar surroundings. They were tired and cranky in the morning.

Harvey had told her he wouldn't get to town until later in the afternoon so he could have supper with them before going back to the ranch. Birdie made all three children take naps, which didn't please six-year-old Steven, but she was firm in her insistence. Their grouchiness was gone when they awoke, and the rest of the day went better. They were excited to see their father ride up on his stallion and ran from the porch to great him chattering about their day.

Harvey stayed after Birdie put the children to bed so they could get better acquainted. They talked about their lives and Birdie had to shoo him away before sunset so he wouldn't have to travel too much in the dark to get home. Her peace continued when the children slept through the night.

The next couple of days went well, also. Each day she loved the children more and they settled in with the rest of the children well. Rather than cling to her and stay by her side, Steven and Mary spent time playing with those of similar age. They no longer feared their father wasn't coming back for them.

Friday brought Noah, Sheriff Newt, Doc Eli and Ben Cutler to the house just after Harvey arrived. He was later than usual since he was staying at the hotel overnight in preparation for he and Birdie to marry on Saturday. He'd worked longer before coming to town.

Harvey and Birdie were sitting on the porch swing that had recently been installed. His arm was draped along the back of the swing behind her, though not holding her. The children were playing with the others in the yard. Knowing the reason for the sudden appearance of the four men, the other women moved from the grouping of chairs near the couple into the house or down onto the grass to give privacy for discussion.

Noah cleared his throat. "So, you both think going through with your plan is still the way to go?"

Birdie looked at Harvey. He smiled at her. "Yes, Pastor, I do," he said. "Birdie has taken superb care of my children. They seem to really like her. Have taken to calling her Ma Bee. I've taken a shine to her, too."

Birdie could feel herself blush. "I've come to love the children in the few days we've had together. Harvey's been a real gentleman, and real respectful to me. I'm hoping you will allow us to marry tomorrow. It's been hard on the children to be away from their pa."

Noah looked at the other three men. "I've been praying every day about this and haven't received any negative answers. It is why you ladies came out here, after all. To get married to our men.

"You're a fine upstanding member of our community, Harvey, and definitely have a need. Birdie, you seem pretty sure you want to take on a man with three children. I have a question for the both of you." He paused. "Have you prayed about this decision?"

"I have, Pastor," Harvey said. "I needed to know if Birdie was the right mother for my children. I prayed all the way home that first night that if God wanted this marriage, the children would be happy and peaceful with staying the rest of the week when I came back that next day. I wanted that to be my sign that God was in favor of us getting married. If they weren't, I was going to tell Birdie I'd changed my mind and take my children home.

"Well, God gave me a firm answer. They were happy and excited when I arrived, and didn't ask if I would take them home. They told me how much fun they were having and how much they liked Miss Birdie as soon as I got here. They didn't even let me dismount before they started telling me."

Birdie leaned back and looked at him. "You never told me that."

"Didn't matter. God confirmed that you're to be my wife and mother to my brood. What He says goes, in my mind." Harvey wrapped his arm around her shoulders.

"What about you, Birdie?" Noah looked at her.

"I knew that first day. I prayed while I was cleaning Jack up and had that peace that passes all understanding. I knew at that moment I was making the right choice. I've prayed every day since, but the peace just gets better and better."

"Sounds like we should have a wedding tomorrow," Ben said.

The other men confirmed the decision. Cheers came through the open window next to them. The curtain was pulled aside. Blanche, Ruth Naylor and Cora Sepal poked their head out.

"I'm sending Ozzie over to Almeda's asking her to make a cake. We'll make tea and lemonade. We can't have our first wedding without some sort of celebration." Blanche ducked back into the room and disappeared from sight.

"I'm so excited. Here comes the bride," sang Cora, then she too left the window.

"How about you let us keep the children here tomorrow night? You two can stay at the hotel and have a bit of privacy before you head back to the ranch," Ruth suggested.

Birdie blushed again and began to protest when Harvey spoke.

"Much obliged to you Miz Naylor. We'll be taking you up on your offer." He squeezed her shoulders slightly and leaned close to whisper in her ear. "Don't worry. I won't pressure you. When you're ready and not before."

Birdie relaxed. It would be nice to get a good night's sleep before moving to the ranch.

"What time do you want the ceremony?" Noah asked.

"What about three o'clock? Jack's up from his nap by then and happy. We'll have time before supper for the reception." Birdie looked at Harvey. "Then we can put the children to bed before we go to the hotel." Her voice faded a bit as she finished speaking. Tomorrow she would leave Sanctuary House for good and spend the night with a man. Whether they consummated or not it was still a nerve-racking thought.

"I think that sounds good," Harvey said. His eyes smiled at her just like his mouth did. "Oh, I brought the children's Sunday clothes. Figured they'd need them for the wedding. And since we'll be staying over they can wear them to church service the next day."

Birdie was impressed that he'd thought of their good clothes.

CHAPTER TWENTY-EIGHT

Birdie's morning was busy the next day. She'd hauled water and given Mary and Jack baths. Harvey had come and taken Steven with him to Hank Johnson's for a bath and haircut. They'd decided on Friday they weren't going to mess with the bride and groom not seeing each other on the wedding day superstition. When there were three young children involved that sort of thing just became nonsense.

They'd had lunch together at the cafe, a sort of pre-wedding family celebration. This sort of spending wouldn't happen often and Birdie was grateful Harvey had suggested they have the treat.

Jack and Mary had been put down for naps early so they would be sure to have enough rest and Harvey had taken Steven with him to the hotel to get ready. The boy was going to stand up with his father. Steven was excited about his important job in the ceremony. Birdie hoped he wasn't disappointed since all it was was standing still.

Laura Duffle arranged Birdie's hair in a fancy do saying that even though she didn't have a new dress for the occasion her hair could be dressed up in a new way. While she was fixing Birdie's hair Laura quietly asked her if she knew what happened between a man and a woman.

"I do. I did live at Sanctuary Place." They both laughed. Given the variety of women who sought refuge there not much wasn't shared about the topic. "Blanche gave me more, um, practical insight last night."

"Good, then I don't need to."

Sooner than Birdie thought possible they were at the church. Mary was jumping up and down with excitement, clutching the small bouquet of flowers that matched the larger one Birdie held in her trembling hands.

Eli had asked if he could walk Birdie down the aisle and give her away. She'd been touched and nearly cried that he had thought of it. Having been cast out from her family at such a young age she'd never dreamt anyone would care enough to do so.

The sound of Joy of Man's Desiring by Johann Sebastian Bach began on the new piano set at the front of the church. The instrument had arrived a few weeks ago as a surprise gift to the church from Nugget Nate Ryder. Blanche Basking knew how to play and was now the official pianist for the church.

Cora, who was standing up with Birdie, urged Mary forward. The little girl ran down aisle and into the first pew where Chloe was. She and Lil-Pen were of an age and had become fast friends over the past few days. Chloe would monitor Mary during the ceremony. Cora gave the bride a hug and slowly walked to the front of the church. Then it was Birdie's turn.

Eli took her hand and placed it on his arm. They walked up the aisle and Birdie made eye contact with Harvey. Her stomach was full of butterflies. Suddenly she wondered about the peace she'd had since Tuesday. Her foot stumbled. Eli's arm held her firmly so she didn't fall.

"Don't worry. Harvey's a good man. I've known him for several years."

The peace settled again and Birdie straightened her back. She lifted her eyes and looked at her groom. His smile was wide and welcoming. She smiled back. A verse from Psalms came to mind. *May the LORD give strength to his people! May the LORD bless his people with peace!*

The peace she'd experienced the past few days cloaked her again. "Let's mosey up to the altar. I've got a man to marry."

A short time later she was walking back up the aisle but on the arm of a different man. She was Mrs. Harvey Hayes, mother to three young children and happy as all get out.

They had the cake and lemonade and tea at Sanctuary House. Tables had been taken into the yard so the warm September day could be enjoyed and the children have space to play and run. The townsfolk slowly headed home and the ladies went on to their various tasks. Birdie didn't have any, though it made her feel guilty. She was assured over and over that they had everything under control.

Harvey and she sat on the porch swing watching the children and chatting. He had his arm around her and she snuggled against him.

"We'll need to head out to the ranch right after dinner tomorrow. We'll need to be all packed up before worship service. I've never been gone this long. My crew is good but small. It ain't fair to leave all the work to them. They've taken on more than they needed to since Mable died."

"I understand. I'm eager to see your ranch. The children are wanting to be home, too."

"I brought the buckboard. It's at the livery." They made plans for the morning to leave as soon as they'd eaten Sunday dinner which they would have at the House. Birdie only had one trunk which was packed with all her things except what she needed for the night and next day. Those were in a carpetbag waiting in her room.

After supper both adults put the children to bed since Harvey was now allowed up to the third floor. Esther, who had no children, was going to sleep in the room with them that night. Harvey picked up Birdie's carpetbag and with one last goodnight to the sleepy ones lying in their beds, he and Birdie left the House.

Birdie was scared, excited, nervous and secure walking beside him. He had his arm wrapped around her waist making sure she didn't trip over the rough dirt of the street. He didn't stop in the lobby but took her directly up the stairs to the second floor and his room.

"I've never been in a hotel before," Birdie said as she waited for him to pull the room key from his pocket and unlock the door.

"Not been in many myself. Not had much need." He unlocked the door then whisked her up in his arms and carried her in.

Setting her on her feet he dropped the carpetbag and turned to shut and lock the door.

Birdie gazed at the four poster bed with its white coverlet. She looked back at Harvey who had come to stand close.

"Birdie, I know I said we'd wait until you were comfortable with me. I just want you to understand I'm ready whenever you are. I'm not going to pressure you, but it's going to be hard on me to wait. I'm a man with a man's urges. I've fathered three children and its been a long time now for me. Not since my wife got sick.

"You're beautiful. I'm wanting you something fierce. I'll honor my pledge to wait if you want. I'm only asking two things. First, that you'll tell me as soon as you are ready. Don't be shy and expect me to know without you saying. And, second, tonight, I'd really like to kiss you like a man kisses his wife. I'll be, well, not satisfied, but as content as I can be with that boon."

Birdie saw the desire and struggle for control in Harvey's eyes. She was nervous but his words and the hands that were holding her face between them so gently eased all her fears.

"Harvey, you don't have to stop at the kiss."

His kiss started out gently then increased with pressure and passion. Soon desire warmed Birdie's body and any fear melted away. Harvey felt her desire and his for her flamed higher. He showered her face with small kisses, and instinctively his hands released all the pins from her hair.

Birdie wasn't sure what she was aching for, just that she needed to be closer to him sooner than it seemed he'd make it. Her hands began pushing his jacket from his shoulders.

When all the pins had been removed and his jacket lay in a heap on the floor Harvey ran his fingers through the tresses then wrapped his arms around her. "Thank you. I promise you delight tonight and always."

~~~~~

As they headed out of town in the buckboard the next day, the children in the bed, Birdie on the seat next to her husband, she smiled. He had fulfilled his promise the night before and that morning. She thought that if they continued the way they started, another child might be in the wagon by this time next year.

One thing was certain. Never, no matter how many children they had, would there be any doubt they were wanted and loved.

CHAPTER TWENTY-NINE

McIlroy's hip still ached but his wound had healed without infection. School had commenced so Dunc was only coming for a few hours after classes were dismissed. He was surprised at how much he missed having the youth around. Just having someone to chat with made the days go more quickly.

Those at the House had celebrated Lil-Pen's fifth and Susan's third birthdays. They were only a few days apart and had been honored together. Dak Levine, the new deputy sheriff, had been present. He was courting Cora. Sheriff Riverby was in attendance, also, as his courtship of Myra Hope was progressing, along with McIlroy's of Chloe.

It was time, McIlroy thought, to speak with her about his intentions and why he hadn't proposed. He figured Newt would be asking Myra to marry him fairly soon. That would put pressure on him to make his own relationship with Chloe more permanent. With that in mind he slipped on a jacket and headed from the warmth of his smithy into the cold October wind.

It was just after two o'clock so the cafe would be empty. He'd eaten there for lunch, very grateful that the ladies allowed him to eat for free. He had made them the shelf brackets they needed and installed them himself. If he was going to marry Chloe, he figured he'd end up doing that sort of thing anyway so might as well start now.

He tapped on the window to get Chloe's attention. She smiled as she looked up from wiping the table and came to open the door for him.

"Hi, what brings you here? Need another piece of pie?"

"Wouldn't turn one down but, no. I have something I want to talk with you about. Didn't want the other ladies listening in or the children… Well, you know. Interrupting." He sat down at the table.

"Okay." The smile had left Chloe's face and doubt entered her eyes.

"It's not that I don't like them or want them around or anything. I want to talk with you about something."

"Okay." She had seated herself across the table from him.

He hated seeing the insecurity in her face. He reached across the table and took her hand. It was trembling.

"Chloe, you know how much I like you. Like Duncan and Lil-Pen, too. I was hoping…" He stopped talking because Chloe's eyes had filled with tears. "Why are you so sad?"

"You don't want to keep courting me. I understand. I'll tell the children. Do you want to still teach Dunc? I know it will disappoint him…"

"No," McIlroy interrupted and gave her hand a comforting squeeze. "I'm not breaking off with you. Not at all." He rubbed his other hand down his face. "I'm making a mess of this." He stood and came around the table. He grabbed a chair and flipped it around to straddle in front of her.

"Chloe, I do want to keep courting you. No, that's not right. I want to marry you and be a father to Dunc and Lil-Pen. There's a problem though. I can't have you moving into my place. It's only one room and, well… You saw it. I don't have furniture or anything. No place for you or the children. Massot is busy building Ben's place and then is going to be doing Eli's.

"I talked with Ben. He's agreed to rent me his apartment above the store, but not until they are in their new house. It's not going to be done until Thanksgiving at the earliest. Maybe not until Christmas.

"That's why I wanted to talk with you today. I think Newt's getting ready to propose to Myra. They can be married as soon as they want. He's got a house. I didn't want you to think I was stringing you along, not mentioning getting married and all. I can't wait to marry you, but have no place for us to live."

He stopped talking when Chloe placed her fingers on his lips. Tears still filled her eyes, but they sparkled and there was a grin on her face.

"Are you asking me if I want to marry you when there is a place for us to live?"

"Well, yeah, I suppose I am."

"Well, I accept. I'm willing to wait until the Cutler's move into their house. Their apartment will be more than fine with me."

McIlroy stood and pushed the chair out of the way drawing her to her feet at the same time. He pulled her to him. "I'm glad. I don't want to wait even a day to make you my wife, but seems I'm going to have to. But I don't have to wait to do this."

He lowered his face and gently pressed his mouth to hers. Then he tickled her lips with his tongue causing hers to open. It was a long moment before he pulled back and released her. He took a shaky breath. He searched her face with his eyes.

"Maybe I need to see if Massot could use some help getting that house done faster."

~~~~~

Newt paced in the jail office. He rubbed his hands down the legs of his pants. He had a ring carefully buttoned into his shirt pocket. Now he just needed to muster up the courage to go and ask Myra to marry him.

"You seem awful nervous, Newt," Deputy Sheriff Dak said. He was seated beside the desk with his feet on it and a coffee mug in his hand.

"Don't you have rounds to make or something?"

"Nope, just got back about five minutes ago." The grin on Dak's face told Newt the younger man was enjoying his discomfort.

Newt stopped his pacing and eyed Dak. "You've been courting Cora. You planning on marrying her?"

"Yep."

"Aren't you nervous about asking?"

"Nope."

Newt stopped pacing and looked at him. "Why not?"

"Already did. She said yes, and we're making plans."

"Congratulations. You never said anything."

"Nope. Decided we want the wedding at Christmas time. It gives me a chance to get to know Cora and especially Susan better. We're going to live in one of the apartments in the cafe, bakery, barber, gun shop building. They aren't finished. Massot's busy building Ben's house. I'm going to ask some of the hands from the Chasing R once they get back from the cattle drive to help me build walls and such. Shouldn't take too long.

"Cora and me, we've ordered some furniture from the catalog at Ben's. Not much, beds, table and chairs, a settee. We'll make do with that until we can afford to buy more."

Newt was dumbstruck. He hadn't really known Dak was that far along in his courting. It didn't seem like the man had been around Sanctuary House all that much. But then, when Newt was there in the evenings Dak would be working.

Dak stood up and smacked Newt on the back. "If you'll take some advice from a younger man… Go ask her and settle the thing. Takes a load off your mind. I can sit here in peace and dream about my wedding night." He sat back down, leaned his chair back putting his booted feet on the desk.

Newt grabbed his hat off the peg by the door and left.

~~~~~

Myra was helping Leah fit a bodice to Traci Fugard. She hadn't been welcoming to the ladies of Sanctuary House. It was obvious from her demeanor that Mrs. Fugard thought they were not fit to be in polite company.

The woman was way too particular if you asked her. No one, did but Myra thought it anyway. Seems the woman wanted to appear more buxom than she really was. Leah was trying to explain that padding the bust would result in a not very flattering drape of the fabric. Traci didn't really care.

The bell over the door jangled and Myra made her escape from the fitting room, making sure the draped entryway didn't reveal anything as she passed through.

"Afternoon, Sheriff. What brings you here?"

"If possible, Miss Hope, I'd like a word with you."

"I knew having these women come to town would lead to problem. I told you that when the idea was first floated, didn't I, Leah?" Traci's voice came through the drapery.

Myra felt her face flush.

"There's no problem, Mrs. Fugard. None at all." Newt raised his voice to be sure to be heard by the busybody. He lowered it and said, "Now must not be a good time. Will you be available to walk this evening?"

Myra flushed again. Newt had been coming at least twice a week ever since he'd first asked to court her but never come to the shop to inquire. He'd just show up, usually after supper but sometimes just in time for the meal.

"Yes." She murmured her reply, not wanting Traci to hear.

"Um, could I possibly take you to the hotel for supper? Just you and me."

Myra placed her hands on her burning cheeks. She nodded knowing her eyes were wide.

"About five-thirty, then?"

She nodded again. Newt grinned at her, then turned and pulled the door open making the bell jangle again.

Myra stood there for a couple of minutes marveling at the thought of having supper in the hotel restaurant. Imagine, ex-prostitute Myra Hope having supper in a fancy place like that, and with a handsome man like Newt Riverby.

When she went back into the fitting room she was met with a sour faced Traci Fugard.

"So, what did he want with you?"

Myra straightened her back and stood as tall as she could. "That, Mrs. Fugard, is none of your business." She glanced at Leah hoping she wasn't in trouble for speaking to a customer in such a manner. Leah, pins in her mouth, was smiling at her.

~~~~~

Newt held the chair for Myra as she sat down. No one had ever done that for her before. It made her feel respected. Not something she felt very often.

"I'd recommend the steak. It's quite good, but then the pork chop is too. I hear their meat comes from Denver on the train everyday." Newt sat across from her and unfolded his napkin placing it on his lap.

"Do you eat here much?" Myra asked.

"Not often. Used to more than now. I eat at the cafe more, but

I can cook, too. Have to, not being married and all."

The look Newt gave her made Myra's face heat again. She thought she had blushed more today than ever in her entire life. Her previous occupation didn't lend itself to a girl blushing very much.

The waiter came and they ordered. Then silence descended over them. Myra thought that was odd since they didn't seem to have trouble chatting during their evening walks. She cleared her throat, then took a drink of water.

Newt fiddled with his silverware. He seemed nervous. It was not an emotion Myra connected with the sheriff. He was always cool and collected. Or at least since they had begun courting. Before that he'd been irritated with her most of the time.

"Myra…" This time it was Newt clearing his throat. "Myra, we've been courting for a while. I've enjoyed our times together and getting to know Troy more. He seems to like me some."

"He does." She wanted to say she did too but kept her mouth shut.

"Myra…" He fumbled with his shirt pocket trying to unbuttoned the button. She took pity on him and stood going to him she deftly worked it through the hole. When she started to go back to her seat Newt took hold of her hand and held her there. He stood up, digging into the pocket. Then he kneeled.

Myra's hands flew to her mouth.

"Myra, will you do me the honor of becoming my wife?" He held a gold band in his hand with a tiny diamond in it. "I know it's not much, but it would mean the world to me if you'd accept this as your wedding ring."

"Oh Newt. Oh Newt. Oh Newt." Nothing else seemed able to come from her.

He chuckled. "Is that a yes or a no?"

"Oh, it's a yes. Of course it's a yes." She was fairly jumping with excitement. She wrapped her arms around him hugging him to her as he knelt in front of her. His head nestled between her breasts until she realized what she was doing. She released him and jumped back. Now her face flamed with embarrassment over her action. She covered it with her hands. Peeking between her fingers she saw a broad smile on his face.

The wait staff and other patrons began cheering and clapping.

~~~~~

Chloe waited in the parlor. She didn't have any chores for the evening so was sort of at loose ends. Lil-Pen was playing outside and Dunc was upstairs doing some homework. He'd been so diligent in his schoolwork. He was loving the time he spent with McIlroy and understood the consequence of not keeping up with his studies.

Heavy steps sounded on the porch and she jumped up. McIlroy was coming for supper tonight. They had decided to tell the children of their plans to wed. Dunc was anxious for the matter to be settled. He wanted McIlroy as his father, though he didn't understand the legal aspects. All he cared about was being able to call him pa.

Chloe opened the door as soon as she got there, nearly being knocked on the forehead by McIlroy's knuckles. She laughed then stepped aside to let him in. She called for Lil-Pen to come. When the girl arrived, she sent her upstairs to tell her brother and then join them in the parlor.

Chloe took McIlroy by the hand and led him into the room and sat next to him on the settee. "Are you nervous?" She asked.

"A wee bit."

She smiled. She knew he was, because of his use of the Scottish 'wee.' "Don't be. They both want you to become part of our family."

Dunc thunked down the stairs at least two if not three at a time and flew around the corner into the room. Lil-Pen called, "Wait for me."

"Hi, McIlroy," Dunc said. "I'm getting my homework done. It'll be all ready for school tomorrow."

Lil-Pen dashed into the room just then and threw herself onto McIlroy's lap. His grunt had Chloe trying to hide her grin. It seemed her daughter had unfortunate aim.

"Settle down." Chloe pulled Lil-Pen off McIlroy and onto her lap. "Have a seat Dunc. Let's chat for a few minutes."

Dunc sat on a chair across the room. Lil-Pen picked at a spot on her dress. Chloe sat silently waiting for McIlroy to say something, anything.

Finally, he cleared his throat. "Dunc, Lil-Pen. Your ma and I had a talk today. We've been courting for a while now and we've decided…"

Duncan jumped up. "Hurray. You're gonna get married and be my pa. And Lil-Pen's, too." He added the last hastily when his sister looked at him funny.

"Well, yes," Chloe said.

Dunc skirted the low table and wrapped his arms around McIlroy. "I can't wait. When's the wedding? This Saturday? Next?"

"Slow down, boy. Hold your horses." McIlroy's words were smothered by the boy's body. Chloe tried to help him extricate himself from her son but Lil-Pen was trying to squeeze into the hug her brother was giving him.

"I take it you're happy with our decision?" Chloe asked the room at large. The answer came from more voices than had been in the room when the discussion started. Now the room was crowded with the other occupants of the House cheering and offering their congratulations.

When things quieted the question of when the wedding would be was again asked.

"Not for a while. We have to wait until Massot is finished with Ben Cutler's house. We're to live in their apartment. So most likely the wedding will be in December," McIlroy said.

There was a general murmur of disappointment.

"That's not too far away. We're already into October. Only two months unless something stops the building."

Esther took that moment to stick her head in and say, "Now that the announcement is done, I only have one thing to say. Supper's ready."

That cleared the room of children very quickly.

Dessert was being served when the front door opened and Myra burst through. She ran into the dining room. Newt followed more slowly, but the smile on his face was just as wide.

"Guess what. Newt and me are gettin' married. He done asked me at the restaurant."

Once again pandemonium broke out. Newt managed to get to the table where McIlroy sat with Lil-Pen on his lap. Troy latched onto his leg so Newt picked him up.

"What do you think, buddy? Can I be your pa?"

"Will you make me a caboose to hook to my locomotive?"

McIlroy and Newt both laughed.

"Sure, son, sure."

CHAPTER THIRTY

Myra and Newt were planning to get married the first Saturday in November. When Dak found out he talked first with Cora then Newt to see if they could move their date up and make it a double wedding. Cora and Myra were both excited with the idea.

Myra was making matching dresses for herself and Cora with one made for, now three year old, Susan from the same fabric. She worked every spare minute on the garments.

As the days got closer, those in the House got more and more excited. When Birdie had gotten married they hadn't had time for the excitement to build. They had almost three weeks to plan this one. It would be pretty much the same with cake served at the reception, but hot apple cider instead of lemonade.

Chloe tried not to be envious of her friends getting married before her, but had to take it to the Lord several times before she was caught up in the general enthusiasm of the residents of the House. She was so very happy for them.

It came as a shock to everyone when Esther up and left town with Trapper Ted, who only came to town twice a year. She saw him on the street and recognized him from when she was young and they'd lived in the same town.

They went to Pastor Preston and said they wanted to get married right then, and if he wouldn't they would head to Denver and find someone who would marry them. They would have been on the trail for several days before arriving so he decided he might as well. They would be living together without the bonds if he didn't.

Noah, Newt, Ben and Eli came to Sanctuary House that evening. They let the rest of the ladies know that sort of thing would not be tolerated. Chloe wondered just what they thought they could do to stop someone, but didn't say it.

Now the entire population of the House was just waiting for the first Saturday in November. The leaves of the trees were turning yellow, red and orange. The air was colder and when it rained it was just plain miserable. Chloe wasn't looking forward to the winter with its freezing temperatures and snow. She was afraid the cafe's income would decrease as people stayed home in bad weather.

Saturday came and the House was alive with more activity than normal. The weddings were to occur at eleven with lunch being held directly after. It was going to be a potluck with everyone attending bringing a dish to contribute.

Myra was nervous and Cora nearly bounced with excitement. Newt had taken a room in the hotel for the night with Troy staying at the House. All Myra's things had been moved to his house the day before as well as most of Troy's.

Dak had moved into the apartment above the gun shop last week and Cora's things were migrating a few at a time. They would spend their wedding night there.

Cora took new linens and made up the bed on Friday. "Dak, you have to sleep on the floor tonight so they'll still be fresh for our wedding night." Her face blushed bright red.

Das grumbled under his breath. Cora thought she heard something about henpecked husbands.

She shot him fierce expression. "You used to sleep on the ground during cattle drives so just quit complaining. It's only one night after all."

Ben and Eli walked the brides down the aisle. Troy stood by Newt and Susan next to her mother. About half way through the service little Susan gave out a scream and launched herself across the platform and pushed Troy off causing him to land on his backside on the floor. Once the tears and outrage of the children was calmed down it was determined that Troy had been making faces and his tongue sticking out at her had been the last straw.

Noah just commented, "Every wedding needs something to

break the tension. This is the first time a brawl has broken out at one of my ceremonies." The resulting laughter did indeed accomplish it.

~~~~~

The dishes were done, the guests out the door and the House residents slipped away to relax after the event. McIlroy took Chloe by the hand to the settee in the parlor. Dunc was off with the Basking boys and Eddie Johnson. Lil-Pen was playing dolls with Susan and Nancy upstairs. The other ladies made sure to give the couple a semblance of privacy by keeping the other children away and going to the various sitting rooms on the upper floors.

"I wish we could have been wed today, as well," McIlroy said placing an arm around her shoulders.

"I do, too." Chloe bit her lip. She needed to tell him how she felt but was unsure of the words. She felt so safe with him. She felt secure in Stones Creek, and Noah made her feel safe, too, but her feelings with McIlroy were different. More intense.

Was it love? She didn't know. She'd never known the love or even the attraction to a man before. Lloyd had only used her. The security she had felt with him had been tenuous at best. On his terms and only when he deemed. She always knew he could throw her away at any time. She and Dunc. As soon as he had died the rest of the gang had thrown them away.

With McIlroy, she had a knowing, a certainty, that he would always be there for her. He would simply be there whenever she needed him. That's what she needed to explain, but she was having trouble finding the words. Tears came to her eyes.

"Auch, honey. What be the matter? What's worrying you?" He searched her eyes with his.

"I can't explain how you make me feel. Ever since that day when I was ten I've been scared. Unsure if I was safe. If there would be enough to eat or if I and then my children would be warm and secure. I don't have that fear anymore. You've taken that from me and given me a place to be. Just like this House and Sanctuary Place have been for the last five years. They've been my security. These places and the Lord.

"Now the Lord has given me you. You've become my

sanctuary. I know I can trust that you will always be here for me. For the children, too. You're there to protect us. You and Noah, but especially you. You are taking on me and Dunc and Lil-Pen. Not many men will do that. Choose to raise another man's children as their own."

"I'm not so special. Newt and Dak both did today. There will be others who will be willing to do the same with the other ladies here who have children." He chuckled. "With five of you married in less than six months, three of you with children, I don't think finding husbands will be much of a chore for the others."

Chloe shook her head. "But you are special to me. That's what I'm trying to tell you. You're my sanctuary. My safe place. The place, the person God sent me to so I could be who He wants me to be. I'm so thankful everyday that I came to Stones Creek. I found Noah, and I found you."

She stopped speaking and just relaxed into the moment. Chloe laid her head on his shoulder and closed her eyes. She sent up a prayer of thanksgiving. No matter what came along she knew McIlroy would be there supporting, protecting and encouraging her, Dunc and Lil-Pen.

CHAPTER THIRTY-ONE

Early December came and Ben's house was nearing completion. Chloe was anxious about getting married, but anticipating it, also. She was definitely attracted to McIlroy but her experiences of the past didn't have her looking forward to repeating them. If nothing halted the progress Chloe and McIlroy would be married on Saturday, December nineteen.

They had spent the last month learning more about each other. She had known he didn't care much about his appearance, but hadn't known he only had two sets of work clothes and one set of good clothes. This she learned from Laura Duffle who did his laundry. She'd tried to encourage him to bring all his dirty laundry together rather than just one set at one time. He told her he did. She'd looked at the meager pile and shaken her head at him. Then she told Chloe.

The next day, after she was done working at the cafe Chloe went to the smithy and hauled McIlroy by the hand over to Ben's store.

"You pick out two more sets of work clothes and one more dress shirt," she instructed.

McIlroy turned red with embarrassment when she held a Union suit up to him, then lay it on the pile of clothes on the counter for Ben to tally up.

Chloe had developed a list of what they would need to start housekeeping but hadn't shown it to McIlroy yet. She didn't want him to have an apoplectic fit. At least not until they were married. She was purchasing what she could in the way of linens and small household items and looking through the catalogs Ben had looking for good quality but low priced furniture.

Almeda had left for the day and Blanche was feeling poorly so Chloe suggested she leave, too. It was drizzling so she didn't think the lunch crowd would be large even though it was a Saturday, when many of the ranch hands came to town to spend their pay.

"I appreciate it, Chloe," Blanche said. "I think I'm coming down with whatever the children had last week." Each day at least one of the children was staying in bed with a fever.

"Dunc is home right now. McIlroy had a job he needed to finish up so he's not going to work today. Would you, please, have him come here? He can do the dishes while I cook and serve." Chloe stirred the pot of chili on the stove then checked on the cornbread baking in the oven.

"Sure. That's a good idea." Blanche wrapped her shawl around her shoulders and placed her bonnet on her head and headed across the alley to the back entry of the House.

A few minutes later, Dunc opened the door and Lil-Pen preceded him into the kitchen.

"Mama," Lil-Pen said. "Can I help, too?"

Chloe smiled at her daughter. She didn't know how much help Lil-Pen could be, but would try to find something.

"You can dry the silverware for me," Dunc said as he ruffled her hair. "That'll help both Ma and me."

"You're right, Dunc, it will." Chloe was so proud of her son for thinking of something simple but vital for Lil-Pen to do. She gave him a hug and then said, "Okay, troops. We've got to get everything ready for the dinner crowd." She gave instructions for the different tasks that needed to be accomplished before what she hoped would be hungry customers arriving for the noon meal.

There were a few early diners, then a large group of hands from one of the area ranches came in. They were kept busy though Chloe had limited the available menu items since she was the only cook that day.

Lil-Pen had gotten bored with drying silverware and was pretending to cook with a few pans and spoons in the corner out of the way by the stove. Chloe didn't mind, understanding the attention span of a five-year-old wasn't that long. Dunc was diligent in keeping up with the dirty dishes.

The dining room cleared of customers and Chloe went out to gather up the dishes from the tables. She looked up as the door opened and the silverware in her hand clattered to the floor. Standing there was Buster King and his brother Amos. She hadn't seen either of them in over five years.

"Howdy, Chloe. Fancy us meeting up with you here in Stones Creek. And you not expecting a baby any more. " The smile on Buster's face spoke of what he wanted of her.

"You can just turn around and leave right now, Buster."

"I don't think so, Chloe. You belong with us, you know, that don't you? We done took you for ours, all those years ago. You don't think just 'cause we left you in Minnesota that you still don't belong to us?" Buster spit tobacco juice onto the floor. He took another step into the room and Amos stepped up beside him.

"We know you're here without your lady friends. Saw the darkie leave and then the other one. You're here all alone ain't you?" This time it was Amos who spoke.

"Yeah, we've been keeping an eye on you for the past couple o' weeks."

Chloe swallowed and prayed. She prayed Dunc wouldn't come out of the kitchen and try to save her. These men would kill him without thinking about it twice. She prayed someone would come in behind them. Prayed that McIlroy or Noah would suddenly enter. Anyone.

~~~~~

Dunc heard the voice and instantly knew who had come into the cafe. The chills that when up his back paralyzed him for a few moments. His first instinct was to rush into the other room and confront them. He ducked down and moved to the wall beside the doorway into the dining room. Then Noah's instructions, as he had taught him to shoot, came back to him.

"Never let your emotions overrule your thinking. If you do, you lose the fight or die or those you want to save die. You have to keep thinking."

Dunc thought. He knew he couldn't take them out by himself.

He could, might be able to, hold them off from hurting or taking his mother until help could arrive, but how to get that help.

He glanced at Lil-Pen. She was tucked up beside the stove, wide eyed. She'd obviously heard the menace in the male voices. He moved as silently as he could to where she sat.

"Lil-Pen," he whispered. "You gotta go get either Uncle Noah or McIlroy. Tell them Ma needs help, right now. Bad men. You need to run there."

As he spoke he picked her up and snuck over to the back door. He took his jacket from the peg, glancing over his shoulder to be sure he couldn't be seen from the dining room. He set Lil-Pen down and wrapped her in the jacket. Buttoning two buttons, he eased the door open just wide enough for her to slip through.

Before he released her he pulled the revolver from the pocket. This time he knew it was loaded and also how to handle it. He'd take down at least one of the men who wanted to steal his mother again before he let that happen.

"Run, tell, but don't come back until we come for you." He gave Lil-Pen a gentle shove. He closed the door not allowing the latch to fall and turned around. He moved to the pass-through window, lifted the gun with both hands and took aim.

"Buster, Amos. You leave now or else." Dunc kept the gun level, aimed right at them.

Both men's eyes left Chloe and turned on him. They began to laugh.

Oh, how he wanted to pull the trigger. He'd been helpless before. Too young to do anything, but now he had the power to do something. His finger shook desperately wanting to squeeze.

Carefully, so his voice wouldn't crack, Dunc cleared his throat. "I've already shot one man protecting my ma. He was a man I liked. You think about what I'm willing to do to you. I don't like you at all."

~~~~~

McIlroy was studying the piece of metal held by his tongs. Newt and Noah were drinking coffee and basically wasting his time. Both men knew he was trying to finish up this order, but with the lousy weather they'd decided his forge supplied both warmth and camaraderie. Oh well, he'd wasted time at both their places of work before so he figured it was their turn.

He was about to shove the metal back into the fire when he heard a crying yell of his name. He looked up and saw Lil-Pen running, then slip and fall in the muddy street. He dropped the tongs and rushed out of the smithy scooping her up into his arms.

"What, Lil-Pen? You're safe now."

"Bad men. At the cafe. Dunc sent me." She was crying and the words came out between sobs.

Noah and Newt were beside him now. McIlroy glanced at them seeing danger and determination in their eyes. They began moving. McIlroy set Lil-Pen down. "You go up the stairs to Vernie. Bang on the door and she'll let you in. Stay there," he instructed her. He watched as she began climbing the stairs. She was still crying, but obeyed.

As they began swiftly moving up the street Noah handed him a Colt six shooter. McIlroy murmured a quick thanks. Newt said he'd go in the back door. Noah nodded, as did McIlroy.

The sheriff veered off to head to the back of the building. McIlroy and Noah continued up the street but didn't use the steps to get onto the boardwalk. They didn't want to alert the men in the cafe.

Noah bent down and hurried to the end of the building then sat on the boardwalk and swung his legs up and stood against the wall. McIlroy did the same in front of the barbershop.

Noah approached from one side, McIlroy from the other. Noah ducked below the window then peeked in and ducked back down. He looked at McIlroy and nodded. He held up two fingers and moved to stand next to him.

"They are looking at the back. I couldn't tell, but I think Dunc's got their attention."

"We need to be sure not to let Chloe be caught in any crossfire."

Noah nodded. "Newt should be in place now. Let's go. We'll holler as we go in. That should bring him in."

McIlroy was shaking inside. He couldn't lose her. She was his future. He'd failed his wife and children before. He wouldn't be able to survive if he failed her, lost her. "You take them. I'll tell

Chloe to get down."

Noah nodded. "Let's go."

They moved quickly but silently to either side of the cafe door. McIlroy looked at Noah and gave a nod. They burst into action.

Noah gave the door a kick and it flew open. As he entered he yelled, "Drop your guns."

At the same time McIlroy yelled, "Chloe, down!" She dropped to the floor. Newt slammed open the back door and came through, not stopping until he was through the swinging doors that separated the kitchen from the dining room.

Buster and Amos simply stood stock still, totally taken by surprise at the arrival of three men pointing revolvers at them. Noah approached from behind and pulled the weapons from their holsters. The outlaws hadn't even tried to draw their weapons. They'd never had a chance. First, Dunc holding them at bay, then the sudden appearance of three men who definitely knew how to handle a gun.

McIlroy skirted around and gathered Chloe in his arms. She was shaking and weeping. She clung to him, nestling her face into his neck.

"You came. You saved me, us."

Dunc had come and knelt beside them wrapping his arms around them both. "Mama, are you all right?"

She released McIlroy with one arm and pulled Dunc close. "Oh, yes. You did exactly the right thing. I'm so proud of you. Where's Lil-Pen?"

"I sent her to get McIlroy and Uncle Noah."

"She's with Vernie," McIlroy said. "She came and told us. We sent her there to be safe."

Suddenly, Chloe was kissing his face. "Thank you, thank you. I was so scared. Dunc, you were so brave and so steady." She pulled back and looked at him, then at Dunc. Then she began to cry again. "I was so scared."

"I need to take these varmints to jail. I know they're wanted in several states," Newt said.

Slowly, McIlroy managed to help Chloe to her feet. He didn't let go of her as she was trembling with the aftermath of her fear.

Dunc stood up, then walked over to Buster who stood a head

taller than the youth. He was handcuffed, as was Amos. Dunc looked at the man who had abandoned him and his mother so many years ago. He looked at Newt. "I don't care if you arrest me for it but…" He made a fist and socked Buster in the face. Blood spurted from the man's nose and mouth. "That's nothing compared to what I want to do to you."

Buster couldn't wipe his face and the blood dripped off his chin onto his shirt. He spit blood and a wad of tobacco onto the floor.

"You be warned, Buster King. You come after my ma again and I'll put a bullet in you just like I did him." Dunc pointed at McIlroy then turned on his heel and marched into the kitchen.

Buster looked at McIlroy.

"Yeah, he did, and he's a much better shot now than he was then."

CHAPTER THIRTY-TWO

The day finally arrived. December nineteen. Today Chloe was going to marry McIlroy. He'd surprised her two days ago telling her to pack her carpetbag as they were going to Denver for several days on a honeymoon. After soothing a disappointed Lil-Pen when she found out she wasn't going along, he'd surprised her again by saying they would be looking at furniture to purchase for their home.

Chloe couldn't believe it. She'd been fretting over the fact that McIlroy wouldn't make final decisions about the tables, chairs and other pieces of furniture she'd found in the catalogs Ben had loaned her. The only things they had ordered were beds. Myra's comment on hearing that had been, "It figures. He's a man, ain't he?"

Ben and his family had moved into their new home a week ago. Chloe had spent two late afternoons scrubbing every wall and floor. She had never had her own home before. She wanted the place to sparkle. Then they'd set up the beds and moved the small table and single chair from McIroy's room into the kitchen. He'd been staying there ever since.

When they moved his clothing, Chloe had found the new work clothes they had purchased still wrapped in the brown paper tied with twine McIlroy had carried from the store. She had placed her hands on her hips and glared at him.

"They were purchased for you to wear not sit on a shelf still wrapped in paper."

McIlroy swallowed. She could tell he was trying to think of

something to say. Some excuse that was good enough to pacify her peak. He opened his mouth then closed it again several times.

"Well?"

"Hum. I wanted to keep them nice for the wedding?"

"You aren't wearing them to the wedding. You're wearing your new shirt and good clothes."

"Uh, didn't want to get them dirty?"

"That's what they are for. Work."

McIlroy looked around the room rather frantically. Then his shoulders sagged. "I just forgot about them. I've worn these work clothes for so long I never gave the new ones a thought. I'm sorry."

Chloe's lips twitched. She tried not to smile but failed. She patted him on the chest. "That's why you need me for a wife. I'll be sure you don't forget."

He'd wrapped his arms around her and stolen a kiss as they heard footsteps coming up the stairs.

She thought about the exchange and how, after he'd told her about the trip to Denver, she'd suggested he pack them to take along. After he wore them for work they'd have burn holes all over and wouldn't be fit to wear to the city.

Now, she was standing at the back of the church. Dunc was going to walk her down the aisle and Lil-Pen was going to stand with her. The girl had wanted to drop flower petals as the flower girl and was disappointed that, since it was December, there were no flowers. She'd suggested pine needles but when she went to gather some the sticky resin convinced her they didn't need them.

Myra had made a new dress for Chloe with fabric she purchased. She had made a matching one for Lil-Pen. It was of striped taffeta in olive, grey blue, cream and marroon. The bodice was buttoned up the front with a double ruffle from each shoulder to the center of the waistband. There was a deep diagonal ruffle at the bottom of the skirt and narrow ruffles on the sleeve cuff. Chloe had never had such a lovely gown. She felt absolutely beautiful. The look in McIlroy's eyes as she walked up the aisle told her he thought the same.

A few days before Chloe had asked McIlroy his first name. She had never heard it. Everyone simply called him McIlroy. He'd turned red and muttered that she'd find out at the ceremony. She'd thought to tease him but the look on his face made her resist.

Noah began the ceremony, though Chloe barely heard the words. She was lost in the look of devotion McIlroy was giving her. Then Noah started the vows.

"Do you Ogilvie Goraidh McIlroy take Chloe…" He had to stop because the laughter from the congregation over rode his words.

McIlroy's stricken expression at the sound of his full name and the laughter tore at her heart. Chloe leaned forward.

"I don't care what your name is. I love you anyway."

His face cleared at her words and he looked at Noah. "Just keep going, Pastor. I don't care if they hear or not. I need to marry this woman and you need to get to it. I may just kiss her before you're through."

They spent the night in their apartment and then caught the early morning westbound train to Denver. Chloe snuggled up to McIlroy on the bench seat as the train climbed the pass between the mountains. "That bed was very comfortable. I slept so well. You made a wise decision in the purchase."

He tipped his head down and looked at her. "Just comfortable for sleeping?"

She smiled. "No. Not just for sleeping."

Chloe nestled into his shoulder. God had been so faithful. He was her ultimate sanctuary, but He'd given Chloe her own personal sanctuary here on Earth.